THE LONG BLUE STARE

THE LONG BLUE STARE

A MONTREAL MURDER MYSTERY

John Charles Gifford

THE LONG BLUE STARE
A MONTREAL MURDER MYSTERY

iUniverse books may be ordered through booksellers or by contacting:

iUniverse
1663 Liberty Drive
Bloomington, IN 47403
www.iuniverse.com
1-800-Authors (1-800-288-4677)

ISBN: 978-1-5320-1665-3 (sc)
ISBN: 978-1-5320-1664-6 (e)

Library of Congress Control Number: 2017905008

Print information available on the last page.

iUniverse rev. date: 04/17/2017

CHAPTER 1

She wasn't the best-looking broad I'd ever seen. It was her smile that caught my attention—and the way she looked at me. She walked in and out of my life in a flash—a sudden streak of lightning in a dark, dismal sky. I saw her for a second time a week later, but it was just a glimpse. The third time I saw her, she was dead. After that, I added her name to a case file I was working on and wrote down what I remembered about her. I didn't have a lot of details, but I would eventually shove, prod, and shoulder what I did have into place later to make sense of things. However, for her, it no longer mattered. It never did to those who were murdered.

I know what you're thinking, and it's not true. I didn't have any romantic intentions toward her. She was part of a much bigger story—the kind that would garner the headlines of all the dailies for days and even weeks. She was the first move in a long game of chess, but I didn't know it at the time. I might just as well tell you about her now before some lout decides to open his mouth too wide and makes chopped liver out of it all.

By the way, the name's Bonifacio Edmondo Wade, but my friends call me Eddie. So do my enemies. I'm thirty-four years old, I've never walked down the aisle, and I run a one-man detective agency out of Mile End, but you can usually find me in most parts of Montreal. I'm licensed by the great province of Quebec, although there was a nasty incident last year when a certain person threatened to pull the aforementioned license. So here's the story without the chopped liver.

I was sitting at the bar of the Flamingo when Billie Holiday finished "Gloomy Sunday." It had been one of those days when nothing went right and you were left looking at the world slantwise. When that happens, every nasty little thing that has ever happened to you comes rushing back all at once and forces itself into crevasses of your brain that you thought had healed, and you feel like an insignificant bug lying on a sidewalk, waiting for someone to walk by and crush you underfoot.

I got off the stool, walked over to the Wurlitzer in the corner, and dropped another nickel into the slot. What was it—the sixth time that night? I'd lost count. It was a Sunday night, when Montreal let her hair down and took her makeup off, and I was gloomy, so the song suited me. The jukebox came to life again, and I returned to my whiskey and pipe at the bar.

Each nightclub in Montreal has its own flavor, its own character—somewhat like cats. Some are warm, cuddly, and furry and sit curled on your lap, content. Others will scratch your eyes out. I liked the soft lighting at the Flamingo, as well as all the chrome, the red leather, and the neon tubes that framed the windows. It was a quiet place where no one caused any trouble; no one would scratch your eyes out. That was where I came when I was in the dumps and I didn't want to see or talk to anyone. Take the barman, Pierre, for example. He always sat on a stool at the end of the bar, minding his own business and reading the latest edition of *La Presse*. Pierre took pride in maintaining a professional distance: far enough to leave me by myself but close enough to talk if I wanted to start a conversation.

I was never the kind of guy who felt sorry for himself, but that was what I was doing that night. My girl, Angel, had dumped me last fall just before I had worked up enough courage to ask her to marry me. Looking back, I realized it was probably for the best. I thought I was over her. I was, in fact, but every so often, she entered my thoughts again, so that night, I found myself sitting there alone, feeling sorry for myself. It was just me and Billie Holiday and "Gloomy Sunday." And, of course, Pierre.

I tipped the shot glass back and asked Pierre for another one—a double this time. It'd save him another trip over to me. He got off his stool and waddled over to me, all three hundred pounds of him, bottle in hand. His white apron covered him from just below his neck down to his ankles, traveling a mountainous terrain. The neon lights reflected off the apron and turned him pinkish blue. He poured the firewater, looked up at me, and winked, and then he returned to his paper. It was a quiet Sunday night at the Flamingo—just the way I liked it.

I looked into the mirror behind the bar again. The broad was still looking at me. Her eyes were flickering over the back of my head, as if she were sizing me up. I wondered how long she'd been doing that. She was no more than twenty-five, with long blonde hair that came down to her shoulders and jumped up at the ends. Her smile was coy—provocative, some might have said—as if we shared a secret. Maybe we did and I just didn't know it. Her makeup was a little too heavy for my taste, but I could tell that under it was a nice face. I was flattered by the attention—what red-blooded Canadian male wouldn't be?—but the mood was all wrong. I smiled back at her to be polite and wondered whether she could see it in the mirror. I thought about swinging around on the stool, but as I said, the mood wasn't there. I didn't want to start something I couldn't follow through on. Nevertheless, there's nothing in this world better than the way a woman looks at you in a certain way, even if you aren't in the mood. It made my heart feel warm.

Angel used to look at me like that a lot, but now her gaze wasn't much more than a pale memory in a worn-out brain. Maybe that was nature's way of protecting me from an eternity of stepping on broken glass with my bare feet. Because of me, she'd taken a bullet to the shoulder. If it had been a few more inches to the left …

Maybe I deserved to have bloody feet. It would have been a penance justly warranted. *Self-flagellation?* I thought, considering a suitable alternative, but I didn't have a whip handy.

I tipped the glass back again and then puffed on my pipe.

Two guys swung the door open and came in, yammering about something. They wore sport jackets without ties. One had a crew cut, and the other had a woolly mop of black hair that hung in his eyes. *McGill boys, probably.* They looked old enough to drink legally but young and stupid enough to make all the wrong moves in life.

Crew Cut said, "Shaddap, will ya?"

His buddy shook his mop back and forth, amused. "You're killing me, man. You're killing me!"

They sidled up to the bar, ordered gin and tonics, and then decided that the far booth in the corner was better. They got up and disappeared.

Yeah, yeah, yeah, I thought. *Have a nice time, fellas—but just keep the chatter down.*

I glanced at the mirror again and saw that Blondie's smile had soured. Her eyes had narrowed, and her lips had pursed.

She waved a hand in front of her face as if she were shooing away an errant fly. The fly was wearing a dark blue three-piece suit and a Panama fedora. He must have sneaked in sometime after the McGill boys. He sat down next to her and took off his hat. He had a headful of red hair. I pegged him for a banker or an accountant, but there was something swarthy about him, and it wasn't his complexion. His hair was slicked back and neatly parted, and it looked orange against the lighting. I was annoyed with him too and wished I had a swatter. He damned well broke the enchantment, so I walked over to the Wurlitzer again and dropped another nickel.

I went back to my drink and relit my pipe. The wisps of smoke rose, and the mirror in front of me became shrouded, but I could see the two behind me in an animated argument with arms flailing every which way and mouths ugly and distorted. They kept their voices low in stage whispers, so I couldn't hear what they were saying. That was good because I didn't want to hear them. I just wanted to sit there and feel sorry for myself.

Before long, I heard a chair scrape the floor and fall backward. I turned around and saw that Blondie had gotten up. She had a bombshell figure in her bright red sleeveless dress. She wore a string of pearls around her neck and matching earrings. Carrottop had gotten up as well, and the argument continued. This time, I could hear them. They made no attempt to keep their voices low. They were shouting—spitting bullets at each other. I could catch about every other word, but none of it made much sense to me. I looked over at Pierre and shrugged. He returned the shrug and went back to his paper, turning to another section, bored. I turned around and sipped my whiskey. There was suddenly a foul smell in the air, like an overturned garbage can in the middle of August. I did not like that. The

Flamingo was supposed to be a quiet joint. Maybe no one had told them.

The scene had the potential of becoming an interesting one-act play, and my curiosity was piqued. I looked at them again over my shoulder and saw that Carrottop had picked up the chair like a gentleman, but he then tried to make her sit in it like a mug, grabbing her roughly by the shoulders. She slapped his face with a cutesy, fast little move of the right hand that would have impressed even Rocky Marciano. The side of his face was suddenly white on its way to becoming several shades of red. He slapped her back, only his slap was harder than hers. Carrottop was no gentleman after all. I could see that the pair of them had the promise of becoming alley cats. The tension was palpable. Maybe if they could just claw each other's eyes out and be done with it, I thought, things might settle down. Instead, she pulled away from him and put her hands to her cheeks, startled and frightened. She let out a small, half-suppressed scream that sounded as if she were about to audition for a bigger one. This was where the director should've shouted, "Cut!"

But he didn't.

The worst thing a guy can do is get between two strangers of the opposite sex when they're fighting. You don't know who they are or what kind of history they have with each other. You don't know what happened the last time they saw each other. Getting involved can backfire on you pretty fast. You might find yourself the object of their hostility in a New York minute. I've been down that road a few times myself. If you haven't, then I'll tell you: it's pretty ugly. However, my mother always told me when I was old enough to understand that a man should treat a woman with respect, no matter the circumstances. I remembered that.

I got off the stool and walked over to them. I stared at Carrottop with the hard kind of stare. His appearance threw me off a bit because of the tailored suit and slicked-back hair. His behavior didn't fit his attire. Guys who dressed well weren't supposed to hit broads, but I knew better. Don't get me wrong. My knuckles don't reach the ground, and I don't go around looking for dragons to slay and fair-haired beauties to rescue. But things happen sometimes, and you can ignore them or not.

I couldn't.

I asked him a question: "Do you believe in heaven and hell?"

He thrust his prognathous jaw up and inventoried me. His suit jacket hung a little too loosely, as if he had lost some weight and forgotten to return to his tailor. His eyes narrowed, and he made a jerky motion with his head that said he didn't understand me. "Whaddya say?"

I didn't want to get into a theological discussion with him, so I made it simple. "Listen," I said. "I don't know what you two are arguing about, and frankly, I don't care. But when a gentleman hits a broad, as you just did a minute ago, he's no longer a gentleman. He's a two-bit punk." I angled my head, narrowed my eyes back at him, and gave him a crooked smirk with my arms akimbo.

Carrottop looked at me as if I had just waltzed into the wrong ballroom. After a long moment, he said, "Why don't you shut your yap? Amscray, you!" A bony finger angled up at my jaw. I think he understood me that time.

He was shorter than I was and weighed about thirty pounds less. He didn't look the type who would stand toe to toe with a person of his own sex, but maybe I was wrong. Sometimes pretty little guys make the lives of women hellholes more so than massive, hairy beasts who chop down trees with their teeth. They slap women around, which gives them the false hope that they can do the same to men.

His skin was pasty white, except for the side of his face where she'd slapped him, which was now pinker than Ray Robinson's Cadillac. His nose was a wafer, thin and long. His eyes were small, dark, and sunken. When I looked into them, I saw the faint glimmer of fire. His hand slowly moved to the inside of his suit coat. That was never a good sign. I'm more sensitive to the behavior of others than most people are. Gestures, facial expressions, dress, and demeanor all have different meanings for me. If you make a living navigating through the seedy side of life, a bad guess can give you a pair of broken knees or cement shoes pretty quickly.

I took one step toward him, grabbed his silk tie at the knot, pulled him toward me, and landed a single blow to his nose. I let go of the tie, and Carrottop dropped to the floor with a thud.

Maybe that wasn't fair of me. Maybe he was reaching into his jacket for a handkerchief. Maybe he wanted to get a notebook and write down my name—the asshole who got in his face at the Flamingo. But maybe he was reaching for something that would've caused more problems than it would've solved. One sudden flash of violence can sometimes prevent an all-out war and more bloodshed. It can turn a man into a boy pretty fast. He loses control of his bladder and can't think straight. Without warning, he turns into a silly, helpless ninny.

Under other circumstances, that punch could have landed me in jail. I had been a prizefighter in another life, and the law still considered my fists the same as weapons. However, there was one exclusionary clause: I could use them to defend myself—which I did in that instance. I think.

Blondie looked down at Carrottop and then over at me. That was when it became dicey. It was the moment of truth.

She could side with him and start pounding me on the chest with her fists and yelling, "You crazy son of a bitch! Whadijya do that for?" Or she could have a sudden sense of appreciation and thank me, her knight in shining armor. She did neither.

"I've got to get out of here" was all she said.

Carrottop was on his back and conscious; he lifted his head off the floor, and it kept bouncing up and down like a bobber on the surface of a lake when the wind comes in. I suspected he might do that for a while, until a fish took the hook and pulled it down. I reached down, slid my hand into his suit coat, and—bingo!—found the handle of a small revolver. My gut feeling had been right. I took it out, popped the cylinder, and let the bullets fall onto his stomach. Then I bent down and placed the gun on his chest. I gave it a gentle pat for good measure. "Don't think it hasn't been charming," I said. His head stopped bobbing, and he watched me with his chin touching his chest, but he didn't move, not even to wipe the blood off his face.

I grabbed my pipe off the bar, knocked the ashes out of it, and then put it in my pocket. I left a fiver for Pierre and walked Blondie to the door. I looked over my shoulder at Pierre as she and I were leaving. He was looking down at Carrottop, scratching his head.

It was late and dark; the neon was intruding into the night. We walked down rue Drummond for a block—as she teetered on her high heels—before she said anything.

"Thank you for helping me."

"Husband or boyfriend?"

"God, no, neither. He's just—" She clammed up again.

We continued to walk a few more blocks until we approached another corner. I was halfway across the street before I noticed that she had stopped there. I turned around and walked back to her. She stood erect, her hands fidgeting in front of her. She looked like a lost, lonely little girl wondering which direction to go. I wish now that I would have told her.

I glanced at my watch and then at a phone booth against a brick building. "I don't mind walking you home. Or I'll call you a taxi. It's getting late."

"No. I'll be okay now. You seem to be a nice man."

I let her believe it.

I reached into my back pocket and took out my wallet. I gave her my card.

"Call me if you need anything," I told her.

I'm just an average guy trying to hustle a living. I sell my services in the marketplace of violence and corruption. This one was free of charge.

She looked down at the card but didn't say anything for what seemed an eternity.

"Thanks, Eddie," she finally said, angling her head up at me. "You've been a swell guy." In the soft light of an overhead streetlamp, her eyes took on a different look than before—imploring rather than teasing, earnest rather than mischievous. A quiet breeze played with her hair. She ran her fingers across her face, combing the strands aside.

She suddenly reached up with both hands, grabbed the back of my head, and brought it down to hers. She was stronger than she looked. Her hands slid to the sides of my face, and she kissed me on the mouth so long and hard that it made my lips hurt. When she let me go, she turned right and ran up the street toward rue Dorchester. I stood there watching her until she was out of sight, wondering whether I'd ever see her again.

There are certain females who are so fragile and sensitive that they become easy marks for the Carrottops of the world. They get slapped and tossed around all their lives. Disaster follows them wherever they go. Once in a while, you have the opportunity to help them, but that's never enough. Oh, they attempt to fight back, but they always end up battered shells of themselves, and there's nothing you can do to prevent that.

Peachy keen.

I walked north a few blocks and hailed a taxi.

CHAPTER 2

The next morning, I had my usual breakfast—a pot of coffee and two orders of toast—at the greasy spoon a few blocks from my office. That got me through most of what interested me in *Le Devoir.* My French was lousy, but I had made a commitment last year to improve it. Reading French-language newspapers was one way to do it. Sadly, hockey season was over, but now baseball was in the air, and the Royals were starting the season off with a series of wins. They'd beat Minneapolis 4–1 at Delorimier Stadium the night before. *Good for them.* They were on the road now, and I made a note to catch their next home game.

I walked up Saint-Urbain to my office, shielding my eyes from the glare of the sun. There was a slight chill in the air, which felt good. I felt good. Life was hunky-dory. As I got the key in the door, I heard my name called. Bruno was washing the windows of the Lion's Den next door. He had a bucket of soapy water beside him and was running a squeegee down the face of the window. I gave him a short wave, unlocked the door, and went in. Bruno owned the bar as well as my office. He was a Kodiak bear who happened to be my landlord as well as my father confessor.

I threw my hat on the coatrack and looked down at my feet. A black cat, her back hunched up, was doing a little ballet dance around me, rubbing her feline flanks against my legs and butting me with her head, making a horrible little sound. Antoinette was chatty that morning, but it wasn't about baseball. It was more immediate and visceral. I had adopted her last fall after her owner was murdered, and we'd since developed a secret language between us. We understood each other. She was indignant about my going out for breakfast without first providing hers. It was unfair of me. She had a feline quality about her that could induce guilt in any human she rubbed against. I walked around the side of my desk, feeling ashamed of myself; opened the bottom drawer; shoved a bottle of Canadian Club aside; and picked up a tin of cat food. She stopped her moaning as I slid her bowl onto the floor.

I went behind my desk, sat down, and put my feet up. I stared at the phone with my hands behind my head. Business had been good that year, but it had slacked off over the past two weeks. I needed a few cases to jump-start my bank account. Don't get me wrong. For the first time in eight years, I was deliriously ahead of the game. However, if work didn't come in, the expenses wouldn't stop, and a nice bank account could take a nosedive faster than a fighter being hit with a solid right hand to the jaw.

My office was modest but clean. I slept in the small room in the back—formally the storage room of the small neighborhood grocery store that had been there before me. There wasn't much more in it than a Hollywood bed without the headboard, but it served me well. Lately, though, I'd considered moving into a real apartment. Living in my office cut down on expenses, but it also had some terrible penalties, especially with women. With the exception of Angel, who didn't give a hoot where I lived, most broads took one look at it, took one look at me, and smiled politely, and the night ended abruptly. Besides, I thought Antoinette felt a little caged in there. A larger apartment would give her more space to find new places to reconnoiter and set up ambushes. Cats needed that. Living outdoors would have been best for her, but I knew she'd have a hard time with the Quebec winters, and I wasn't sure how she would fare with all the roaming toms. She was petite and had never lived outdoors. A girl had to protect herself.

The phone suddenly jumped up. So did I. I reached for the receiver.

"Wade Detective Agency," I said casually.

"Is that you, Eddie? Bradford Wilcox here."

"A ghost out of the past. Where've you been hiding, Brad?"

Wilcox was one of the key figures at the Guarantee Company of Quebec. I'd known him for years and had periodically done work for him. We'd become good friends, but we'd lost contact with each other that past year.

"Not hiding, Eddie. In the same office of the same building, doing the same job. I think I'll have my funeral here. Send flowers to my secretary. She'll know where to put them. Speaking of jobs, are you free to take on a case? It'll be worth your time. If you're a good boy, there could even be a bonus in it for you."

"Gee whiz, Brad, I don't know about that. I've been really busy lately. I'd have to look at my schedule. Can you hold on a bit?"

I set the receiver down, opened a drawer, shuffled some papers so that he could hear the sound on his end, and then picked up the receiver again.

"Yeah, Brad, I think I can squeeze you in."

"Squeeze me in, huh? If I remember correctly, Mr. Wade, you did that little routine of yours with me before, which can only mean that you're as free as a con artist just released from Bordeaux. Can you come over in the next hour? I'll brief you then. This is a hot one, Eddie. You'll need to get on it right away."

I told him I'd be leaving in five minutes and hung up. Before I got my hat and pipe, Antoinette and I did a little jig around my desk. I was certain Brad had mentioned the word *bonus*.

I sat in a comfortable brown leather chair in Bradford Wilcox's office. The room was small but nicely furnished, with wooden paneling, bookshelves set into the walls, and a nice little bar behind his desk. He sat with one haunch on his mahogany desk, facing me. He wore a dark gray gabardine suit with six-pleated high-rise trousers, a white shirt, and a green tie with two golf clubs on it, crossed like M1 rifles.

"What's on your mind, Brad?" I pulled out my Dunhill billiard and filled it with a burley blend.

"Sleep." He folded his arms across his chest. His eyes drooped down at me. "I'm not getting enough of it these days. One hundred thousand simoleons are keeping me up at night."

"That's a reasonable fee for my services, Brad. What'll I have to do for it?" I lit my pipe and puffed a few times, sending a cloud of smoke between us.

"You're as good as they come, Eddie, but not that good."

Wilcox was in his late forties. He had jet-black hair combed to the side with a sharp part on the right side. He had a pencil mustache and wore silver wire-rimmed glasses that would have made him look ten years older had he any gray hair. Most people who met him for the first time pegged him for the serious type, as if he were a Crown attorney ready to send someone to the gallows, but they put him on the wrong peg. The truth was, he had a helluva keen sense of humor, and he used it even at the most inappropriate of times. We'd spent hours over whiskey trying to outdo each other. However, that day, there didn't seem to be a trace of humor.

"So give me the lowdown, Brad."

"The yokel's name is Philippe Belanger, and he embezzled one hundred thousand dollars from his clients at Spence and Belanger Investment Brokerage."

"Did he confess to it?"

"He did not."

"The police are probably better than me at getting confessions out of people."

"That very well may be true, if they had him. He's a runner, Eddie. Completely disappeared. Jumped his bail. He's on the lam."

"So what are you pitching? You want me to find him and the money he stole?"

"That's right. I want you to find the son of a bitch and bring him in."

"I'm not one to turn down a case," I told him. I paused to take a few puffs from my pipe. "Especially when a bonus is offered, but I'm sure the police could track him down faster than me. With that kind of dough, they probably have an APB out on him."

"They're on the case now, but you know them. Whoever's been assigned to it will more than likely be juggling a half dozen other cases at the same time. Belanger will have the loot spent and be looking for his next caper before they nail him. It's worth what we're willing to pay to have one man looking for him full-time. Of course, my first thought was you."

"I see your point."

Wilcox walked behind his desk, sat down, opened a file, and sorted through a handful of papers. He looked up at me and then leaned back in his chair.

"How do you figure it, Eddie? A firm like Spence and Belanger goes along for years without a spot on their record, and then bang—one of them turns sour and throws up all over them."

"That's what makes prizefighting, I guess."

"It's also what gives bonding companies headaches and sleepless nights. We hold a fidelity bond on the brokerage firm. It's insurance protection that covers them for losses that they incur as a result of fraudulent acts by employees."

"Right. Give me the particulars." I took out a notebook and pen. I supposed that meant I was taking the case on.

Brad reached over to his ashtray, retrieved his half-spent cigar, and put a match to it. "It's all in here." He slid the folder at me. "The whole rotten story. Spence and Belanger Investment. Really high-class clientele."

"A partnership?"

"Oh yeah. Michael Spence is the other partner. Thirty-six years old. A pillar of society."

"Married?"

"No, a widower. His wife died three or four years ago."

"And this Philippe Belanger is his partner. Equal partners, I assume."

"That's right. They started the firm back in 1941. He's also thirty-six. Big fellow, clean cut, and educated. Played varsity hockey at McGill. He had everything in his favor: looks, personality, intelligence, ability, and a profitable career. Why, Eddie? Why a guy like that?"

"You're asking the wrong fellow, Brad. I've seen enough embezzlers to know they come in all shapes, sizes, and pedigrees."

"What turns a man sour like that?"

Brad had been in the insurance business long enough to know the answer to that question. Maybe after all those years, he was still stunned to find that a person with everything in the world would risk it all for even more.

"You know the stock answers to that. Gambling debts or a woman. Or both. Desperation generates madness, an insane kind of energy. Makes people do reckless things. By the way, is Belanger married?"

"Yes. No kids." He grimaced. "That's another thing I can't figure out. As you said, one of the reasons for embezzlement is another woman. If that was Belanger's reason, the guy's nuttier that a salted nut bar." Brad drew on his cigar and started to smile but ended up smirking. "Why anyone with a wife like Juliette Belanger would even look at another woman is beyond me."

"It's like that, hmm?"

"It's like that. She's a goddess, Eddie—a real-honest-to-goodness Greek goddess. And besides that, she appears to be a really fine lady. Very refined. I interviewed her myself. So did the Crown attorney's office. You'll be talking to her, so you'll see for yourself."

"When a man leaves his wife for another woman," I said, "it usually has nothing to do with looks. He begins scratching an itch that's been bothering him for years. He begins looking for something new—something less familiar. He becomes a man who's not restrained by the things that restrain the rest of us. There are complex women out there who have subtle powers to make men do all sorts of foolish things. Men end up falling over themselves in order to please these women. Sometimes they steal; sometimes they even kill. The prisons are full of the self-deluded. But we're getting ahead of ourselves. Now, about the money that's missing."

"One hundred thousand smackers, more or less. Currencies, checks, negotiable securities."

"Look, a theft like that doesn't just happen overnight. It must have been going on for a long time." Embezzlement was like an empty barrel sitting in the rain. Little drops would eventually fill it to the brim.

"It was."

"How did Belanger manage it?"

"Well, Spence can fill you in on that better than I can."

"He must be ready to kill Belanger. Any way this turns out, the firm's going to take a hit."

"That's the other thing. I think Spence still believes that there's been some kind of error, accounting or otherwise. He's not completely with us on Belanger's guilt. I think he's pretty concerned about the firm's name and reputation. That's completely understandable, but he's been more than cooperative."

"Well, maybe he's got something there. Maybe Belanger is innocent."

Brad got up, walked to the front of the desk, and sat down where he'd been before. "You'd better save yourself some time, Eddie. Just answer one question for me: Would an innocent man jump bail?"

CHAPTER 3

A car was pulling out in front of the Hardcastle Office Building on rue Dorchester, which housed Spence and Belanger Investment Brokers, and I slid the black Ford coupe into the space. It was a fine day. The sun was out, there was a light breeze, and I was gainfully employed on a case. It wasn't exactly a case of a missing person, since the subject of the investigation had jumped bail and was deliberately on the lam, evading the police, but Philippe Belanger was missing nonetheless. I had a gut feeling that I was going to earn my fees. I was glad Brad had told me I'd be reimbursed for any expenses I incurred along the way. When you take on a client, you have to be clear who's paying the expenses. I learned that lesson the hard way with my first job as an investigator. After I finished a four-day case, my expenses nearly equaled the fee I charged. Because a stipulation about expenses wasn't written into the contract, I found that I had worked for free.

I thought about walking two blocks to Slitkin's and Slotkin's for lunch, but I wasn't hungry enough. Besides, I wanted to interview Michael Spence as soon as possible. One hundred thousand bucks was a lot of money, and the longer a case like this went on, the worse the odds of finding it were. I took the elevator up to the top floor. The office I was looking for stared at me from the opposite side as the doors slid open. The door to the office was open, and I saw a man starting to turn around.

Michael Spence was a handsome, tan man of thirty-six. The tan looked too deep for that time of the year. *Florida getaways, perhaps, in between well-to-do clients.* His hair was long, wavy, and black. Given the business he was in, I was surprised not to see a bit of gray in the mix. I'd expected to find him in a $300 suit; instead, he was dressed casually in khaki slacks, a blue sports shirt, and a camel-colored jacket.

"You must be Mr. Wade," he said. "Mr. Wilcox phoned and said you were coming over."

He extended his hand to me, and we shook. His grip was strong, but his palm felt cold in mine. He had a pleasant enough smile—the same one, I suspected, he showed his clients—but I could tell it was forced. If it had been genuine, his eyes would have narrowed somewhat, and the sides would have wrinkled. I didn't stand in judgment, though. If I had been duped out of a hundred grand, I might not want to see anyone, let alone smile at anyone.

"Call me Eddie. You must be Michael Spence."

"Yes. Just Mike or Spence is fine. Let's go to my office and talk. I gave Chantal some time off while I try to handle this crisis. She's my secretary and runs the office."

I followed him through the reception area, down a short corridor, and into his office. It was efficient looking but lacked any personal touches that might reveal something about the personality of the person who worked there. Two sturdy leather-bound wooden chairs lined one wall, and I sat in one. He remained standing.

"I was just going to have a brandy. Can I pour two?"

I nodded.

He walked behind his desk and slid back a door that sat on metal tracks. An array of liquor bottles sat on top of a cabinet. He picked one up and poured some into two snifters. He walked back to me with a slow, geriatric gait. He had a thousand pounds of misery on his shoulders, and it showed—one hundred thousand pounds, to be exact. He sat down next to me, reached over and gave me the brandy, crossed one leg over the other, and sighed.

"I just can't believe it, Eddie. Phil Belanger, of all people. He's like a brother to me."

"How long have you been partners with him?" I asked, and then I sipped the brandy.

"We started the firm thirteen years ago. We've known each other since college. This whole thing just doesn't make sense."

"When something doesn't make sense, rest assured that some of the facts are missing. Let's see. That would have made you around twenty-three at the time, right? That's pretty young to start an investment firm, isn't it, especially with limited experience?"

"You're right. It was." He threw the brandy back and finished it in a couple of gulps. "Things just fell into place. The previous owner of this firm was retiring, and we were lucky to get some financial backing, so we had hundreds of existing clients from the very start. As I said, we were lucky, but we both worked hard to maintain the business and to expand it. And now this. It could ruin us. And Juliette. Poor Juliette." He took his leg off the other, put his elbows on his knees, and covered his face with his hands. He was a very upset man.

"His wife?"

"That's right. His wife." He sat back in the chair again. "If I ever saw a perfect marriage, that was it. As far as I can see, she's all that a man could want."

"Maybe not for Philippe Belanger."

"Yeah, well, maybe not. I just don't understand it." He shook his head.

"Do you know whether he was seeing another woman?"

He threw his head back; the shocked look on his face was genuine. "God, no. Not Phil. He was totally dedicated to her. He'd never cheat on her."

"You never figured he'd embezzle from his clients, but he did."

He looked at me for a long moment to confirm that I was right, but he didn't say anything.

"How was Belanger able to get away with the theft?" I asked.

"Our firm has always been able to maintain an excellent relationship with our clients. We specialize in the high end, if you know what I mean. We go out of our way to nurture a trusting relationship. We know our clients well, and they know us. We know the markets well, and we do a lot of buying and selling for them, sometimes very fast. We're good at what we do. Trust and confidence are a two-way street at this firm. I think Phil used that to juggle figures."

"And that's what Belanger did? Mr. Wilcox believes that you think your partner could be innocent."

"At first, I did, but after he jumped bail, well, it doesn't seem so now."

"Explain just how he juggled the figures."

"Phil specialized in clients who had growth investments—you know, long term. They buy and hold for a long time. The clients feed the machine periodically and expect their money to grow over a period of ten or twenty years or longer. And it does.

I found out about what Phil had done after one of his clients decided to liquidate on short notice."

"And the account came up short."

"Yes, quite short. I, of course, ordered an immediate full-scale audit. The firm I hired discovered that a good number of Phil's clients came up short of funds. I reported it straightaway. That's when the Crown attorney became involved. The rest you know."

"Yes."

Spence reached over to a small table near him and placed a hand on a stack of folders.

"Here are the files on his accounts. He recorded each transaction clearly and carefully. He wrote memos on all of them."

"These memos are in his handwriting?"

"Yes, they are."

"May I take a couple of them with me?"

"Yes, by all means."

Spence took a few files from the pile, opened them, and gave me three of Belanger's memos.

"As I understand it, Belanger wouldn't talk after his arrest," I said.

"That was the most frustrating part of it. I wish he had given us some kind of explanation, some reason for it. But he refused to say anything in his defense whatsoever. I arranged for his bail and tried to do what I could, but—"

"But he jumped bail." I drank some more of the brandy. It was warm and smooth.

"Yes, I'm afraid so."

"This was four days ago, as I understand."

"Yes."

"Are there any other brokers working for this firm?"

"No, it's just Phil and me. We're a small firm. Hiring anyone else wouldn't have been justified."

"How about your secretary? Does she have access to your client files?"

"Only if we give one to her to type up any correspondence, and then she returns it right away. The files are kept in a walk-in safe. Phil and I are the only ones who have the combination."

"One more thing. Had Belanger acted differently lately? Anything out of the ordinary? Some strange behavior in any way?"

"I hadn't noticed anything lately, but apparently, his wife, Juliette, had. I had dinner with them at their house about three weeks before this happened. Juliette took me aside and asked me whether I'd noticed any change in Phil lately."

"Change?"

"Yes, she said that he seemed moody and preoccupied. That made me realize that yes, I had noticed he was a bit tense around the office. Apparently, he told her that he'd been working extra hard. I shrugged it off. I suppose I made a mistake. Perhaps I should have followed up on that. But this is the last thing I'd ever think of him doing."

"Yes, I suppose it would be. I wouldn't beat yourself up over it. It took a lot of planning. He was obviously determined."

He looked at me mournfully, worried. I'd have been worried too in his place. The future was indeed dim for any investment firm accused of embezzlement.

"That's all for now," I said. "Here's my card. Please let me know if you think of anything else. Even the smallest of things might be important. I'll keep in close contact with you until I find him. If he tries to contact you, notify me immediately."

"Yes, of course. But do me a favor, will you, after you find Phil?"

"What's that?"

"Ask him why."

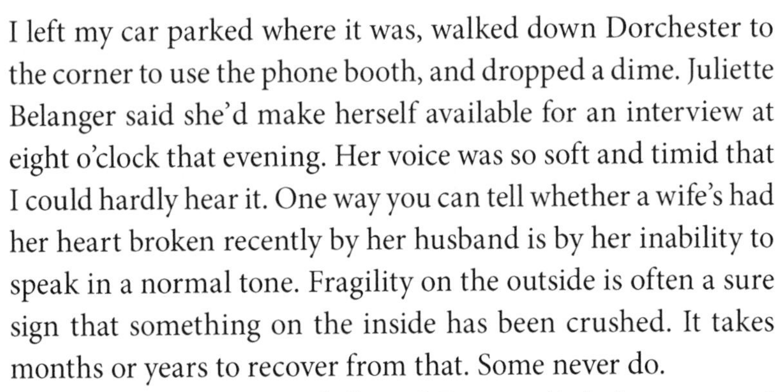

I left my car parked where it was, walked down Dorchester to the corner to use the phone booth, and dropped a dime. Juliette Belanger said she'd make herself available for an interview at eight o'clock that evening. Her voice was so soft and timid that I could hardly hear it. One way you can tell whether a wife's had her heart broken recently by her husband is by her inability to speak in a normal tone. Fragility on the outside is often a sure sign that something on the inside has been crushed. It takes months or years to recover from that. Some never do.

I had some time to kill, and I was a little hungry, so I continued down Dorchester and walked into Slitkin's and Slotkin's for a bite to eat. Most of the lunch crowd was gone, but there were still a fair number of people seated. As I walked in, I noticed the bald head and the cigar smoke of a man sitting in a booth with his back to me. That could only be one person.

"You old reprobate," I said as I slid into the seat opposite him. "You still prowling the streets, leering at young women? I thought you'd be retired by now."

"My soul was irrevocably damned long ago, Eddie. It's nice to be able to do as I damn well please and not have to worry about hellfire. I'm going to hell anyway." He puffed a few times on his cigar and then said, "Prowling the streets, leering at young women—if this is how you talk to me to my face, what do you say about me behind my back?"

"Get up and walk ahead of me, and you'll see."

Jake Asher had been a crime reporter for the *Gazette* for nearly thirty years and had an encyclopedic knowledge of the seedy side of life in Montreal. He'd mingled with every known hood in the city, but he maintained that it hadn't rubbed off on him. I had my doubts. He was also buddy-buddy with the police, which put him in a unique position. He was probably the only guy in Montreal comfortable enough to have breakfast with the chief of police and dinner with the local Mafia don.

I ordered a hamburger and french-fried potatoes, and we caught up a bit while I ate. I hadn't seen much of him since we'd worked on the tram murder case last fall. He'd been my main source of information since I'd gotten my private license. He was short, bald, and fast on his feet when he had to be. As a person, I found him fascinating. He was the only chunk of real estate left in this world unexplored by the National Geographic Society. He wanted to know what I was working on now, and I told him in general terms, because I had only the basic facts at that point, and I hadn't come to any conclusions yet.

"You get a bang out of taking cases like that, hmm?"

"They pay the bills. Besides, this case comes with a hefty bonus." I paused for a moment and then said, "Let me ask you a question."

"How did I know this was coming?" He grabbed his cigar that he had placed in an ashtray, knocked the ash from the end, and relit it. "Okay, shoot."

"I don't want any lectures, Jake, just some of your thoughts."

"I don't have any to hand out. Lectures, that is. My thoughts are a dime a dozen, but maybe you can't afford that."

"If you were a partner in an investment firm and had a beautiful wife and a house in Outremont and embezzled one hundred thousand dollars, where would you go?"

"Probably above Timmins about twenty miles to do a little hunting and fishing in the wilds of Ontario."

"No, seriously. Where would you go?"

"Actually, I would've arranged a nice little nest ahead of time for myself right here in Montreal. Stock up on things I'd need. I'd stay there—say, four to six months—until the heat was off me a little. You know, keep my head down out of the line of fire. Make 'em think I'd made for Vegas or Mexico. Then I'd pay off the appropriate people at the port and take one of those big cargo ships to Europe. The trip wouldn't be like a luxury liner, but I'd have little choice. That kind of dough would go a long way in France. I'd change my appearance a little—maybe grow a beard and wear different clothes. Stay under the radar. Keep outta trouble. You could lead a good life there." He angled his head a little at me and then said, "Finding some schmuck who doesn't want to be found, even here in Montreal, can be a little tricky, Eddie, especially if money isn't an issue."

"I once had a case of a magician who made a girl disappear and then couldn't find her. It took me two hours."

"Oh, I forgot you're a genius—a real Shylock Holmes. If you exclude the possibility that his wife or his partner was involved in this gambit, then what you have is a puzzlement, Eddie—a gen-u-wine, honest-to-goodness puzzlement."

"That's worth at least fifty cents."

"It'll take more than that to get me drunk. What do you want from me?" he asked, hunching his shoulders. "I'm just a casual observer of life."

We ordered a couple of Molsons and then chatted about nothing in particular until he announced he needed to get to work. He didn't want to miss out on a mugging, knifing, drug deal gone wrong, or wife shooting her husband because he manhandled her once too often.

"By the way, where'd you find that girl who disappeared?" he asked, putting on his hat and adjusting his tie.

"In the closet of the dressing room in the same building where they performed—drunk and asleep."

"Aha, I told you!" He pointed a chubby finger at me. "Stick close to home."

CHAPTER 4

Her house wasn't far from my Mile End office. I drove south on rue Saint-Urbain, turned right onto avenue du Mont-Royal, continued on for another three blocks, and then made another right onto chemin de la Côte-Sainte-Catherine, looking for 550 in the Outremont neighborhood. The houses were old and stately, and the people who lived in them were old and stately—some of the wealthiest of Montreal's French tycoons. As they died off, they were replaced by the same breed, only younger and some with families. This was the new strain, the driving force behind the capitalist engine, the entrepreneurs who took risks in order to bring innovation to industries and the economy through creative destruction. Wealth begot wealth. Someone had to keep those old houses going.

On the rare occasions when I found myself in Outremont, I was usually there to interview someone for a case. The curse of the wealthy was that they seemed to get their knickers in a twist as much as the rest of us, maybe more so. I guess that made them like everyone else. I'd untwisted a few of them in the past, but as a general rule, I got in and out of the area quickly. If you wandered around the neighborhood in the wrong kind of clothes, you'd be taken for a vagrant. There'd be eyes peeking through drapes and calls made to the police, sure enough. The reality was this: you could find as much numbness and despair there as you could find in the darkness of the squalid, narrow streets and alleyways of skid row. The only difference was that there, you had to sift through window dressings before it became apparent.

I found the house at a corner, resting lugubriously on a small mound, set back far enough from the sidewalk to have elbow room from the rest of humanity. Two old maples with complicated root systems were on the property, their leafy crowns overhanging the roof. The house was stone, two shades. It had two stories and a white wooden wraparound porch that had probably been built a few decades after the house was constructed. A small green oxidized-copper dome topped a minaret-style tower in the back, thrusting out of one corner. I guessed the house was about three thousand square feet, which meant it had at least five bedrooms and three bathrooms.

That was one hell of a house for two people.

I walked up the long path to the front door. The porch light was on. I looked at my watch. It was five minutes till eight. I posited a tentative idea: Belanger had bought the house to keep up with the lifestyle of his job. Time had ticked away. He'd found making the payments difficult. He'd schemed. A clever idea had popped into his head: he'd embezzle the money from the firm and then replace it over time before anyone became wise. The portfolios Belanger managed were long-term investments, after all. Then the earthquake had come forth—someone had decided to liquidate his assets. *Not in good, old Philippe's plan.* The earth had opened up wide, and he'd disappeared. *We shall see.*

I knocked on the door. Someone pulled it back at once.

"Mr. Wade," she said, "I'm Juliette Belanger. Please come in."

Bradford Wilcox had said she was beautiful. He'd said she was like a Greek goddess. He'd said I'd see for myself. He'd been miserably wrong. I saw for myself. A Greek goddess would have paled in comparison. Her beauty could have launched the ships of the Greek navy and several others as well.

She led me down a long hallway with a narrow Persian runner in the middle of it. The paintings along the walls all had heavy gilt frames that probably cost more than the paintings themselves, although I couldn't say that for certain. She opened a pair of doors with stained glass in shades of rose and green, and I trailed behind her into a room that rounded at the far end—part of the tower I'd seen outside, I guessed. I sat down on a white leather couch whose shape followed the contour of the curved wall behind it, undoubtedly made especially for that. I was in a sitting room in Versailles, waiting to interview the queen consort herself. People who bought houses they couldn't afford usually furnished them on the cheap, often times buying used and having relatives chip in. I saw none of that there. The chairs and tables looked like the nineteenth-century French provincial furniture I'd seen in other houses of the wealthy in Outremont. The pieces all had cabriole legs with scalloped carvings that terminated into ball-and-claw feet. No, there was nothing cheap there.

"Can I offer you a drink? I was going to have one myself. Whiskey?"

My mouth had been dry, but now I was on the verge of drooling. I nodded a polite yes.

She turned around and went opposite the fireplace to a Burmese teak cabinet set against a wall. It was nicely oiled, which made the tight grain stand out. I watched her from behind. She was one gorgeous blonde. She was wearing a white blouse and dark blue pants that flared out at the bottom. Her round behind was perfect. She had on an expensive necklace with matching earrings but no makeup. Her hair fell down to her shoulders. She looked over one shoulder at me.

"Ice?"

"No, plain is fine. Thanks." I raised my eyebrows and smiled with my lips closed.

She was so dangerously thin that she would've knocked a fellow off his barstool with one glance. But everything about her was understated. Nothing about her was coarse or flashy, as you might expect to find with some women of wealth. She had the appearance and mannerisms of a woman who would have felt comfortable at cocktail parties at the best mansions in Montreal as well as in a third-grade classroom, teaching the little tykes a basic lesson in arithmetic. She had the utmost class and style. If Philippe Belanger had left her for another woman, he was a foolish man.

Some men do that, of course. They get bored with their trophy wives because these women no longer retain the mystery necessary to sustain the fantasies of their reckless husbands. One woman doesn't seem to be enough for them. They crave the excitement of the forbidden. These husbands are driven by a complex set of DNA that lures them with a seductive genetic dominance they cannot or will not control. They begin to see members of the opposite sex in terms of biology, as their means of survival and immortality. The replacements are rarely as beautiful as the wives they cheat on and finally leave—the trashier, the better. It's their unconscious attempt to punish themselves for the misery they hand out. Some men want to destroy for the sake of destroying, or they destroy because their wives are fragile and beautiful, and they can't contend with that any longer. What they don't understand is that they can't destroy their wives; they can only change them, and it's usually into humiliated and pitiful relics of their former selves. Their hunt begins and won't stop until the first shovel of earth is tossed onto them six feet under, leaving behind violence and heartache. The male of the species is a dreadful creature.

She handed me the drink and sat down on a chair to the side of the couch, facing me. She knew why I was there. I sipped the whiskey and waited for her to speak. She glanced several times up at me and down at her drink, never focusing her eyes completely on me. Her expression was a mixture of sadness and pity—maybe for herself. When she realized I wasn't going to say anything until she did, she spoke.

"I don't know whether there's anything I can tell you that I haven't already told the Crown attorney's office, Mr. Wade." She had a trace of a French accent. Perhaps she was old French Canadian stock—*pure laine.* Beneath her beauty were the ravages of a terrible storm.

Tread lightly, Eddie. Tread lightly.

"Please call me Eddie," I said. If you establish a casual, informal conversation and forgo the harsh, starched-collar interview, the person usually says a lot more than what he or she intends. Little things can slip out before the person is even aware of it.

"If you call me Juliette."

"Fair enough," I said. "I was just brought into this case, Juliette, and I haven't had the chance to read your interview at city hall. But I did talk to Michael Spence and got a pretty good idea of what happened. What I'd like from you is more personal information about your husband. What kind of person was he?" I took out my notebook and a pen.

Her eyes were blue and intense, yet they had a sadness and depth behind them that suggested they had been hollowed out by pain that faded deep into a nightmare. Her long fingers combed away a few strands of hair from her forehead, as if they had gotten in the way of her thoughts. "I guess I'm the wrong one to answer that question, Eddie. I thought I knew Phil better than anyone in the world. I guess I didn't know him at all. It's funny how you can live with someone for years …" Her voice trailed off. It was soft, vulnerable, and innocent. It made my stomach ache from the pain she must have been feeling.

It's one of the ripe, ancient questions of humanity: How deeply can you really dive into the heart or soul of another human being? What depth can you go to before your lungs begin to burst and you have to race to the surface for air? Answer me that, and you'll get to live the rest of your dandy life in peace and contentment.

"I can tell you what kind of man I thought he was," she said. "He was a loving husband who showed me the kind of attention a man should show his wife. He was compassionate. He liked people and showed them respect, no matter who they were or where they came from. He'd help people he barely knew. I'm not really a churchgoer, Eddie. Maybe I should be, but I'm not. But Phil insisted we go to Mass every week. It's hard for me to think of him as something other than that, but I guess he was."

"The best of us get fooled sometimes in our lives, Juliette. No need to feel ashamed about that. Which church did you go to? Can you give me the name of the priest?"

"Yes, we attended the Church of the Madonna della Difesa. Phil didn't see too much of the parish priest, but he'd made friends with another priest. I forget what his title is, but his name is Father Joseph Segretti."

Joe Segretti—Little Joey—was a childhood friend of mine. We'd grown up together in the Italian section of the city not far from the Jean-Talon Market. We'd been close as kids, but we hadn't seen each other since his parents had sent him away to a preseminary school for boys who thought they had a vocation.

"Why did you go so far? There are others closer."

"Phil had become friends with Father Segretti. He met him somewhere; I can't remember just where. Then we started to go to his church. Phil felt comfortable with him, I guess. Sometimes he would even attend Mass during the week, if he could manage it. He donated quite a bit of money to Father Segretti to help him take care of the bums around the parish. Phil really did have a good heart."

"Tell me something about his routines—what he liked to do and maybe some of the places he'd go. What did he do outside of work?"

"Well, he liked dancing—we both did. We'd go out on a Friday or Saturday night, you know, so Phil could unwind from the week. Outside of that, he liked to play cards—you know, gamble. It was just a hobby, so to speak, but he did have a passion for it. Other than that, Phil was dedicated to his work. Most nights, you'd find him in his office here at home or at work, going over accounts, making sure he was doing the best for his clients." She put her head down and looked as if she were in the first stage of spilling her emotions onto the floor. She shook her head slightly and then regained control. Pride and nostalgia struggled in her expression.

"Where'd he gamble?"

"I don't know. I never went with him. That was part of his life that I wasn't involved with. I'm not particularly interested in it myself. I didn't really approve of it, but I kept it to myself. It was a harmless pastime. I don't think he ever won or lost much. He was just sort of excited by it. He started to gamble a few years ago. He told me he liked the risk involved in it. It never involved our personal finances, so I said, 'What's the harm?' and left it at that."

"If he didn't gamble with your personal finances, what'd he use?"

She was surprised by that question and briefly confused by it.

"I assumed he used pocket change. He took care of all our bills—our financial obligations. I suppose I should look into that, huh?"

"I think that would be wise. Had you noticed any change in his behavior in the last few months? Maybe in his attitude about things in general? Did he seem depressed?"

"Well, he had been moody lately, preoccupied, as if he had something on his mind all the time. He told me that work had been very busy. He did spend a lot of nights at the office, the main office downtown. I guess being a partner means you've got to put in the time to have a successful business. And then there was this thing about our trip."

"What's that?"

"You see, Phil doesn't like to travel. He hates being away. He doesn't even have a passport. That's been the only point of contention in our marriage. I've always wanted to return to Paris. I went there during the summer before my last year in college many years ago. I had really forgotten about it until recently, when the urge to go returned. He promised me that we'd go soon. I guess to make me feel better, he planned a short vacation for us in New York. Everything was set, the hotel was booked, and we made arrangements for someone to stay here and watch things. Just before we were to leave, he said that something had come up at work, and he couldn't go just now. But he insisted that I go by myself. I didn't want to, but he was adamant about it. I was gone for two weeks, and when I returned, I found out about all of this."

To me, this information—along with the nights she said he worked at the office—added up to an affair or at least the time he needed to cook the books.

"Juliette, do you have any idea where your husband could be?"

"I have no idea. I just don't know. His parents are deceased, and he doesn't have any relatives as far as I know."

I asked her for a recent picture of him. She got up, walked a few steps to the fireplace, and took a framed photo off the mantel. She stared at it for a moment and then pulled the picture from the frame and gave it to me. There was a good angle of his face from the right distance, with Juliet beside him.

"Eddie, is there any chance he's innocent? Any chance that this is one big mistake?"

"I don't know. I guess we'll just have to find him first to answer that."

I gave her my card and told her I'd be contacting her again, and in the meantime, she should call me if she thought of anything else that could help locate her husband. I also told her to call me immediately should he contact her.

"I'll let myself out," I said to her. I got up and started walking toward the stained-glass doors. Before I got more than a few feet away, she called to me.

"Eddie, can I ask you a question?"

I turned around. "Certainly."

In a dreamy, faraway voice, she asked, "What do you think about in the middle of the night, when you're sitting alone with the lights turned off, and all you can hear is the wind rustling the leaves outside?"

"I don't understand the question," I said, perplexed.

"Oh, it doesn't matter. Good night, Eddie."

We'll just have to find him first. Those words had come off my lips pretty easily, but I had to leave her with some hope. I'd made it sound almost effortless. I didn't want to tell her what it was going to be like to try to track him down with nowhere definite to start.

The case had begun to take shape, and the details started to spin around inside my head faster than a spider at a weaving convention, as cases always did in the beginning. I knew I was going to get little sleep until it was resolved one way or another, so I drove back into town. I parked in a lot along Sainte-Catherine, crossed the street, and walked into the Sans Souci.

After my eyes adjusted to the lighting, I saw Henri Salvador onstage just as he finished playing the last chords on his guitar. The cabaret was jammed that night, and I couldn't find an empty table. There weren't any stools at the bar either, but I noticed a space at the end of it, so I zigzagged around the tables, avoiding knocking into people holding drinks, and made my way to the bar. I wedged myself between the wall and a broad who was sitting with her back to me, chatting with someone. Her hands were flailing as she talked, and I had to duck several times for my own safety. Henri had apparently seen me come in, because I noticed him walking toward me, stopping at every table en route to shake hands. As he lived in Paris, he wasn't in town often. The Sans Souci usually placed ads in the city papers whenever he was there, but this time, they hadn't. He and the main attraction were scheduled to play a gig in New York, and this was just an unannounced one-night stopover in Montreal. He had dropped me a note about it last month.

Henri had honed his skills well, hobnobbing with musicians like Django Reinhardt in the smoke-filled cabarets in Montmartre and Pigalle. When the Nazi tanks had rolled up the Champs-Élysées, he'd fled to Montreal. There, he'd become quite a sensation as a regular in the French nightclubs throughout the city. On his nights off, he could be found at the Forum, either taking in a Canadiens' game or watching a boxing match. That was where we'd met. He liked boxing, and I liked French jazz, so we'd become friends. We'd seen a lot of each other until I joined the army and left for Europe. At the end of the war, he'd returned to Paris. Now he was a big shot. I had heard he was even in a few movies.

We ordered drinks and talked for a half hour, catching up. We hadn't seen each other in several years. At one point during the conversation, my eyes wandered over his shoulder and landed on a guy sitting near the stage. He had red hair and a bandage over his nose. It was Carrottop, the guy with whom I'd had a run-in at the Flamingo the night before. He was sitting at a table with a short, husky bald guy I had never seen before.

The lights flickered briefly, which meant the entertainment would resume momentarily. Henri and I hugged each other, and then he made his way to the stage. I looked over at Carrottop again and saw that he was glaring at me. The guy had a short fuse, and I didn't want to second-guess him. Besides, more than likely, he was packing a rod. The last thing I wanted was a commotion there, and I sensed this guy was capable of starting one. I threw back my drink and aimed myself at the door.

Henri played a few introductory chords on his guitar, and the main attraction came onstage. With the door half open, I looked back over my shoulder just as Madame Piaf started singing her first notes.

CHAPTER 5

Who was Philippe Belanger? Was he a husband; lover; partner in an investment firm; small-time philanthropist; and all-around solid, good guy? Or was he a conniver, embezzler, and duplicitous fugitive on the run? The evidence suggested he was all those things.

Wilcox had asked me what made a person go sour. I had given him a simple response; however, the real answer was complicated. It required a journey into the deep recesses of the human soul. Along the way, you had to stumble and fall many times over obstacles. Once you reached the cavern, you might forever remain floundering outside the entrance, unable to penetrate it, unable to ever fully know what was inside.

Maybe Belanger was sour from the beginning. Maybe he sought righteous behavior to shroud his darkness. Maybe the virtuous life was his lifelong quest, though he knew that eventually, he would stumble and end up the person he was at the beginning—a destiny laid out for him by some inevitable, indifferent swirling mass of molecules.

The toughest part about trying to find a person who was on the lam was knowing where to start. You could go to the people who knew him the best; some might know where he was or even be helping him elude the authorities. But if he was smart, he wouldn't be within a five-mile radius of them, because that was where the police would go first. Belanger didn't have a passport, so it was unlikely he would have gone to Europe.

That just left all of North America.

Belanger was hot. There was an APB out on him, so the local and provincial police as well as the RCMP would be on constant alert. The border guards would be especially watchful. Because of the amount of money he had stolen, Belanger would be a high priority. Jake Asher had been on the mark. The best thing for him to do was lie low. That was what Jake would have done, and that was what I would have done. Of the 2.728 billion people in the world, only 1,367,000 of them were right there in Montreal. That narrowed it down.

The trouble with someone who spent a great deal of time at his job, as Belanger had, was that he didn't leave many footprints around town. He could change his appearance, rent a bug-infested room somewhere in the city, and keep to himself. However, he'd have to eat eventually, and when he did, people would see him, whether he was disguised or not. Besides, staying alone—isolated from others—could get on a person's nerves pretty quickly. Sooner or later, he'd have to take a chance and go out, or he'd go stir-crazy.

I had to conclude that there were people in Montreal—strangers—who had already seen Philippe Belanger since he had been on the run. Perhaps someone knew exactly where he was staying but hadn't connected him to the person the authorities were after. The idea of standing at the corner of Sainte-Catherine and Stanley with an armful of his pictures and handing them out to passersby had occurred to me. Other than that, I could see no viable way of getting to those people.

His picture was plastered in the newspapers, both English and French. If Belanger were hiding out in the city, he was probably smart enough to disguise his appearance. *Where do I start looking for a guy who left no footprints and may or may not look like his picture?* I had no idea where to begin.

The phone rang on my desk, and I picked it up. It was Michael Spence, Belanger's partner. He sounded excited.

"I saw him last night around nine. I tried to call you but got no answer."

"You saw Belanger?"

"That's right. I know it was him."

"Where?"

"I worked late, going through the files, calling clients, and reassuring them that their investments were fine. I decided to walk partway home—you know, just to unwind and relax a bit. Then I felt hungry and went up Drummond near Sherbrooke to the 400 Club for a steak. I walked in and saw him sitting at the bar. His hair was short—sort of a crew cut, I guess—and he was wearing thick black horn-rimmed glasses. He looked a lot different, but I know it was Phil Belanger. No mistake about it."

"Did he see you?"

"No, I don't think so. I ducked around a column and looked again just to make sure it was him. The lights were low, but I could still make him out—the way he sat, his mannerisms. It was Phil all right. No mistake about it."

"What'd you do then?"

"I left and used the pay phone outside to call you. But as I said, there was no answer."

"Okay, that's good. It's the only lead I have right now. Don't go there again for any reason. If he was Belanger and he sees you, you'll only scare him off. I'll go there tonight and see what I can find. He doesn't know me."

I hung up the receiver. I jotted a note to myself. One of the things I planned to do but never got around to was subscribing to an answering service. I could afford to hire a secretary now, but an answering service seemed less complicated. I leaned back in my chair and put a match to my pipe. I watched the smoke rise to meet the streams of sunlight slanting in through the slats of the Venetian blinds. I then shifted my eyes and scanned my office. It could have been a murky stage setting in one of those private-eye movies from the '40s. I wondered which Hollywood star would play me. I imagined him, featureless, sitting at my desk, waiting for a lead to come in, and throwing back a whiskey or two.

Most of the time, I had to scratch and claw for days and weeks for a good lead on a case, but sometimes one just fell into my lap.

At eight o'clock that night, I drove over to the 400 Club and parked in the side lot. If this was where Belanger decided to have his meals and drinks, maybe he was staying at a hotel or rooming house nearby. I walked into the club and waited at the door for my eyes to adjust to the lighting. The bar was off to the left, with tables arranged on the right. They had linen tablecloths on them, so I knew the menu was probably pricy, but Belanger wouldn't have to worry much about that.

The lighting was low. I walked to the bar, pulled out a stool, and sat down. There was one guy nursing a drink six stools to my left, and only four or five tables had people sitting at them. I supposed at that time of night, business was getting a little slow.

"Black Horse ale," I told the barman. He brought a bottle and glass and set them down on a couple of cardboard coasters.

He had the shoulders and arms of a longshoreman and the face of a professional gambler, but he seemed friendly enough.

"I'm looking for a guy who was in last night," I said. I pulled out Belanger's picture and slid it to him. "He looks something like this, but his hair is cut short, and he wears thick black glasses. His name is Philippe Belanger."

He picked the photo up and gave it a cursory glance. "Could've been here, bud, but you couldn't prove it by me. Wasn't working last night." He held the picture out again and looked longer this time, rubbing his other hand across his sandpapered chin. "But any other time, never saw the face, and the name don't ring a bell." He slid the photograph back to me.

"Who was on last night?" I asked, pouring some of the beer into my glass.

"My brother-in-law, but he took off for Toronto this morning for a little R and R. Can you believe it? Toronto, when New York's closer by train? From the way you talk, sounds like you've got a beef with this guy, eh? You don't look like a bill collector."

"No, nothing like that. I owe him some money, and I'm just trying to track him down."

"Yeah, with a picture and all. Must be some kind of money. Maybe he owes you, eh?" He threw his hands up with the palms facing me. "None of my business, though."

"Yeah, maybe."

He went back to whatever he was doing. I took my glass and slid down the bar to a harmless-looking fellow sitting alone. A nicely dressed man in his fifties sat looking at his beer with his hat shoved back on his head. He must not have seen me, because he jumped a little when I sat down next to him.

"Hello. *Bonsoir,* if you please," he said, slurring the words. I guessed he'd been drinking for a while and had passed through several stages of drunkenness, settling into a kind of wide-eyed phony sobriety that I had become familiar with at one time or another in my own life.

"Hi. You come here often?"

"Whenebber I'm in town. I sell Autolite car parts to dealers across Quebec and Ontario. Are you a dealer?" The thought that he could make a sale made his brows jump.

"Not that kind. I'm looking for someone. I was wondering whether you know a Philippe Belanger, by any chance." I showed him the picture and explained how Belanger looked now.

His back straightened, as if that physical movement would assist his thinking. He squinted at the picture, holding it with both hands and extending his arms. After repeating the phrase "Let's see now" about half a dozen times, he finally gave it up.

"I once knew a Philippe Belanger in Quebec City; a Philippe Belanger in Drummondville; a Philippe Belanger in La Chine; a Philippe Belanger in Kingston; and, oh yes, a Philippe Belanger in Chateauguay. And one in Plattsburgh too. Does that count?" He had a remarkable memory for his level of intoxication.

"I suppose it counts for him."

"But none of them looked like this guy." As an afterthought, he said, "You sure you're not a dealer?"

I cut the conversation short, thanked him, and went back to my stool. I decided I would stay there for a few hours to see what happened. I didn't want the barman to get his knickers in a twist, so I ordered another ale and nursed both of them. I wanted to be clearheaded. If Belanger had truly been there last night, he might return eventually. If he didn't show up that night, I'd have to come back there tomorrow night, and every night after that, until he did. On the other hand, I knew I could be wasting my time. However, it was the only lead I had.

About a half hour later, a sleazy, skinny guy slid up to me on the next stool. He wore a dark purple suit, a yellow tie, and a black porkpie hat with the front turned up. He had pockmarks on his face as deep as the potholes on rue Dorchester. From his appearance, I could tell he lived by no code of the civilized world. He navigated through life by instinct only. He had *con man* written across his mug.

"You Eddie Wade?"

"What will I get if I am?"

"Information that you'll be happy to have." His voice was smooth and low, and he spoke as fast as a bookie taking bets from a long line of people five minutes before a race.

"The hell you say. And what might that be?" I looked at him closer. "Who are you?"

I knew a lot of hoodlums in Montreal, but I'd never seen this one before. Maybe he was from New York or Chicago. Hoods running from the law came north to Montreal to lie low. Or they went to St. Paul if they didn't want to cross the border. He was definitely not from Toronto. I could spot people from Toronto a mile away.

"Manny Trocadero. It's around the street that you're looking for someone."

"News travels fast."

"Before you can get your shoes on in the morning, my friend."

"What information?"

"You're looking for someone, and I know just where he's at."

"Someone's always looking for someone else in this town."

"Yeah, but nobody's going to find this Belanger fellow without me telling him."

That caught my attention. I looked at my ale for a moment and then back at him. He was playing the con artist's game. I just didn't know which one.

"You know where he is?" I drew the words out slowly, as if I didn't much care.

"Just as sure as I know I'm at the 400 Club, talking to Eddie Wade."

"Where is he?"

"Not so fast, my friend. Information like this comes with a price. Quid pro quo, baby. How bad do you want to find him?"

I took a swig of the ale, ran the back of my hand across my mouth, and angled my head at him. "Listen, we can throw jabs and bob and weave and duck until the cows come home, but it won't do you any good, and it won't do me any good. Just tell me how much you want, and we'll get this little show on the road."

"A C-note should do it fine."

"For that, you better keep talking. And it better be straight—no twists, *baby*."

"The guy you want checked into the rooming house I stay at. I recognized him from his picture in the paper. I buddied up to him. He was unfriendly at first, but I have a special talent for making friends pretty fast, especially with a guy trying to stay in the shadows."

A scam, I thought. Thousands of people had seen Belanger's picture in the paper by now. I wondered how this punk had gotten my name and found out I was looking for Belanger.

"Before I give you a hundred bucks, I need to see some proof."

"That's what I like about you, Eddie Wade. You look after yourself. Proof? Not a problem, my friend. Manny will give you proof."

"What's he look like?"

"Tall and athletic. Sandy-brown hair. Like in the papers. But now he's got one of those crew cuts and wears glasses. Big black ones. It's the same guy, though. I'm one for details. The face is the same. No doubt about that."

"Okay, I need proof you know where he's at before I fork over that much money."

"You stay right here." He patted me on the shoulder. "Don't you move an inch, and old Manny will return with undeniable proof. Just give me an hour."

He did a Fred Astaire to the door, the metal cleats on his heels leaving an echo behind.

I had a bad feeling in my gut about this Trocadero character, but it wasn't going to cost me anything except the price of another drink to find out whether he had proof that he knew where Belanger was. He did know that Belanger had changed his appearance, so that was a good sign that he wasn't handing me a line. I asked the barman for another ale. He brought it over.

"You know that guy?" he asked me.

"No, just met him."

"A little piece of advice: stay away from him. He's bad news."

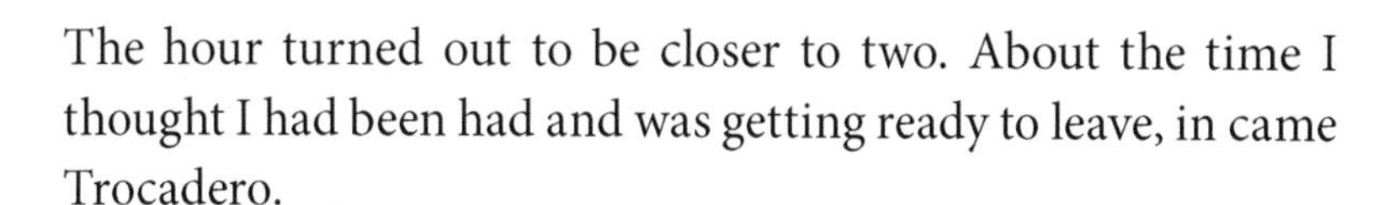

The hour turned out to be closer to two. About the time I thought I had been had and was getting ready to leave, in came Trocadero.

"You said one hour. It's been two. This better be good, or you're going to see what Eddie Wade looks like when he's angry."

"Why you got to be so nasty about this? Cool your jets, my friend. What Manny says, Manny delivers on."

He took a crumpled piece of paper from his pocket and gave it to me. I pressed it flat on the top of the bar and read it. It was a half-written note to Belanger's wife. Then I took one of the memos I had gotten from Michael Spence and compared the handwriting. I wasn't an expert, but I could tell they were probably written by the same man. The loops in some of the letters looked the same, as well as the angle of the writing. The *i*'s were dotted the same way. At any rate, the two pieces of writing were close enough for me to part with a hundred bucks.

"Okay, I'm convinced, Trocadero." I took my wallet out and gave him a hundred-dollar bill. He snatched it out of my hand and put it in his pocket. I took a gulp of ale and set the glass down. "Lead on, Macduff. Let's go." I started to get off the stool but stopped.

"Not so fast now, Eddie Wade. That's going to cost you a little more moola. It's the cost of doing business with Manny Trocadero. That little C-note was to get your attention and trust. A little taste of the appetizer before the main course. But Manny's got expenses, you know. Like I said, quid pro quo."

I reached over, grabbed his shirt in my fist, and pulled him closer to me, within a few inches of my face. The drinks were beginning to have an effect me.

"Expenses, huh?" I said in a stage whisper. "I do believe that Manny's getting a little too greedy now. You know what happens to people who get a little too greedy? They get flushed down the toilet. That's my quid pro quo." I let go of his shirt, and he ran a hand down the middle, flattening out the wrinkles. "You want to get flushed down the toilet, Manny Trocadero?"

"Calm down there, son. Calm down. Manny says he's got some proof, and he brings it. That's what you paid for. Manny says he can take you to Belanger, and he can take you. All you have to do is ask yourself how bad you want this guy. He stole a shit house full of moola. Ask your company if they think five hundred bucks is worth getting back the one hundred Gs he stole."

I stared at him with a scowl on my face. The dirty rat had me. There was little I could do short of breaking his arm or leg, but even that wouldn't guarantee he would take me to Belanger.

"How'd you know I was looking for him? How'd you know I was here?"

"I can't very well share all my little secrets, now, can I? I wouldn't have any left for myself."

That remark left the scowl firmly on my face.

"Can you still take me to him tomorrow?"

"Manny can certainly do that, Eddie Wade. The guy's hotter than an afternoon sun in the middle of August. He ain't goin' nowhere."

"I'll have to check whether they'll pay that much." I reached for my wallet and took out my card. "Call me tomorrow at ten."

"Morning or night?"

"Tomorrow morning. If they agree, you can take me there tomorrow night."

"Manny says it's been a pleasure, Mr. Wade." He reached into his pocket and then slapped two bits onto the bar. "Whyntcha do us both a favor and have a drink on me? Maybe it'll change that disposition of yours a little. Anyone ever tell you that you are inclined toward aggressive behavior?"

CHAPTER 6

I stopped at Schwartz's Deli on the Main for a smoked beef sandwich and then took Duluth to avenue du Parc, turned right at the east end of Mont Royal, and cut north. There was a strip of wide-open grass in that area, just as the mountain began its incline. When I was growing up, it looked different. There was an underbrush of shrubs, saplings, and low vines as you approached the taller trees of the urban forest. I used to hide among them, sometimes playing cowboys and Indians with my friends. It was a mystical little piece of the city, where we could let our imaginations run wild. The older kids used them as well to hook up with their girlfriends at night and to do unspeakable things there. Drunken adults did the same thing on their way home after the bars closed. I'm sure it had been going on since the Iroquoians greeted Cartier in Hochelaga. A few years ago, the morality squad got fed up with the whole thing and had the area cut down to grass, thereby turning all of us into a righteous citizenry.

I had phoned Bradford Wilcox at his office early that morning and gotten his stamp of approval for the $500 that Manny Trocadero demanded to take me to where Belanger was staying. He'd even reimburse my C-note. "Just add it to your expense account," he had told me, which had been music to my ears. Trocadero had phoned just before ten, and we'd made arrangements to meet back at the 400 Club at nine that night. I'd then phoned Michael Spence to let him know what was going on. I'd reminded him to stay away from the club. If he happened to show up, it could spoil the whole plan.

I turned left onto chemin de la Côte-Sainte-Catherine on my way to see Juliette Belanger. I felt sorry for her. She was hard done by and deserved to have an update on her husband's whereabouts. Her world had fallen out from under her. I was trying to set it right, but the best I could do was to give her a clear picture of where she was at. Her life would never be the same, regardless of how this situation turned out. Whether she decided to stay with him was her decision to make. At least she'd have some clear choices. With Belanger on the lam now, her life was in limbo.

I knocked on the door and waited. There was no answer. I could see through a window to the right of the door the soft light of a table lamp. I knocked several more times with the same result. I started to head back to my car, when I heard the door being pulled back slowly. I turned around, and she was standing there, shy and timid, her arms folded around her waist. Her eyes were red but without the tears. *Poor Juliette indeed.*

She showed me to the same sitting room as before. We both sat down on the couch. I explained what had happened last night. She held her hands on her lap and listened intently to me. She looked even more fragile than she had the last time I saw her.

"Who is this man? Can he be trusted?"

"His name is Manny Trocadero." I swallowed and then continued. "Juliette, I'll level with you. He's a con artist—a swindler. I didn't trust him then, and I don't trust him now. But he did have some undeniable evidence that what he told me about your husband was true."

"What was it, Eddie?"

"He gave me a letter that Phil had written to you. It looks as if he started to write to you and then changed his mind. I compared the handwriting with a memo that he wrote from work. I believe they're the same. Trocadero found it in his room, crumpled up."

She came to life again. She placed a hand on my shoulder. "Where is it? I want to see it."

I hesitated to give it to her. I'd brought it up only as a way to show her that I might be able to get my hands on her husband that night—that it really was him.

"I don't think it's a good idea, Juliette."

"No, I want to see it! I know his handwriting. I could tell you absolutely whether Phil wrote it."

I took the letter out of the inside pocket of my suit coat and gave it to her. She looked at it, then at me, and then back at the letter with an expression of uncertainty, as if anticipating that if she read it, it might self-immolate in her hands. After a few moments, she unfolded it and read it aloud:

> *My dearest Juliette,*
>
> *I know what you must be going through right now. I won't ask you for your forgiveness. I don't deserve it. The best thing you can do is to forget about me and the years we've spent together. Once I'm settled, I'll send you enough money to live on. I'm afraid*

you'll have to sell the house, though. Please don't look for me. You see, I've found som

She looked up at me. Her face was strangely neutral. I couldn't read it.

"I don't believe it," she said as she rose from the couch. "This is not the Phil that I know."

"Is that his handwriting?" I got up and stood beside her.

"Yes, the handwriting is his, but the words aren't."

"People do change, Juliette. It happens all the time, and it happens to the people we'd least expect."

"Not to Phil. Not to us."

I took her by the shoulders. She needed comfort and a clear dose of reality. "People come and go in our lives, Juliette. Some stay longer than others. The reasons they come are sometimes apparent. There's no easy answer why they leave. No one knows why the lights go out."

She drew herself into me and began to sob on my shoulder. They were hard, terrible, gut-wrenching sobs that jerked her whole body. I held her firmly, with one hand on the back of her head. After a few minutes, the sobs subsided. She pushed away from me and seemed embarrassed by what she had done.

"I'm sorry. I feel like a fool. Please forgive me."

"There's no need to feel that way, Juliette. You've been hurt by someone you love."

"I just can't believe this is happening. We had a good marriage. This just isn't like Phil. None of it—the stolen money, this letter. There's got to be something else."

I could see that the wheels were spinning. She wanted to do something—or go somewhere.

"What time are you going tonight, Eddie?" she asked.

"I'm meeting Trocadero at nine, and then he's taking me to Phil."

"I want to go with you. I want to see Phil tonight."

"Juliette, I don't think that's a good idea."

"Please take me with you! I need to see him tonight. I need to talk this out with him before the police have him. This has got to be one big mistake. There's got to be more to it. I can get him to tell me the truth."

I still didn't think it was a good idea, but at the very least, I didn't think it would harm anything. Perhaps it might even do her some good. By all accounts, Belanger wasn't a violent man. By facing him directly, she might once and for all accept him as the person she never knew. She'd had psychic damage done to her by someone she loved. That was sometimes worse than being slapped around. She was precariously balancing on a tightrope. I didn't want her to fall off. I felt I owed her something.

A storm was passing overhead. She wanted to face it. That was good. But I knew the courage she was mustering could suddenly, without warning, change into a terrible anxiety that would leave her paralyzed. She needed my help. Without it, she could just as easily close the shutters and lock the doors forever. I'd seen that with other women. She needed help to see that the storm was temporary; it would pass her by, and she would be able to open the shutters once again, peek outside, and see a hint of the sun and clear skies and feel the breeze against her face. Without help, she could rush into the basement to take cover and never surface again. Too many women lived subterranean lives.

I told her I'd pick her up at eight thirty that night.

Strangely enough, the 400 Club was once a gathering place for the blue bloods of Montreal society. The society crowd had since moved on, and now it was a place for the upper end of the commoners in the Montreal social stratification. History was repeating itself. You could change the country, the ethnic makeup of the group, and what the nobility did, but the process always remained the same. The aristocrats favored a particular style of clothing and then discarded it when they were bored with it. The social group just under them copied the style because it made them feel more blue-blooded. The clothes eventually ended up in the bargain basement at Morgan's for the peons. It was the same with nightclubs. In another ten years, the 400 Club could be a cheap dive on skid row.

Juliette and I sat at a table near the side wall, in clear view of the entrance. We listened to a guy dressed in a black tux play a piano and sing. A sleepy-eyed redhead wearing a tight-fitting lime-green silk dress leaned an arm on the upright, swooning over him, with a whiskey in one hand. His collar was open, and he was singing "Sweet Georgia Brown." I liked it better when Satchmo sang it. "Georgia claimed her; Georgia named her."

We had ordered drinks, and we sat nursing them.

"I wonder why Phil came here, Eddie. We never came here at all."

"Maybe he felt he wouldn't be noticed. Maybe it's close to where he's staying. It's hard to be cooped up in a room without going out. This place was probably just convenient for him. Nothing more."

"Eddie, I want to thank you for taking me with you. I don't know what will happen when he sees me. Maybe he won't even want to talk to me. Whatever happens, I want you to know that I appreciate what you've done. It was very sweet of you." She was going to say something more, but we both noticed the front door opening.

Trocadero was on time. He spotted us and then walked over to the table. He pulled out a chair and sat down.

"Well, well, well. Who's the gorgeous broad?" He leered at Juliette, making her feel uncomfortable.

"Cut the crap, Trocadero, and tell me your plan."

"Aren't we the sensitive one now? I see you still got your attitude, my friend. Luckily, I'm not the kind who's easily offended." He leaned across the table toward me. "Okay, I talked to him. I'm supposed to be getting him a passport with another picture—you know, short hair and black glasses—and another name on it. I told him I'd make arrangements for him to slip away in one of those cargo ships at the port. He's supposed to meet me in my room at midnight. I told him I'd take him to someone who could take his picture. After that, I'd fix up a passport for him and take him to the ship. Here's the address of the rooming house." He handed me a piece of paper. "Room 306. Key's above the door. I'll meet you there at eleven thirty. Don't do anything until I get there, or we'll scare him off. He's the jumpy type, and he's kind of paranoid right now, if you know what I mean." He looked at Juliette with a cruel smile, and I kicked his knee under the table. "Hey, what'd you do that for, big guy? You keeping her for yourself?"

"Shut up, Trocadero, and get out of here."

"Wait, now, Eddie boy. We have some unfinished financial business to take care of. Didn't we talk about my little old fee for services rendered?"

"You'll get your money in your room when we get there."

"Okay, okay, but I hope you'll come with a different attitude than what you're displaying before this lovely blonde dish sitting next to you. And I might add that you have a remarkable talent for spoiling a guy's fun."

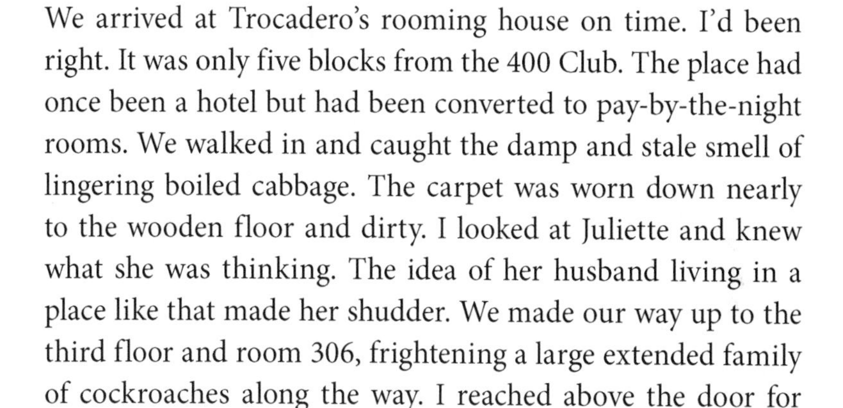

We arrived at Trocadero's rooming house on time. I'd been right. It was only five blocks from the 400 Club. The place had once been a hotel but had been converted to pay-by-the-night rooms. We walked in and caught the damp and stale smell of lingering boiled cabbage. The carpet was worn down nearly to the wooden floor and dirty. I looked at Juliette and knew what she was thinking. The idea of her husband living in a place like that made her shudder. We made our way up to the third floor and room 306, frightening a large extended family of cockroaches along the way. I reached above the door for the key and stuck it in the lock. We went in. Besides a wooden table with four chairs in the middle of the room and a bed up against a wall, it was empty. There wasn't anything that suggested Trocadero lived there. I didn't like it. We sat down at the table and waited. Juliette looked down at her lap, wrung her hands, and then looked up at me.

"Now that I'm here, I'm not sure what to say to him. If it's all true, if he really did embezzle the money and find another woman, I don't know what I could say. What can a person say to that?"

"At least he'll see for himself what it's done to you."

"If he's guilty, as the Crown attorney thinks he is, maybe he won't care."

I had no response to that. There was a long moment of silence.

"Are you going to hurt him? He's not a violent man," she said.

"That's not my intent. If he doesn't try to escape, there'll be no need for that."

"Do you have a—"

"A gun? Yes. I don't expect to need it."

There was more silence with more wringing of the hands.

Finally, she said, "We had plans for the future, you know. We were—oh, never mind. It doesn't make any difference now."

At twelve, there was no Trocadero and no Belanger. At that point, we were running out of conversation. I talked about a few past cases I had worked on. She talked about some of the charities she had worked on. At twelve thirty, there was still no sign of them. She was curious about my misshapen nose, so I gave her the lowdown on my brief boxing career. After that, we listened to a couple in the next room spitting venom at each other, until we heard a door slam shut. It became quiet again, except for the occasional whimpering of a female voice.

We waited until one o'clock before I decided for sure that we had been scammed. I couldn't understand it, though. Trocadero hadn't gotten his money. Maybe he had thought I'd give him the $500 at the club, and when I hadn't, he'd had to drop the con game. Still, he knew that Belanger had changed his appearance. He must have had some contact with him to know that. And then there was the letter. I couldn't figure it out.

I took Juliette home and then drove back to the 400 Club. I didn't know what I expected to find there, but I was too wound up to return to my office just yet. A block away from the club, I came across two police cars and a crowd standing near them. I drove by slowly, trying to catch what was happening. There were too many people blocking my view. I decided to move on because the cops didn't need anyone rubbernecking an accident or a crime scene or whatever it was. I started to speed up, when

I noticed Jack Macalister's mug above the heads of the crowd. I drove to the lot of the 400 Club, parked there, and walked back.

I had to push my way through the onlookers, who didn't appreciate being pushed. You have to be decisive, or you'll never get to where you're going. One fellow tipped the brim of my hat in the back with his finger, and it went forward, almost down to my eyes, nearly falling off my head. Bulldoze your way through a crowd, and that's what you get; it was his gesture in response to my rudeness. I set the hat straight on my head again and ignored him. He threw some unkind words in my direction, but I snubbed him by not responding. Finally, I made it to a clearing at an alley between two redbrick buildings and saw a body covered with a sheet. Macalister swung his head in my direction and noticed me.

"Eddie, long time no see."

"What happened?"

"Small-time petty criminal. Someone put a small hole in the back of his head and took off most of his face."

Jack Macalister and I had gone to high school together. Toward the end of the war, just as the draft was gearing up, we had gone south and joined the American army. We'd served in Europe in the same unit. I had saved his life once and had been doing penance ever since. He believed he had to repay me. He didn't, but I couldn't convince him of that. He'd joined the Montreal police force when he'd returned, and he was now Detective Sergeant Macalister.

I looked over at the body and said to him, "Do you mind?"

We walked over to it, and Jack leaned down, took hold of the two ends of the sheet above the head, and raised it, making sure it blocked the view of the people closest to us. I went around to the front and looked down. Jack was right. The victim's face was a mess—but not so much so that I couldn't recognize him and his yellow tie and purple suit. His porkpie hat lay on its crown a few feet from us. Jack covered him again, and we walked to one of the prowl cars near the front of the alley and leaned against it.

"You know him then?" I asked Jack, taking out my pipe and filling it.

"We all know him, Eddie. Manny Trocadero. Two-bit hood. This is the middle of his turf." He gestured with his hands. "He probably scammed the wrong person this time. We all knew Manny was going to end up like this sooner or later. I think he knew it too. He kept pressing his luck. I guess tonight his luck ran out." He looked at me for a moment and then said, "I saw the telltale sign of recognition on your face when I lifted the sheet. You knew the guy?"

"I knew the guy." I put a match to the pipe.

I also knew that the entire police force was aware of the embezzlement case involving the Spence and Belanger Investment firm and that there was an APB out on Philippe Belanger. I explained to Jack what had gone down that night with both Trocadero and Belanger and how I'd gotten tied up in the whole thing.

"As I said, Eddie, Trocadero scammed the wrong person one too many times."

"I thought when he hadn't shown up at the rooming house that it was just a big scam to get the money. But Trocadero did have a letter written by Belanger, and his wife verified that it was her husband's handwriting. And Trocadero knew that Belanger had gotten a crew cut and wore black glasses. Belanger's partner at the firm gave the same description after seeing him at the 400 Club. And when I told Trocadero that he'd get his money at the rooming house, he didn't kick up a storm about it. He seemed as if he'd expected to get it there." I paused for a moment. "Maybe Belanger sensed that Trocadero was double-crossing him."

"Well, at least we now know that Belanger's in town. I'll call Lieutenant Drummond right away and notify him. It seems that our mild-mannered investment broker is now an embezzler and a murderer."

"Yeah, it sure does." I looked toward the body, puffing away on my pipe and thinking about Juliette Belanger.

CHAPTER 7

The next morning, I phoned Bradford Wilcox from my office to update him on the case. He was the one writing my check, after all. He was giddy about not having to fork over the five hundred smackers but felt bad about Trocadero getting a slug in the back of the head. Or maybe he felt bad because I hadn't apprehended Belanger. I couldn't tell. Anyway, I wasn't particularly broken up over Trocadero. Granted, he hadn't deserved to die as he had. Some people did merit being on the receiving end of a revolver, but probably not him. Then again, it wasn't as if he was an upstanding citizen. He had been traveling down a dark road for a long time, doing the dance of death, whether he knew it or not. I wondered for a moment whether he'd have a funeral. Would his parents be there? Did he have a wife or children? Would they weep over his casket and say, "Daddy's never coming back"? Petty criminals were still part of the human race, and I believed they deserved something at their departure time. I also believed I owed them a modicum of gratitude because they helped keep me in business. There would always be others to take Trocadero's place and keep the wolf from my door.

After the chat with Wilcox, I drove downtown to talk to Michael Spence at his Dorchester Street office. I wanted to ask him a few more questions, and I also wanted to probe him further about his elusive partner.

"There's no doubt now that Belanger is still in Montreal," I said to him. "You saw him; so did Trocadero."

"Eddie, I can't believe he killed that man. That is so unlike Phil. I can't imagine him hurting anyone. I just can't believe it. He's not a violent man."

My patience was wearing thin with Spence. Belanger was his partner and friend. He was also an embezzler and possibly a murderer. That was a hard pill for Spence to swallow. Maybe he wasn't taking enough water with the pill, and it got stuck in his throat.

"You couldn't imagine him stealing a hundred grand either, but the evidence points in his direction. He had a motive to kill Trocadero. He knew who Belanger was. Belanger must have somehow found out that Trocadero was conning him, and he couldn't let him get away with it, and he couldn't let him go. He probably felt desperate and trapped and thought he had no choice."

"I suppose you're right, Eddie. But still ..." He lowered his head and shook it in disbelief.

"Now he's wanted for the big *M*. He's probably guessed that, so it's going to be harder to find him, because he's going to hunker down somewhere other than that rooming house. Trying to get out of Montreal is going to be difficult for him but not impossible. The border's too risky. He could still be considering the cargo ships docked in the port, but without contacts and with no passport, that could be dicey. But he does have money, so it's still a possibility that he could bribe his way out of the country. There are a lot of honest, hardworking citizens in the right places who wouldn't have a problem responding to cold, hard cash. The letter he started to write to Juliette and never finished seemed to suggest that he found someone else. If that's the case, she could be helping him. They could be planning to leave together. Husband and wife. Brother and sister. Cousins. A boss and secretary off on a business trip. New identities. All sorts of possibilities. It won't be easy finding him."

"I didn't want to bring this up because of Juliette, but I guess it doesn't matter anymore. I know he had been seeing someone else. At least I think he had." He looked at me sheepishly for my response.

I was surprised and peeved that he hadn't told me this before now. There's always some little piece of information they never tell you. I get sick of it. It costs money and time.

"Go on," I said, not too politely.

"At least a half dozen times, I heard him talking to someone on the phone in the office. Of course, I only heard one side of the conversations, but he was always—well, you know—more than friendly."

"How do you know it wasn't Juliette?"

"I could tell whenever Phil spoke to her. He would always use the same tone of voice. And I could tell because of the conversations themselves—the things he would talk to her about. But when he spoke to this particular person, he was like a little kid. You know, the puppy-love things that teenagers would say."

"Did you hear anything important?"

"Only one time. In one conversation, I overheard him making arrangements to meet whomever he was talking to. Wait—he did say her name once. Marguerite, I believe. Yes, that was it—Marguerite. He never said her last name. And he mentioned something about her hair as well. It was blonde."

Like his wife's, I thought.

"Did he say where he wanted to meet this person?"

"They were planning to meet at the Bellevue Casino. Something about dancing." He looked me straight in the eyes, as if he had a sudden attack of guilt. "I want to make it clear that I did not deliberately listen to his conversations. His office is next to mine, and voices carry. I'm sure he could hear me as well, whenever I talked to clients."

"What else haven't you told me?" I said, irritated.

"You have every right to be angry with me," he said gently. "No, there's nothing else."

I couldn't help feeling a little sorry for him. He had been trying to protect Belanger's wife. Any way you looked at this case, Michael Spence was going to take a hit.

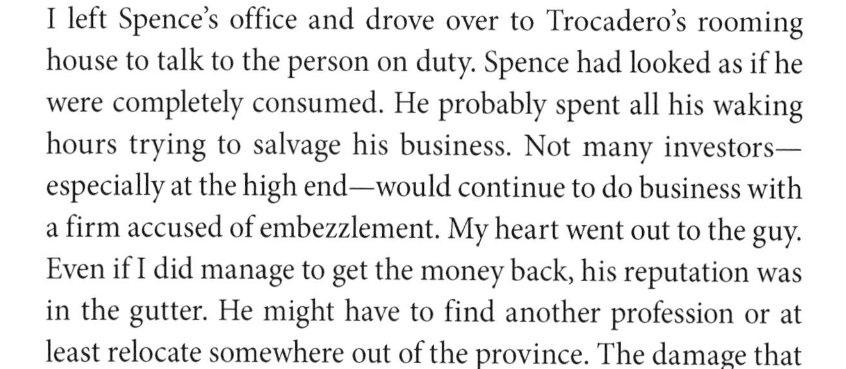

I left Spence's office and drove over to Trocadero's rooming house to talk to the person on duty. Spence had looked as if he were completely consumed. He probably spent all his waking hours trying to salvage his business. Not many investors—especially at the high end—would continue to do business with a firm accused of embezzlement. My heart went out to the guy. Even if I did manage to get the money back, his reputation was in the gutter. He might have to find another profession or at least relocate somewhere out of the province. The damage that Belanger had done was not likely to be undone.

I walked into the rooming house and got the same whiff of boiled cabbage. There was a short guy sitting behind the counter, drinking coffee and reading a newspaper. He was fat and bald on the top of his head, with gray hair running along the sides that made him look as if he had missed his appointment at the barber about two years ago. He sported a thin mustache and had drooping eyes. He wore a white shirt that had seen too much bleach and brown trousers. His stomach hung over his belt and hid it from view. His forearms were two pieces of hairy kiln-dried hickory. I placed him at about fifty years old. But he was friendly enough and chatty and happened to be the owner of that dump. That was the kind of person I liked to interview: friendly and chatty.

I showed him my license and took out Belanger's photo.

"That's his picture, but he's got a crew cut now and wears black glasses. I have reason to believe he's stayed here recently. The name's Philippe Belanger, but he could be using another name."

"Ah, yes indeedy, sir. He is a registered guest, but I have not seen him here." There seemed to be a tenth-of-a-second pause between words when he spoke, which made his speech slightly mechanical, and he pronounced the letter *a* as a hard vowel. Words did not readily flow out of his mouth; they escaped at intervals.

"Then you didn't do the registration yourself."

"No, sir, I did not do the registration myself. Not with him, that is. You see, this gorgeous blonde tomato came in and rented the room for him. No disrespect to the lady, but she was very beautiful. She did not take my breath away, on account of I am a married man, but she definitely would have. The lady paid in cash, and I gave her the key."

"When did she rent it?"

"She rented the room a little over a week ago." He picked up a log from his desk and looked at it. "On June 2, to be exact. She paid for a month, and I gave her a receipt."

"What room was it?"

He looked at the log again. "She rented room number 306."

I didn't have any more questions for him, so I thanked him and went out to my car to think. The blonde could have been the same person Spence had overheard Belanger talking to, Marguerite. I suspected she had hooked up with Belanger and was looking out for him. But room 306 was Trocadero's room, the one that Juliette and I had gone to the night before. Had Trocadero been somehow involved with Belanger and decided to double-cross him? Maybe he and Marguerite had teamed up.

Spence had said that Belanger and Marguerite had planned to meet at the Bellevue Casino. I decided to go there that night to snoop around. If I could find Marguerite, perhaps I could find Belanger as well.

CHAPTER 8

It was nearly eight o'clock when I pulled into the parking lot beside the Bellevue Casino on rue Ontario and Bleury. It had been four days since I'd taken on the case, and I had no substantial leads on Belanger's whereabouts. Small ones had been spinning in no particular direction. If Belanger had taken Marguerite there, maybe someone would remember them. I remembered that Juliette Belanger had told me that she and her husband enjoyed going out to dance. I had forgotten to ask where. It was a little piece of information I'd have to follow up on later.

Angel was a born dancer. She oozed rhythm—a true terpsichorean delight. She would dance anywhere to any music. I was clueless on the dance floor, but after being with her for five years, I could hold my own now. We'd practiced in my office to an all-night radio station for months before she worked up enough courage to be seen with me in public. With her long legs, she was magnificent to watch. The only thing that had prevented her from a brilliant career was her height; she was too short to go the professional route. She had known all the places in town to go, places where the really great dancers hung out. At the top of her list was the Bellevue Casino, the largest and best of the dance halls. That was where she'd drag me. I wouldn't say it was the swankiest in the city, but it sure was the liveliest. It drew the best entertainers from Paris, New York, and Chicago, and the price was right. As the owner, Harry Holmok, would always say, "Fifty cents to get in, and fifty cents for the beer."

I went there that night to poke around. If that was where the Belangers used go, maybe Philippe Belanger had retained some of his old habits. Maybe in his current state of isolation, he comes here, sits at a corner table, and remembers the life he gave up. It was a long shot but worth a try. At the very least, maybe I could get a lead on Marguerite.

As I walked to the entrance, I noticed a poster by the side of the door, advertising Abbe Lane and Xavier Cugat. They were sure to bring in a crowd that night. Their first show wasn't until nine thirty, so I had time to check the place out. Bix Belair and his band would be onstage playing waltzes and paso dobles until then, with hundreds of dancers on the floor. I paid my fifty cents and went up to the balcony to get a good look at the main floor. At capacity, it could hold seven hundred easily. I looked down at the stage, where the Glorious Bellevue Lovelies were dancing up a storm, with the most popular chorus girl in Montreal, Lola Sully, lighting up the stage with her beauty. *Ooh-la-la!* I saw the back of Bix's head in front of the girls as he conducted his band. The acoustics were top notch, so I could hear every note they played. I ordered a gin and tonic, and ten minutes later, the barman gave me a pink drink in a tall glass with a greenish-yellow mermaid swizzle stick in it and the words *Bellevue Casino* running up the side. As long as it had some alcohol in it, I didn't care. I paid him and took the drink on a little trip around the balcony, trying to look inconspicuous as I checked out the merry partygoers, especially the blonde ones.

The chorus girls had finished their routine below, and an intelligent-looking chimp called Zippy took the stage with a less-intelligent-looking man wearing a toupee that I could easily detect, even from that distance. The duo was one of the casino's less memorable acts, but people generally liked a little variety, including some animal acts. Their programming, however, was normally sophisticated and was designed by Nathalia and George Komorov, who had previously worked at the Cabaret Latin Quarter in New York on Broadway and the Folies Bergère in Paris. There was an interesting array of jolly characters upstairs, but I wasn't particularly interested in any of them, so I went back downstairs with my unidentifiable pink drink in hand.

As I rounded the stairs below, the crowd was pressing through the entrance as if rushing into Morgan's for a close-out sale, no doubt coming there to see the husband-wife team of Lane and Cugat and to dance to some Latin rhythms. There were tables to the left and right of me, with a huge dance floor in the middle. Zippy had finished his routine, and the people politely clapped. The band was taking a break, and I noticed Bix walking toward the bar off to the right. I followed the wall around to the bar, because there were fewer people there to shoulder my way through. Bix was talking to a few people sitting at tables along the way, so I waited at the bar with my drink. A guy wearing a white suit and a lime-green tie sat next to me and flashed me a smile. He looked down at my drink and then up again at me, caught my eye for a fraction of a second, and then looked away. I glanced over my shoulder and saw the main room filling up.

"Come here often?"

I swung my head to my right. He had inched closer to me. His smiled was fixed, his eyes swooning. He seemed like a nice guy, but he was driving down the wrong road and about to crash. I turned around on my stool to face him, put my hand on his shoulder, and pointed a finger at a guy who looked like the Canadian wrestling champion, who was standing by himself near a table.

"I do indeed. With him—always! Should I make the introductions?"

His smile faded, his lips twitched, and he said that would not be necessary. He excused himself. *Deed finished. No harm done. Plenty more to choose from.* I hoped he didn't get himself into a bind with the next one.

Bix came over and leaned into the bar. He was nearly as tall as I, with a headful of dark hair combed back, a pencil mustache, a bowtie, and a charming personality—a real Hollywood matinee idol. He was delighted to see me. He ordered a drink, grabbed my arm, and led me to one of the empty tables along the side.

"Cugat brings his own band, so I won't be up until he breaks."

We chatted for a while, bringing each other up to speed on our lives. Although he worked nights in the entertainment business, he was a devoted family man and doted on his wife and kids. He used to pilot a Cessna 180 with pontoons, and we had spent many hours together in the wilds of Quebec, pulling fish out of lakes. After a while, I walked the conversation over to what I had come there for.

"I'm looking for someone, Bix. You might have read about him in the papers recently." I pulled out the photo of Belanger and his wife. "Philippe Belanger. That's his wife." I pointed.

"He doesn't look familiar, but hey, a lot of people come here. But the lady—how can you disremember a woman like that?"

"How often is she here?"

"Maybe once a week. She's always with someone, of course, but when you see her, you don't exactly focus on who she's with. It could be him, but you couldn't prove it by me. By the way, this picture doesn't do her justice."

I looked over Bix's shoulder at a short, stocky bald guy sitting behind him about four tables down. He was puffing away on a cigar. Two tall, ugly brutes in dark suits sat on either side of him. I had seen him once before a few nights ago at the Sans Souci, sitting at a table with the redheaded guy whose nose I had tried to rearrange.

"Bix, turn around slowly, and look at the bald guy with the cigar."

He did so and then turned back to me.

"Carmine Galante. Comes in a lot for the entertainment. Never dances. He's a nice guy, but don't cross him. Rumor has it he's connected."

Abbe Lane was singing and doing a fancy movement that looked like the steps of the cha-cha, a new dance that was gaining popularity in the city.

"Well, I'll be. Eddie Wade himself. Hello, my little darling boy."

I looked around, and Colette was standing over us with a Speed Graphic in her hands. Her short, curly dishwater-blonde ringlets bounced when she talked. She was wearing what looked like a bathing suit with shiny sequins, probably something from the wardrobe room backstage. Her high heels made her long legs look even longer. She was the photo gal, taking and selling souvenir photographs of the customers. We'd dated a few times, but we'd never clicked as anything more than friends.

Bix got up, stood behind me, and then squatted a little with a hand on my shoulder.

"Click away, baby doll," he said.

She aimed the camera and clicked away. Bix excused himself to do a bit of socializing. As he was turning around to leave, I grabbed his arm and asked him if, by any chance, he knew a blonde by the name of Marguerite. He said that besides his seventy-three-year-old aunt who lived near Lac Sept-Îles, whose hair was now gray, he didn't.

I turned around to Colette and asked her to sit down for a minute.

"Can't talk too much, Eddie," she said, pulling out a chair. "With a crowd like this, I'll be busy right until closing time."

"Just a quick question, Colette. Do you keep copies of all the photos you take, even when someone buys one?"

She nodded, and then she grimaced. "God, you should see the boxes in the back. We keep the negatives and make one print. If a customer wants one, we develop another one for the file. Most of them end up wanting a few more—you know, especially the Yanks—for friends and relatives. They're all numbered and dated and then stored. Why you asking, Eddie?"

"I'm looking for someone who may have had his picture taken. If I come back another day, do you mind if I snoop a little?"

"Snoop all you want, but come back much earlier in the day, before we open the doors."

"You're a sweetheart, Colette."

"Yeah, I hear that line all the time. And you should hear the song-and-dance routines that follow it. Gotta go!" She got up.

"One more question." I pulled Belanger's picture out of my jacket.

"Sorry. Gotta go!"

She shuffled away on her heels, taking short steps, her cute little tush wiggling behind her. If the Belangers came there often, Colette likely would have taken their picture at one time or another. Maybe I'd find that Belanger had been photographed with a blonde other than his wife.

I looked over at Carmine Galante again but cut my gaze short. The two bozos on either side of him were staring at me at the same time. I finished my pink drink and left, with Abbe Lane's melodious voice singing something in Spanish in the background.

I took Bluery to Parc, which ran on the east side of Mont Royal, on my way to my office. The clouds covered the moon, so it was particularly dark. An unlit strip ran around Mont Royal Park, so it wasn't difficult to see the headlights of the car behind me. The lights were increasing in size and intensity to such an extent that I figured the driver was either a drunken dolt or driving a carload of his buddies and a girl they were showing off for in some kind of twisted fertility rite that the male of the species often succumbs to when behind the wheel of a three-thousand-pound weapon. Either way, the best thing you can do to avoid being a traffic statistic is to pull over and let them pass you. After that, you can drive a few blocks, stop at a phone booth, call the police, and tell them where to find the upturned car resting on its roof. Oh, and don't forget to send an ambulance.

I pulled the car close to the curb and slowed down to a crawl. The beams of light focused right and then straightened out again directly behind me. They were getting bigger and brighter. I gripped the wheel with both hands and held it tightly, bracing myself for the impact. The car pushed me forward violently. I looked into the rearview mirror and then braced myself again. My car lurched forward upon impact, and the rear end landed above the curb and twisted to the right diagonally.

The engine died. I looked over my left shoulder through the open window. The other car was pulling around me fast. I caught a glimpse of the person behind the wheel. I also caught a glimpse of an extended arm with a hand grasping a gun. I quickly swung myself to the right and stretched out on the seat, just as the window on the passenger side exploded over my head, spewing shards of glass over me.

CHAPTER 9

I walked back to my office in Mile End from Mont Royal. I felt as if I had just been run through an electric daiquiri maker, but I was in one piece. An empty taxi slowed down at some point when the driver saw me, but I waved him on. The weather was cool, and I needed the time to decompress and think.

I couldn't have identified the driver who had just run me off the road and taken a potshot at me even if he'd been standing in front of me naked and waving his hands in my face. I could identify, however, the pair of black-framed glasses he was wearing. My first thought was Philippe Belanger. So were my second and third thoughts. If that had been him in the car, then it was obvious he knew I was looking for him, and he was trying to dissuade me from further investigation. A gun usually has an uncanny knack to do just that. If he had killed Trocadero, it was unlikely he would stop short of that with me.

Once in my office, I stood under a cold shower for ten minutes. I dried myself off, opened a tin of cat food, fed Antoinette, and then turned on the radio. The station was in the middle of a *Gunsmoke* episode. I grimaced and then turned the dial until some music was playing. I poured two fingers of whiskey into a glass and took it over to the couch. I stretched out, leaning my back against the arm. I gulped down half the glass. My mouth and throat were on fire, but in no time, I dozed off with the soft melody of Oscar Peterson in my ears.

The next morning, Friday, June 11, I called a nearby garage. I had the driver swing around to the office to pick me up first. The Ford coupe was still in the sad position I'd left it in the night before. The driver towed the car to the shop as I tried to calculate the cost of restoring her. Every time you're ahead in the game and you get too cocky, someone throws a knuckleball and strikes you out.

The owner of the garage was a middle-aged man named Jacques. He looked the car over with a critical eye and concluded that it needed extensive rear-end work. He looked up at me from on his knees. "Accelerate in the wrong gear?" The doors wouldn't close properly, so he'd have to repair them as well. There might be some engine damage and loose wiring from the pounding it got, but he couldn't tell until he had a closer look under the hood. "With the work I have to do on the other cars here," he told me with an apologetic look and a crooked grin, "she's going to be out of commission for a couple of weeks."

I asked him if he had a loaner there that I could use in the meantime. He considered that.

We walked outside, and he pointed a greasy, crooked, bent finger at an old gray 1946 Packard. Car production had stopped during the war, and most auto manufacturers south of the border had converted their machinery to military production in 1942. There was no such animal as a '43, '44 or '45 model. After the war, it had taken them several years to catch up. A 1946 Packard was essentially the same thing as a 1942, with a few fancy knobs and buttons. I told Jacques I'd pay him a daily rate, but he wouldn't hear of it. He had kept my Ford in top condition since I'd bought it, and he looked at it as a surgeon looked down at an old friend on the operating table. I had some errands to do downtown, so we said good-bye. Jacques would phone me if he discovered anything he hadn't anticipated over the estimate he had given me.

I got into the gray beast, aimed it south on Saint-Urbain, and drove into town. After I finished doing some personal errands, I had a sandwich at Ben's Deli on Maisonneuve, trying to determine whether their smoked meat was as good as Schwartz's. After deliberating for the time it took me to eat it, I shrugged and concluded that it was too close to call. I wiped some yellow mustard off my tie, left a tip, went out to the Packard, and then drove to the Guarantee Company to update Bradford Wilcox on the case. He was concerned about what had happened the night before and wanted me to report it to the police. I told him it wasn't necessary. I couldn't identify the driver or the car; it had happened too fast. I didn't tell him that the driver wore black glasses or that I thought it was Belanger. Knowing Brad as I did, I believed he might have taken me off the case, fearing I was in danger. If the driver had been Belanger—well, the police were already looking for him. It was after six when I left. Brad was going to take the elevator down with me but then remembered something he had to do. Most people in the office building quit work at five, so I went down to the main floor alone in the elevator.

As I was walking through the lobby, I saw Ruth to the right of me, on her hands and knees, scrubbing the marble floor. She wore a drab brown uniform that pulled up slightly on her calves. Her boxy black shoes had scrapes on the leather, and the heels were worn down on the outside. I walked over to her. Her face was pink and sweaty.

"Isn't retirement around the corner?" I asked her, squatting down to close the distance between us.

She looked up, her face angled at me. "I'm afraid it's around the corner and down a half mile," she said, slightly out of breath. "Hi, Eddie. You must be on a case with Mr. Wilcox."

"I am. You look a little tired, Ruth. What say you take a break? I'll go next door and buy some sandwiches and coffee, and we'll have a nice little chat."

"You're a jewel, Eddie." She stopped to catch her breath. "I'd love to, but I had a doctor's appointment this afternoon and came in late. I'm behind as it is. Can you give me a rain check on that? It'll give us a chance to catch up on things."

"You bet, Ruth. You'll be seeing a lot of me for the next while."

Ruth had worked in the building since I started doing investigative work with the Guarantee Company. Over time, I'd discovered that she'd been working with the cleaning crew since 1934. She'd spent twenty years scrubbing the same floor, washing the same walls, and cleaning the same wash basins and toilet bowls. I felt ashamed and belittled because I didn't know her last name, where she lived, or whether she had a husband waiting for her when she finished work. She picked up candy wrappers that others threw; wiped up coffee spills from the floor, dropped from paper cups when the shoulders of people streaming back and forth rubbed against each other; and cleaned up cigarette butts that men in expensive suits ground into the marble. To most people in the office complex, she was invisible, doing invisible work at night, like thousands of others in the city. She kept it clean at night, while we busied ourselves by dirtying it in the day. We were easily identifiable; we were the ones with the looks of indifference on our faces.

I didn't like the way she looked. She was breathing too hard for what she was doing. There was too much exertion on that sixty-something-year-old body of hers. Age lines ran up both sides of her face and across her forehead. I wondered what the doctor had told her.

People would leave tips if the service was good at a restaurant or bar. It was expected. Why not leave one for a scrub lady in an office building? I started to reach for my wallet but stopped. Ruth did her work for a predetermined salary. She was a dignified woman of character. I did know enough about her to recognize that she would consider a tip an insult. I left my wallet where it was.

We said good-bye, and I walked toward the entrance, where the negro night guard stood. At six o'clock, he locked the doors, and he would let out anyone working late as he or she came. With keys in one hand, he tipped the visor of his hat to me with the other as I approached, and then he looked behind me over my shoulder with a shocked look on his face. "Oh my Lord," he said, his voice barely audible, touching his fingertips to his chin.

I turned around to see Ruth lying facedown on the floor. The guard and I ran over to her. I raised one wrist and checked her pulse. When I couldn't find it, I felt the side of her neck for the carotid artery. I felt none there either. I stood over her and grabbed her shoulders, and the guard and I turned her over onto her back. I put my ear to her nose and listened for any breathing. When I didn't hear it, I put one hand on top of the other on her chest and started compressions, as I had learned in the army. I told the guard to call an ambulance and tell them to be prepared for a heart attack victim. When he returned, I was leaning over her with my head just above her. I looked up at him.

"She's dead."

He again said, "Oh my Lord," and then he took his hat off and held it down at his side.

After the doctor and his partner strapped Ruth to the gurney and took her away, I stood there where she had died. Her rag and brush were still on the floor; the bucket of water was a foot away. *So this is how it ends*, I thought. I looked down at the marble tile. It was still wet near the rag. *No pain. No suffering. Just gone. The invisible become even more so. Turn off the lights; close the door on your way out.* Tomorrow the candy wrappers would be there, along with the cigarette butts ground into the floor. Someone else would pick them up.

I turned to leave, and one of the other cleaning women—a short negro lady—approached me.

"Are yous Mr. Wade?"

I said I was.

"I figured you was. Ruth had described you once. She always talked about the nice gentleman who stopped to talk to her. Yous got to tell her son, Mr. Wade. She has no one else."

"Do you know how I can reach him?"

"I don't ever knowed his name, on account of whenever she talks about him, she juz calls him 'my son.' We should go downstairs to her locker. Her purse and clothes is in it. Maybe there's something in it to help you."

I followed her across the lobby to a door off to the side. It had a rectangular black sign with white letters on it: Employees Only. She unlocked it, and we went downstairs. She took me down a long hallway with cement blocks on one side and rows of horizontal pipes on the other. It was steamy hot. We entered a doorless room with lockers along one side. She took me to Ruth's locker, which had a flimsy little lock on it.

"She muz has the key on her," she said.

I took a little tool from the inside pocket of my jacket, put one end in the lock, and fiddled with it for about ten seconds, until I got it open. Ruth's purse was there—a small, dainty type—along with a pair of shoes, a flower-patterned dress, and a lightweight blue spring jacket. I opened the purse. There were keys inside; I assumed they were house keys. Also, I found an envelope and a comb. There was nothing else. I looked at the envelope. It was a utility bill with her name and address printed on it in bold typewritten letters. It was addressed to Miss Ruth Adler.

"I's afraid wez has to go now. I has to gets back to work. But I want you to know that Ruthy was very dear to us here. She was one of us. Wez loved her dearly. I can't believe she gone."

"I'll try to track down her son. I'll take her things with me."

"Dats fine, Mr. Wade. Yous a good man. Juz like Ruthy says you was."

"What's your name, by the way?"

"Agnes."

"Your last name?"

"Montjoy. Agnes Montjoy. Dats my full name, if'n you puts a *T* in the middle."

"Thank you, Agnes T. Montjoy."

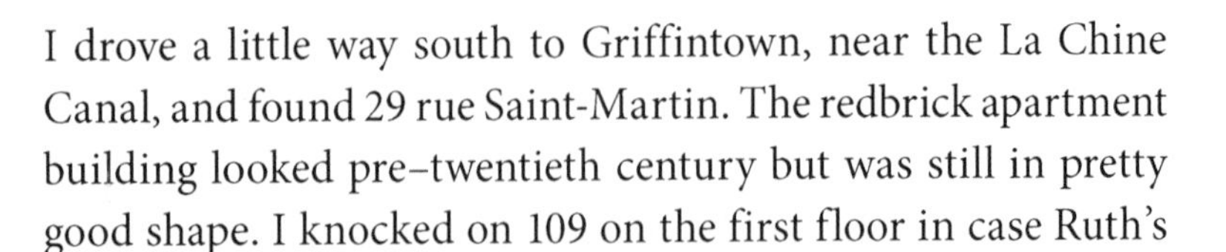

I drove a little way south to Griffintown, near the La Chine Canal, and found 29 rue Saint-Martin. The redbrick apartment building looked pre-twentieth century but was still in pretty good shape. I knocked on 109 on the first floor in case Ruth's son was there. I waited a reasonable amount of time before letting myself. I reached to the left and found the light switch. The room was small but tidy. There was a square table with a blue oilcloth over it by the window opposite me. I walked over to it and set her purse and clothes on it. A door to the right led into a small bedroom. To the left of the table was a narrow kitchen too small to eat in, with a stove and refrigerator. A wooden bureau stained dark brown, with nicks along the edges, was against one wall. A small couch and matching armchair of unidentifiable fabric, which looked well used but comfortable, took up most of the main room. Unless he slept on the couch, I didn't think Ruth's son lived there. Besides, nothing in the room suggested that a male lived there.

There was a quick knock on the door, and a man pushed it open. I hadn't closed it all the way.

"Who are you?" he asked accusingly. "What are you doing—casing the place?" His right hand grasped a baseball bat tightly. He let it hang down the length of his leg.

"The name's Eddie Wade. I'm looking for Ruth's son. Who are you?"

"I'm the concierge. I look after Ruth. What are you—a bill collector? You don't look like someone who'd be associating with her son. Besides, you should be asking Ruth where her son is instead of breaking into her apartment."

He stood sideways with his back to the door, waiting for me to leave. He was as big as I was and outweighed me by at least twenty pounds. His hand was still tight on the bat, the muscles in the forearm rippling.

"I didn't break in," I said. "I have her keys." I paused briefly to consider how I was going word what I was about to say next. If he looked after Ruth, that meant he was probably close to her. I decided to be direct with him. "Ruth died at work less than two hours ago. I have her belongings. I'm trying to track down her son to tell him."

The look of shock on his face was genuine.

"My God," he said. "Jesus, Mary, and Joseph. Ruthy's dead?" He leaned the bat against the wall by the door and stared at me, at the carpet, and then back at me.

"I'm sorry to bring you the news. You look as if you were fond of her."

"She's a sweet old lady, sort of like my second mother. How?"

"Heart attack. Do you know how I can find her son?"

The expression of sorrow on his face changed into disgust. "That no-good, dirty rat. The bum lived off poor Ruthy for years. He took money from her that she couldn't afford. I tried to tell her that she had to look after herself, that he was old enough to make it in the world by himself. All she said was that he was her only son, and she had only one life to live."

"Do you know where he lives?"

"I don't know, and I don't care. He didn't deserve such a wonderful mother like Ruthy. He can burn in hell for all I care."

"If you don't mind, I'll have a look around. Maybe I'll find something here."

"What should I do with all her things? The furniture, her clothes—I can't just get rid of these things, not Ruthy's. It would be blasphemous."

"I suppose her son will take care of things, but I have to find him first. What's his name?"

"Ezra Adler. Just ask around for the biggest asshole in town, and someone's bound to tell you."

He left it at that. I told him I'd let him know when I found Ruth's son so that the apartment would be taken care of. I went into the bedroom and looked under, above, and through everything but came up with nothing. When I returned to the living room, a young lady, maybe in her early to midtwenties, stood facing me, her arms wrapped around her waist.

"My father just told me the news. Can't say I'm too sorry." She threw her head back, trying to get the hair out of her face. When that didn't work, she tried it again, only harder. That did the trick. She wore blue jeans, a white blouse, and black sneakers. She might have been pretty but for the ugly look on her face.

"You should be more respectful of the dead. She's not even in the grave yet."

"I'm sorry, but I didn't like Ruth—the way she treated Ezra. Tried to keep him a little boy. She never let him grow up and become a man. No wonder he never did anything with his life, always being dependent on that old witch."

The expression on my face compelled her to look away from me.

"Do you know where I can find him? He needs to be told."

She swung her head around to me again but avoided eye contact. "I haven't seen him around here in months. He used to hang around the Montreal Pool Room." She seemed to be talking to my tie. "I had a real crush on him at one time. But I decided that he was never going to stop clinging to his mother's apron strings, so I broke it off. It's a shame, but a girl's got to watch out for herself and not get tangled up with the wrong guy. Know what I mean?" Her eyes flittered up at mine for a split second, as if she were expecting confirmation. Then she lowered the boom on me. "It's all his mother's fault."

Either she was dumb, or she was going to be a hard nut to crack. I decided it wasn't worth my time or effort.

"If you find him, tell him Tizzy says eh." She pointed to a photo on the wall. "That's a picture of him and Ruth. It's about five years old, but he looks about the same. Maybe a few pounds more."

After she left, I searched the kitchen and bathroom and came up with nothing. I walked back into the living room and took the photo off the wall. Ruth looked good. She was wearing a nice Sunday dress and a little hat. I tried to discern something about the character of her son from his expression but came up empty. His face looked vaguely familiar, but I couldn't place it. I put the photo back on the wall, tilting it slightly with one finger guiding the wire to the top of the nail, when I saw that something was taped to the back of the frame. I turned it over and discovered it was a bankbook. I took it off, placed the frame on the table, and sat down. I flipped through the pages to the back. It was a savings account with the Bank of Montreal. The balance startled me: $15,006.60. I paged through it again. At one point, the balance had been fifty dollars. Then there had been a series of withdrawals, leaving a balance of six dollars. Then there had been periodic deposits of $1,000 each. I couldn't imagine where Ruth would have gotten that much money. For good measure, I slipped the book into the inner pocket of my jacket.

Maybe there was more to Ruth Adler than met the eye.

CHAPTER 10

The next evening, I drove to boulevard Saint-Laurent. Montrealers call it the Main, the dividing line between the east and west sections of the city, between the two solitudes, the French and the English, where communication remains rusty, as does the will to communicate. There, communication is like a circus act in which one balances on a plank with legs stretched out on either side of a fulcrum. If there's too much weight on one side, it goes down, and then some kind of recurring cultural crisis sparks all over again. Those who refuse to become performers, whether from the east or the west, stand with their hands akimbo, their heads tilted back, and smirks on their faces, despising those who do. They rail, quack, and bray, and then they return to their dark, isolated fortifications and rebuild their walls to protect themselves from the other. It is one of the few instances in the history of humanity where no one remains indifferent.

I stopped the Packard in front of the Montreal Pool Room, got out, and walked in. I inhaled the aroma of fried potatoes, steamies, and lost innocence. Whoever invented the term *greasy spoon* had the poolroom in mind. I'd been shoveling down hot dogs there with my friends since I was a punk kid, and I loved every minute of it. The hotdogeria was long and narrow and on the verge of being declared a disaster zone by the local government, with the eating part up front and two billiard tables in the back, both of which were in use. I hadn't eaten supper, so I sat down on a stool and ordered fries, a hot dog, and a bottle of spruce beer. The guy behind the counter who took my order was tall and had hunched shoulders, dark brown hair cut sharply across his eyebrows, and elephant ears on either side of his head. He was about thirty-five, I guessed. He said nary a word to me. When he brought the food, I said nary a word to him.

Whatever the poolroom lacked in their run-down furnishings, they made up with their food. Both the fries and hot dog were satisfying. "A seedy kind of goodness," Jake Asher had once said to me.

Mr. Personality leaned over the counter at the other end, examining his fingernails. I needed information from him, and I knew it wasn't going to be easy to get.

I cleared my throat. "Ahem."

He looked closer at the row of nails. I cleared my throat again, only louder.

"Ahem!"

He twisted his head slowly in my direction with a blank expression on his mug. I lifted one finger vertically, bent it several times, and smiled. A good smile at the right time goes a long way. He walked languidly to the side where I sat, looking annoyed at being disturbed. This was turning out to be a bad Hollywood script.

"I wonder whether you can help me with something. By the way, I really enjoyed the food."

He knuckled his eyes. He looked like an adult version of one of the Dead End Kids in the movies. He waited for me to say something more.

"I'm looking for a fella. About five foot nine, black hair, a little on the hefty side. His name is Ezra Adler."

"Never heard of 'im."

I took my wallet out to pay the bill.

"Here's for the food." I handed him a twenty. "Keep the change." He didn't look like the type who would cough up anything for less than that.

His hand moved faster than a long-tailed cat under a rocker. "He comes in every day for an hour or so before he goes to work. You look like a cop, but you ain't one, are you?"

"What time might that be?"

"Eight. At night."

"Do you know where he works?"

"Naw. He never said."

I looked at my watch. It was seven thirty. I pulled a fiver out of my wallet and set it on the counter. "You never saw me, right?" I said. "There was no one here looking for him."

He snatched the bill and gave me a conspiratorial wink as I was leaving.

I inched my car back about three doors down from where I'd parked. I had a good view of the poolroom from every angle. I tapped the tips of my fingers on the top of the steering wheel. It wouldn't make him come any faster, but it gave me something to do. Only a few people are born with patience. The rest of us have to learn it. In my case, the army taught me well. After three years of "Hurry up and wait," you have it down pat. The trick is to focus your mind elsewhere.

I looked at my watch. It was eight o'clock, and there was no sign of Ezra Adler. I started to sing "Rags to Riches" and was surprised that I knew all the words. Before I could finish it a second time, I saw him walking up the street, coming my way. He was shorter than I'd thought he'd be, but it was definitely the same face I'd seen in the photo. He hooked a left and went into the poolroom.

I went through the lyrics of a half dozen other songs by the time it was nine o'clock. On schedule, Adler came out, looked up and down the Main, and started to walk from whence he'd come. I eased the car forward when he got about a half block away. He put up an arm and hailed a taxi when he got to Dorchester. I followed the car, going west. When it got to Peel, the taxi turned right. I made the same turn cautiously and stopped. I watched Ezra lean toward the window of the taxi, paying the driver. He crossed the street and went into the Windsor Hotel. I inched the car forward, parked directly across the street at Dominion Square, and followed him in.

The Windsor Hotel was one of those places reserved for the rich and powerful. A couple of decades ago, the queen mother and her hubby, George VI, had stayed there on one of their infrequent trips to the Dominion. I figured Adler must work there. That was the only way he could get into a place like that. I walked through the rotunda and saw him turn left toward the elevators. It was quiet, with only a few people milling about. Three uniformed clerks were behind the main desk, busy with whatever hotel clerks did. They paid no attention to me.

As Adler got into an elevator and the doors closed, I walked over to it and looked above at the arrow. It stopped on seven, the top floor. I knew from other visits there that this was the north annex. I took one of the elevators up. There was just one long hallway and nothing else. He must have gone into one of the rooms. Maybe he didn't work there after all. But what would a mama's boy who lived off the meager earnings of a charwoman and couldn't make his own way in the world be doing in a room in one of the most prestigious hotels in Montreal? My interest was piqued enough for me to hang around to find out.

A plush leather lounge chair, the kind you can sink into and disappear, sat at one end of the hallway, with a small, highly polished mahogany desk beside it. On the desk were a phone and some magazines laid out like a fan. I sat down, grabbed one of the magazines, and started to page through it, starting with the back cover, pretending I was the house dick. That's one of the great phenomena of the human race—reading a magazine from back to front.

As I was paging through it, I came across an ad for Henri, Henri, my hat shop on rue Sainte-Catherine. My hat was becoming shabby, and I had spent many hours in deep contemplation, considering whether or not to replace it. Any serious hat wearer would discern the anguish that would entail. The problem was that a shabby hat was also the most comfortable one. By the time a hat became tattered and scruffy, it was an old friend with a history. A new hat required you to start all over with the introductions and the awkward conversations. It would take an inordinate amount of time before you'd be comfortable with each other. Unfortunately, prospective clients didn't like to hire someone wearing a ragtag hat. I made a mental note to pay the shop a visit.

After about fifteen minutes, I heard the elevator bell ding. A well-dressed older gentleman got out, turned left, and went down to one of the rooms. He rapped on the door lightly: two quick knocks, a single one, and then two quick ones again. The door opened, and he went inside. The room was on the other side of the hallway, so I walked down to see the number. It was 705. I went back to my magazine and continued flipping through the pages. Ten minutes later, the elevator bell sounded again. This time, four men got out. One was noticeably older than the others, with a headful of silver hair. He was telling them a story with an amused look on his face, while the others hovered around him, laughing and making all the appropriate sounds and gestures afforded to someone of a higher status. They were all dressed like lawyers or chief magistrates off on a night of fun and games. They stopped in front of 705, and one of them used the same coded knock.

It wasn't as busy as Grand Central Station, but something was definitely happening in that room, and I had to find out what Ezra Adler was doing there if, in fact, that was the room he had gone into. I walked down the hallway, straightening out my collar and adjusting my tie. I used the same knock as those before me. The door had a tiny peephole, a judas window, so I smiled at it. Someone pulled back the door, and I was face-to-face with Ezra Adler. He looked at me in much the same way a car salesman looks at the rusted trade-in you just drove up in. When the salesman's eyebrows knot in the middle, you know you're not going to get what your car is worth.

"First time here, sir?" he said.

He caught me off guard; I had to think of something to say right away before the door slammed in my face.

"Friend of mine says this is where the action is," I said, as if I knew what I was talking about. He inventoried me up and down with a steady look of uncertainty that lasted a bit too long for my taste. However, his expression suddenly changed, and he took a long step backward. My first assessment of him from the picture in Ruth's apartment had been correct. His face looked familiar, but I still couldn't place it.

"May I take your hat?" he said, and I gave it to him. "You'll find the tables and wheel in front of you and additional tables to the left in the main bedroom. Please enjoy the complimentary drinks. The washrooms are at either end of the suite. Enjoy your evening, sir."

I walked a couple of steps in and stopped. I found myself in a gambling joint. No, *joint* was the wrong word. The suite, by virtue of the fact that it was in the Windsor, was already classy. Whoever had rented it had a terrific starting point with which to begin. Adding elegant touches here and there had brought it up several notches to the chic level. I wondered whether the management knew they had an illegal activity going on up on the seventh floor.

I had to laugh at the whole thing. While provincial government huntsman Pacifique Plante had been ferreting out and raiding the working-class establishments, the blind pigs, these high-class gambling enterprises were springing up across the city and flourishing. There was still a lot of money flowing into Montreal, especially from the States. Plante might shut down the little guys, but he wouldn't touch places like the one I found myself in, because certain people in the city made an awful lot of money from them. Someone would put a bullet in his brain first.

A tall young girl, probably not much older than eighteen, walked over to me with a highly polished silver tray in her hand. She had long, dark, coppery reddish-brown hair that came down past her shoulders. Her skin was Cinderella white. She was wearing a tight-fitting, sleeveless crimson dress, the bottom of which dragged on the floor as she walked. There was a cute little bow pinned on the right side, near her breast. Her lips were painted the same color as her dress. She had that smoky bedroom expression on her face that I'd seen on older, more experienced women. It said, "Come in, dear sir, so we can fleece you for all you're worth." The look didn't suit her.

"Champagne, sir?" she said with a cutesy smile.

I took a flute off the tray. "You should be at home with your mammy and daddy. You might get yourself into trouble here if you're not careful."

She walked away with her smile rigidly in place.

I told myself to behave. I was there to snoop around, not to mind young ladies. *Check your white horse in at the door, Eddie boy.*

With glass in hand, I began walking around the suite, observing the lay of the land. In front of me was a roulette wheel, with four men seated in front of the layout. I looked between two shoulders and got accusing looks, so I moved on. There were four card tables in that room, two on each side of the wheel, and four more in an adjacent bedroom to the left. They were all full. *With an operation like this, the hotel must be getting a slice of the pie*, I thought. Behind the roulette wheel was a long black leather couch. Teak end tables sat on either side, with silver art deco lamps on them. Off to the right, beyond one of the gambling tables, there were two large, comfortable-looking overstuffed armchairs. A matching art deco pole lamp sat between them, its glass shade turned up, redirecting the light to the ceiling. The room was quiet, full, and classy. There were few conversations, and those who were talking spoke in whispers, their faces as serious as heart attacks. It was readily apparent to me that there was a hell of a lot of Montreal money in that suite.

I decided I'd better start acting the part of the gambler before someone began looking over his shoulder at me once too often and became suspicious. I had about a hundred bucks in my wallet, which I knew wouldn't last long. I wasn't what you'd call a seasoned gambler. My being there wasn't part of the Belanger case, so I wouldn't be able to write off any losses in the expense account. When a place gives away the booze, you know the stakes are going to be high. I walked over to the roulette wheel and situated myself behind the layout, making sure I could see the door and Ezra Adler. Roulette's a game in which you can win big with little money, so I hoped my money would last a little longer there than at one of the card tables. However you look at it, though, it's still a carnival game of chance. The people sitting at the wheel were the beginners, perhaps afraid of losing their money. The big spenders were sitting at the tables, where more skill was involved. I glanced through the door leading into the other room and recognized a face. I had never met him, but I'd seen him around town enough to know that he was the chief of the Montreal police force. I had a feeling the place wasn't going to be raided that night, but with Plante on the loose, you never knew.

I looked down at the wheel and saw a single green zero slot, which meant that it was a thirty-six-numbered European wheel. That told me the house edge was 2.7. I'd expected a double-zero American wheel, because the edge was twice that. It looked as if they wanted to treat their customers well at the wheel and find other ways to relieve them of their cash at the tables. I took two twenties from my wallet, gave them to the croupier, and asked for blue chips. I know, I know—big spender!

"What value, sir?"

"A dollar."

He shoved two columns of blue chips, twenty in each, over to me and then placed a button on my color as a reminder to him that each chip was worth a buck.

"What's the maximum bet?"

"None, sir. No minimum as well. You can bet whatever you want." He was a man of about fifty, with gray hair combed back and a David Niven mustache. His face was dignified. Proper behavior was important to him. His tuxedo jacket lay across the stool behind him.

The employees there, including Ezra Adler, the gatekeeper, were as professional and well dressed as you would see in any glitzy casino in Europe. Whoever was running the place knew what he was doing to attract the cream of Montreal's crop.

Roulette is simply a game of chance; no skill is needed or required. However, there is a way to give yourself a little edge. I made a relatively safe bet; I placed a chip on 1–18 for even money. After the other two men beside me made their bets, the croupier waved a magic hand over the layout and said, "No more bets," and then he spun the wheel in one direction and threw the little white ball onto the track at the top in the opposite direction. We waited for gravity to pull the ball down into one of the numbered pockets.

Gambling is the grand metaphor of life. In thirty minutes or less, you can experience what might otherwise take you a lifetime: struggles, victories, catastrophes, pain, and joy. The roulette wheel spins your life around, and the little white ball falls either in the placid streets of English Westmont or French Outremont or in the gutters of a skid row. Dreams are lost, won, and then lost again, and, baby, it's all chance and stacked against you.

"We have number eleven, gentlemen," the croupier said. Reaching over, he placed a marker on the number.

I'd won.

The croupier removed the losing bets of the other two and paid me. He removed the marker, and I took my bet off the layout. I was pleased with myself.

I played it safe again and made another outside bet on the second twelve numbers and won on number fourteen, red, with a payoff of 2–1. The third time, I made a split bet, numbers

31 and 29, with a 17–1 payoff. He spun the wheel, and I won again with 29. I made sure to tip him after each win. I wasn't really there for the gambling, but I realized how winning could get under your skin, with your heart pumping blood madly throughout your body. You begin to think that some little creature in the universe has looked down upon you with favor, anointing you with some special oil. It's only at the end that you realize it was only playing a little prank on you, but by then, it's too late.

I had a friend who was a gambler at heart. He once told me that the roulette wheel was not randomly perfect; if you made small bets, played at the same wheel, and paid attention to the winning numbers long enough, you could win big money. "All wheels are biased," he said. "Some numbers come up more frequently than what probability would dictate, some numbers come up less frequently, and others come up almost never." The legs of the table could be unbalanced slightly, throwing off the wheel. The size and weight of the ball could make a difference, as well as the wear of the track where the ball was spun. The ball bearings on which the wheel spun would wear eventually, tilting the wheel slightly. He said that between nine and twelve numbers on any given wheel came up the most times. "Find them, and you can cash in."

To my surprise, my winnings sparked inside me and ignited that old human trait of greed. It made me nearly forget why I'd come there in the first place. My next bet was a street bet, numbers 22, 23, and 24. He spun; I won on 22 with a payout of 11–1. I was feeling pretty good about myself and gaining confidence, so I made a straight-up bet: chips on seventeen with a payout of 35–1. It paid the most, but it was also the most difficult to win. He spun, and I lost—big.

I decided to cash in my chips. I nearly broke even because I had been playing with their money. I got up as the cutesy redhead was passing by with her tray, and I grabbed another flute. I took a sip while looking over at Adler as he was opening the door. A nice-looking blonde came in. She walked over to my left and stopped at the beginning of the hallway, where I assumed the other bedrooms were. A short bald man smoking a cigar appeared from the hallway, and he greeted her with a kiss on the cheek. I recognized both of them. The guy was Carmine Galante, whom I had seen at the Bellevue Casino and at the Sans Souci with Carrottop. The blonde was the woman I had saved from Carrottop at the Flamingo club last week. Another woman, with black hair, appeared from the hallway and joined them. They talked for a couple of minutes and walked down the hallway and out of sight.

This was starting to become interesting. I had verified with Jake Asher at the *Gazette* what Bix Belair had told me about Galante. Jake knew him. He was a New York mobster who had partnered up with Vittorio "the Egg" Coppoletta, the Mafia boss who controlled most of Montreal. Galante had his hands in everything in the city but never left any fingerprints. He had been in town for the past two years. Jake called the pair the Little Napoleons of Montreal. I knew a lot of hoodlums in Montreal, but I had never seen Galante before. Maybe I hadn't gone to the right places. Small-time hoods on the lam came there to lie low, especially those from New York and Chicago. They usually tried to blend in and didn't cause problems. Apparently, Galante was not small time. Perhaps he and Coppoletta were running the place together. I'd had a run-in with Coppoletta last year, and I was not looking forward to having another one any time soon. I wondered how Carrottop fit into things.

I decided to leave, so I walked over to Adler for my shabby hat. "What time do things wind down here?" I asked him.

"Usually between four and five, depending," he said while reaching behind him.

"I need to get some more cash. I'll be back."

"Yes, sir. Just knock like before," he said. "We'll be here."

CHAPTER 11

I left the Windsor, crossed rue Peel to the Packard, got my black Dunhill lovat and tobacco pouch from the glove compartment, and then turned around and walked to Dominion Square, which was five steps in front of me. I found a bench with a good view of the front entrance of the hotel. The clouds covered part of the moon, and the pole lamps in the square were dim, but there was enough light reflecting from the surrounding streets and buildings for me to pack my pipe. In a few hours, Ezra Adler would be leaving. I had a few questions to ask him, and I suspected I'd find the answers interesting. Jack Macalister, my buddy on the police force, had once told me that when interrogating a suspect, he would never ask a question he didn't already know the answer to. That was all well and dandy. As a principle, there was some merit to that. But when the river is brown and murky and you need to cross it now, you can't wait until it clears up. You cross it one careful step at a time.

There was little traffic on the streets, and I didn't see another soul in the square. I put a match to the bowl and puffed to get it going, making little *pah* sounds. Then I tamped the ash down with the broad end of a nail and relit it.

After a few minutes, I heard someone walking slowly to my left. I craned my neck to see who it was. A well-dressed man of about sixty walked by me without an acknowledgment and sat on the bench to my right. I glanced at the hotel entrance. All was quiet. It was too early for the place to be folding up. I then took a quick look at the guy to my right. He looked straight ahead, never giving any indication that I existed. It was about two o'clock in the morning. There were no other people around. It was quiet. We sat about ten feet from each other. The silence felt awkward to me, so I decided to say something for no other reason than to acknowledge that another fellow human being was in the same universe and within earshot.

"Bonjour, monsieur. Nice morning, hmm?"

He looked slightly to his right, away from me, at the bronze statue of Wilfrid Laurier, who wasn't saying much of anything either. He sighed once, straightened his back a little, and then said to the former prime minister, "That, my friend, is not a fact. It is simply your opinion, and the current rate for opinions is a dime a dozen."

The same rate as Jake Asher's opinions. I was glad to know that Jake hadn't ripped me off. I swung my head toward Wilfrid as well.

"For two bits, I'd say your old lady had enough of your supercilious attitude that she's been living with for the last forty years and threw your ass out of the house, and you've been wandering around for the last six hours, trying to figure out how you got yourself in all that muck with her, right up to your fancy gold watch chain on your waist."

He turned his head slowly in my direction; his eyes narrowed and riveted on me. For about ten seconds, he stared without saying a word. I had difficulty reading his face. His expression wasn't that of shock or distain. I'd seen enough shocked and disdainful looks directed at me to know the difference. It wasn't anger either. It looked like a combination of all three, plus a little something else thrown into the mix to give it a unique air. Suddenly, his hands went down to his stomach, his head went forward and then backward, and he started to hoot and holler in an attack of uncontrollable laughter. I watched him curiously until he was finished.

"My Lord," he said finally, the laughter diminishing in intensity but still strong enough to give his stomach muscles a workout, "you are one brazen son of a bitch. I haven't had anyone talk to me like that in I don't know how long."

One bout of laughter must not have suited him, for he went into another one, but this time, it was shorter. When he finally finished, he got up, walked a few steps to my bench, and sat down. I glanced again at the hotel entrance and then looked at him. He had a bushy gray mustache under his nose and wore wire-rimmed glasses. I sensed that he had regained control of himself, but every so often, he'd jerk his head every which way slightly, as if trying to fight off another attack.

"Mind if I join you?" He pulled a pipe out of his jacket, filled it, lit it, and puffed away. "A pipe man is a thinking man. But my thoughts this morning are not good, my friend. What should I call you?"

"Eddie Wade."

"Frederick Churchill. No relation to Winston."

He ran the words together as if that were his full name. I'd initiated this interaction because I thought it was rude to sit ten feet away from another human being in the early hours of the morning with no one else around and not at least say something; however, I wasn't looking for a long conversation—or a distraction. Ezra Adler was going to walk through the doors of the Windsor Hotel, and I didn't want to miss him because I'd engaged an elderly man in a discussion.

"Have you ever reached a point in your life, Eddie, where you thought you had everything worked out? A point where you had all the answers? Yes, of course you have. There are two critical periods in one's life when that happens." He stopped to relight his pipe. His next words came out in puffs. "The first time it hits you is roughly between the ages of fifteen and twenty-five. Certainly you've experienced that. It lasts awhile and gets you into hot water until you come to your senses or some catastrophe happens to wake you up. Then you go through a long period where you are unburdened by having all the answers. The second time you fall prey to this psychological malady is at the age of fifty or thereabouts. But be forewarned, my friend: you may never extricate yourself from its hideous hold on you. I'm fifty-four, and I'm the department chair in philosophy at McGill. I've studied and taught the thoughts of the best minds in Western civilization. And yet it all comes down to this: I don't know a damn thing about life at all. I have no answers about anything."

"Did the wife leave you?"

"Yes, but not willingly. She's buried on Mont Royal. Five years and three months ago. A long, drawn-out, painful affair. God rest her soul."

"Sorry."

"It's my son. He's the one person on earth that I thought I knew—I mean really knew. I reared him; my wife and I both did. Unlike many fathers, I gave him part of myself every day as he went through the stages of life and developed into manhood. He turned into a fine young man, got married, had two children, and taught at McGill with me in the same department. We couldn't have been any closer. We had lunch every day and talked about his life at home and at the university. I saw the grandchildren part of nearly every weekend. If I don't know him, by God, then I am incapable of knowing anyone else, including myself. And then, two days ago, he did something that made me question the very foundations of the universe."

"What'd he do—rob a bank?"

"That would have been preferable. He just disappeared."

"That seems to be catching on these days."

"Oh, he left a letter for Maggie and one for me, essentially explaining the same thing to us both. But we have no idea where he went. He said he thought he was merely existing rather than actually living—that life was just passing him by. He explained that he had a recurring dream of himself on his deathbed, examining the life he had led and enumerating all the regrets, the missed opportunities. He said that the dream was an omen and that if he didn't act now, he would find himself on that deathbed, cataloging all the things he should have done. The thought of that was unbearable. So like some useless little irresponsible dolt, he abandoned his family, he abandoned me, he abandoned the life he worked hard to attain, and he fled to God knows where. It would serve him well if he went straight to hell. Better yet, maybe he'll end up in France."

He relit his pipe. I sensed he hadn't finished, so I kept my trap shut.

"I thought I had imparted him with a solid code of ethics, a solid foundation of knowing right from wrong. That was one topic we'd talked about ever since he was sixteen: what it meant to be a man. Anyone who knows him knows him as a fine, upstanding young man who takes responsibility seriously. But his actions now confirm that I never really knew him at all. I was fooled. So now I'm sitting here questioning the very fabric of my own life. If I could be fooled by him, someone I knew so well, then what more in my life have I been fooled by?"

I asked myself that same question from time to time. I had no satisfactory answer.

I'll be honest with you. I found Frederick Churchill intimidating, and I'm not easily intimidated. He was obviously looking for a response from me, maybe even some kind of advice. But who was I to give it? I was just a high school graduate, a former pug, and a private dick. I found it audacious to even consider imparting any wisdom I might or might not have had to him, a philosophy professor, but that was what I did.

"Listen, Fred," I said. "I'm not married, I don't have any children, and I never went to university, but I do know a little about human nature. Parents can impart the best wisdom in the world to their children. Sometimes it sticks, and sometimes it doesn't. You can blame yourself for your son's behavior if it makes you feel better. You might even find it necessary, but in the end, it's not going to change anything. It's nearly impossible to know what's going on inside the soul of another human being, but it gives us a certain comfort to think we do. We all have a great big storage bin inside ourselves where we keep our thoughts and our secrets. Sometimes we share little pieces of it with others. Most of what's inside the bin, we don't share at all, because it would be too great of an embarrassment. There's even a nice little portion of it whose existence we don't even acknowledge to ourselves. It would be dreadful knowledge. Go ahead and grieve for your son. You earned that right, but I wouldn't beat yourself up over it too badly. Your son is an adult, and he made his choices. He'll have to live with them. You can't control that." My intent wasn't to lecture him, but I think that was how it must have sounded to him.

He turned his head to me, and I saw the saddest face I had ever seen on a grown man. He looked at me as if I were a priest who had just given him absolution. But he was wrong. He didn't need absolution. He had simply taken the sins of his son onto himself, and that was a hard burden for anyone to carry around for too long. All he needed was to unburden himself to a complete stranger he'd probably never see again.

"His sins are a punishment for my past transgression. Repayment, so to speak."

"Come again?"

"It doesn't matter. It's not important."

He got up and extended his hand to me. We shook, and then he quietly walked away. Aromatic tobacco trailed behind him.

I had thought of Juliette Belanger while he was talking—another victim of cowardice and deceit. It does our hearts good to believe we can dig way down into another person's soul. Infrequently, some can. More times than not, we fail dreadfully.

About thirty minutes later, some of the men I had seen gambling came through the doors of the Windsor. A few minutes later, there were more, talking loudly and laughing. One, an older man, got into a limousine; the others climbed into taxis parked in a row by the curb. I walked to my car and waited. Soon after, two women came out with Ezra Adler trailing behind them. The women got into a taxi, and Adler got into the one behind it. The first taxi went straight to Dorchester and turned left. Adler's made a U-turn and drove north.

I waited until the car was a block away before I started to follow it. At Sherbrooke, it turned right. I continued to follow it, making sure to keep well behind. There was little traffic, so the driver and Adler could spot me easily if they had any reason to look behind them. After fifteen minutes or so, the taxi made a right turn onto rue Nicolet. I slowed down as I approached the intersection and then eased the car around the corner. As I did so, I spotted Adler walking up to an apartment house as the taxi drove on. I parked the car at the opposite curb and quickly walked up the sidewalk leading to the building. I pulled the front door back just enough to squeeze through and then placed one of my business cards between the catch so it wouldn't make noise when it closed. I saw Adler fumbling with his keys with his back to me about halfway down the hallway. There was a strip of carpet covering most of the wooden floor, so I walked toward him without him hearing me. When he stuck the key in the lock and opened the door, I placed my hands on his back, shoved him inside, and closed the door behind me.

"What the—"

The streetlights streaming through the blinds cast shadows in the room. I turned him around and pushed him onto a couch, and then I reached near the door and flipped the light switch. We made eye contact. I waited a few seconds for his own lights to go on.

"You! I knew there was something fishy about you. What do you want? Why are you here?"

I took out my semiautomatic, pushed the safety with my thumb, and chambered a round. I reached back, grabbed a wooden chair, and swung it around, straddling it. I rested my arms on the back with the gun in my hand.

"Here's how it's going to work, Ezra. I'm going to be the one who asks the questions, and you're going to be the one who answers them. A word of caution, though: I'm a goddamn human lie detector. If the bells and whistles go off, it won't go down very well for you."

"You're either a cop or a … I don't have nothing to say to you of any interest." He moistened his lips with his tongue and tried to size me up.

He had a thick neck and black hair and wore an expensive suit, but he was just a poolroom cowboy who tried to dress like a gentleman, and it didn't work. His assessment of me—either a cop or a hood—was predictable. Either way, he didn't look intimidated. I wondered why. Maybe with customers like the chief of police and Carmine Galante in the gambling establishment, he felt sure of himself.

"The hell you say."

I got up, set the gun on the chair, and walked a few yards toward him. I stood over him, grabbed the knot of his silk tie with one hand, and started to twist it. His head went back a little, and his hands grabbed at my fist. I kept turning the tie until his face became purple and he made a gagging sound. I held it in place for a few seconds while putting my other hand on his forehead, pushing his head back into the couch. His eyes were wide and bulging.

I eased up slightly. "I'm giving you a little glimpse of hell, Ezra. It's going to turn you into a believer. You're going to answer some questions, and if you do it nice and honest-like, I'll leave, and you can make yourself some hot milk and get ready for bed. If you understand what I'm saying, just nod."

He nodded his head with quick, sharp little movements.

The tie-twisting routine usually worked well with most guys. I released him and sat back down, gun in hand. He held his neck with both hands, panting.

I got down to business straightaway. "Who runs that nice little operation? Who's the head honcho?"

He scratched his head like a Yankee outfielder. I started to get up.

"Okay, okay." He held his hands out in front of him as if he were trying to stop a moving truck. "God, he's going to kill me if I talk. You got to believe me. He'll kill me."

"You should be more concerned with what I'm going to do if you don't."

"His name's Carmine Galante. He was there tonight."

"Who's the broad who came in last? The blonde who was talking to Galante."

"Marguerite Levesque. She's there to entertain if any of the customers want a little release from the stress of gambling. You know, if they're losing. She takes 'em into one of the bedrooms. It's complimentary. On the house."

Her name rang a bell. Michael Spence had told me that Philippe Belanger was seeing someone named Marguerite, and Juliette had told me that Belanger liked to gamble. Things were starting to fall into place. I took the photo of Belanger out and showed it to him.

"Do you know him?"

"Sure. He gambles there, but I haven't seen him recently."

"Do you ever read the papers?"

"Not if I can help it."

"Where can I find Marguerite?"

"Jesus, the boss is going to kill me if he ever finds out I opened my mouth. She lives at the Winchester Apartments. I don't know the apartment number. We shared a taxi one night, and the driver drove her home first."

I didn't have any more questions for him, at least not at the moment. However, there was one thing I had to tell him that I wasn't looking forward to. Ezra Adler was a two-bit punk, but he was still a human being. I put the safety back on and put the gun away.

"I've got some bad news for you. Your mother died last night."

I expected to see shock on his mug, but I was disappointed. It looked more like panic. I took the bankbook out of my pocket and held it up so he could see it. Panic turned into relief. His eyes were glued to the bankbook. Then he must have wondered what I was doing with it, because the look of panic returned.

"Don't worry, Ezra. It's safe. I thought this might be yours. Your pay, no doubt. Why did you put the money into her account?"

"It was safer there. My mother thought she had only six dollars left in it. She hasn't used it for a long time." As an afterthought, he asked, "How'd she die?"

It would have done my heart good to pistol-whip this two-bit ugly mug. He could have used some of the money to make Ruth's life a little easier. Instead of pistol-whipping him, I tossed the bankbook to him.

"A heart attack at work. I knew her. She was a fine woman."

To that, he said nothing.

"If you've been lying to me, Ezra, I'm going to come looking for you. There's not a place in this lovely city of ours that'll be safe for you."

The overhead light fell on him like an ugly truth. He looked like someone who had just finished the dance of death and lived to tell about it. He looked up at me, and I could tell he was holding back sobs. I couldn't tell whether the sobs were because his mother had died or because he'd survived a close call with me. I left before he embarrassed himself.

I drove back to my office as the sun was just peeking over the horizon.

CHAPTER 12

Sundays are my days to unclog the debris that accumulates in my head during the week. A daily shower doesn't quite wash away the gunk of my beloved city, not even with 20 Mule Team Borax. I'm not trying to be cute. Cynicism doesn't run in my blood. I wouldn't live in any other city, except for New York, my birthplace. I would still be there if the old man hadn't jumped ship and left my mother and me stranded and penniless in Brooklyn. After that, my Italian Canadian mother returned to Montreal with me in tow, and I've been here ever since. Canada gave me citizenship, and Montreal adopted me. The streets of Little Italy were hard, and life growing up on rue Saint-Dominique, near the Jean-Talon market, wasn't always easy. Maybe I had a right to be cynical about life. Many of the kids I grew up with ended up cynical adults, and I saw what it did to them. But it never took hold in me.

I know you're asking yourself, "How can Eddie Wade, a private investigator who sees the contemptuous side of human nature daily, not be cynical and distrustful?" The answer is easy. Most people have good hearts and would give a guy a dime for a cup of coffee. If I went around town distrustful of the motives of everyone I met, it would take little time for me to sink into the dregs of humanity. The harm it would do to me would be irreparable. But don't let that fool you; give me a reason to be wary of you, and I'll be wary. Give me a reason to be skeptical of you, and I'll be on you like ugly on a rat. Giving people the benefit of a doubt, however, always seemed reasonable to me.

Because of my job, I spend a great deal of time away from my office. That wouldn't necessarily be a problem, but I have a cat to look after, and lately, I've begun to feel guilty about leaving Antoinette alone so much. Last year, I was a witness to a murder that took place on a tram. During the course of the investigation, I interviewed Madame Madeleine Pépin, a little old lady in her eighties who lived alone with Antoinette as her only companion. A Mafia button man broke into her apartment, tied her to a chair, and made a big mess while looking for something she never had. At some point, as he was rummaging through her things, Madame Pépin's heart gave out. It was murder any way you spin it. My intent was to keep Antoinette only until I found a more suitable home for her. I never got around to it, and now I've become attached to her. I think she might even like me, but you can never be sure with felines. They mostly tolerate humans.

That morning, after she finished her breakfast, she and I had a lengthy discussion. As we talked it out—my guilt, that is—she groomed herself, pretending she didn't care whether she was alone most of the time. After all, she told me, she slept eighteen hours a day. What was the big deal about being alone? I told her I disagreed. A companion who was around the office more than I was would do her a world of good. She had never been an outdoor cat, and I wasn't certain she'd fair well if I let her roam the neighborhood. At that, she licked the top of one paw and then washed her face with it, feigning disinterest. She then turned around with her tail up and walked away, leaving me to see what she thought of my idea. I checked the hours of the Canadian Society for the Prevention of Cruelty to Animals. It was open on Sundays from one o'clock to five. I planned to go there later in the day, whether mademoiselle liked it or not.

However, that Sunday, at least the morning, wasn't going to be my own. The embezzlement case demanded I stay with it till the end. I had a gut feeling that this Marguerite Levesque would be useful. If she was having an affair with Belanger, she might be able to lead me to him. If she wasn't, she could have some important information she might not even know she had that could lead me to him. I put my hat on, grabbed a pipe out of the rack, hesitated, put it back, grabbed another one, felt around my suit coat pocket for my tobacco pouch, extended one hand to the doorknob, and then stopped dead in my tracks when the phone rang. I swung around to my desk and picked up the receiver.

"Wade Detective Agency," I said.

"Drummond here. I hope I'm not bothering you, Mr. Wade."

"Not at the moment, but the day's not over yet. What's up?"

There was a long pause on the other end.

"I have this little problem here, and I'm wondering if you could meet up with me. I'm at 301 Ontario, at the corner of Saint-Lawrence. You'll see a prowl car outside when you get here."

Drummond was, in fact, the ineradicable Max Drummond, chief of homicide of the Montreal Police force. For most of my professional life, Drummond had been a pain in the ass. Once upon a time, I had a wound. The blood vessels around it constricted to prevent blood loss. Platelets rose to the surface of the bloodstream, helping the wound to clot. A scab formed, protecting it from infection. It wasn't fully healed, but it was on its way. Every time that happened, Drummond would pick the scab off, and it became infected again. This happened again and again over the course of nine years. With Drummond removing the scab before it fell off naturally, the wound never healed the right way, and it left a nice little scar. However, the scar led me to a case that he was involved with, and I discovered something about him that he would never want the Crown attorney's office to know. Now Drummond was no longer a pain in the ass. He was polite to me. He even called me Mister rather than the usual Shit Bird.

"What happened?"

"Can't discuss it on the phone. I'll give you the details when you get here."

"Right now?"

"If you wouldn't mind, Mr. Wade."

I told him I'd leave right away and hung up. Then something smacked me in the face: the address. I reached into my pocket for Marguerite's address: the Winchester Apartments, 301 Ontario.

I eased the Packard around the corner on Ontario and stopped across the street from the apartment building, in front of the Dreamland Café. I winced when I saw the café. It had been several years since I had been there. Looking back, I think I had been subconsciously avoiding it—you know, as one avoids stepping in excrement on a sidewalk. About three years ago, on a nice, lazy summer evening, I was sitting in Dreamland, way in the back, eating supper and listening to a small band playing up front. Most of the musicians were from the Belmont Park Orchestra. They did little gigs now and again around town on their days off. Right in the middle of "Frenesí," which I supposed was appropriate, as the word was Spanish for *frenzy*, in walked a palooka, flashing two barrels. He ordered us all in a businesslike way to make a contribution to his general welfare by putting all our valuables in a gunnysack he'd brought in with him. I had my .45 strapped around me, but there were too many people in the café for me to do much. He hadn't done anything with his guns other than waving them around, and I didn't want to encourage him to shoot up the place.

When an American tourist, a big hunk of a man, threw a chair at the gunsel, Rex, the drummer, made a wild dash for cover behind the bar. The gunsel unintentionally fired and hit him in the right ear. He then fled, leaving behind his empty gunnysack. I ran to the door, but he had disappeared. Many who had witnessed the murder said it was the Mafia. It wasn't. It was strictly an amateur job. It wasn't the mob's MO. That was little consolation for Rex, though.

I had never gone back there after that evening.

Drummond was waiting for me outside the apartment house. A few uniforms were with him, and a small crowd had formed. I made my way over to him. He stood as tall as I did, and he was wearing a wrinkled brown suit. He had me by about ten pounds, but it was mostly flab under his clothes. His fedora sat on the back of his head. It looked better than mine.

"Let's go upstairs," he said with his head down, not making eye contact.

I followed him up, catching whiffs of Brylcreem as I did.

We entered an apartment. It was small and tidy but hardly enough room for Drummond, two uniformed constables, and me. Marguerite Levesque was stretched out on her back on the living room floor. Her blonde hair fanned out around her head. Her arms were parallel to her shoulders, extending out on either side. Her left leg was straight; her right one was bent slightly.

The eyes that had been sizing me up at the Flamingo just a week ago were now fixed on the ceiling. Her mouth was open about an inch, the bottom lip slightly contorted. Her front teeth were smudged with red lipstick. She was wearing a cute little yellow dress with blue, red, and green spring flowers on it. A knife was sticking out of her ribcage. The hilt had thick, coarse black tape wrapped around it and was nearly touching her stomach. There was a small, gelatinous mass of purple-black blood around the blade. The knife had been pushed upward into her heart. It would have been a fast, nearly painless death. That accounted for the lack of blood. Whoever had done it knew what he was doing. Whoever had done it knew her well. He hadn't wanted to cause her any more pain than he had to. Nothing in the apartment told me there had been a struggle. The killer had concealed the knife until the last moment.

"She's dead," Drummond said.

"I can see that," I said, still staring at her. I reached down and touched the side of her face. "She's been that way for a while."

"The reason I called you here is because I found this in her purse." He handed me a card. "It has the name Wade Detective Agency on it. I thought you could enlighten me a little."

"Let's go get a cup of coffee and sit down. It'll take a little time."

We walked down the street a block away to a dingy neighborhood bar. We sat in the booth nearest the door and ordered coffee. I began telling him everything I knew about her and explained why I thought she was somehow involved in the Belanger case. I had never liked Drummond, and I still didn't, but he was a good homicide detective, and I had wanted to draw him into the case even before then, because I thought he could be useful.

"I don't think it's a coincidence that just when I began hunting Belanger down, two people whom I now believe were connected to him somehow turned up dead. And then I was run off the road by a guy with black glasses who also decided to take a potshot at me." I paused to sip the rancid coffee and then said, "Trocadero and the girl could have been in on it with Belanger."

"Or not."

"Or not, but I think it's worth considering."

"I've been investigating murders in this city long enough to know that you shouldn't put your eggs in one basket." His eyes were puffy and tired. Lines ran up his cheeks and across his forehead. He shook a cigarette from his pack and lit one but didn't offer one to me. He put the pack down near his cup and placed the book of matches on top of it.

"But you have to admit that the murders point in Belanger's direction."

"I do, enough to involve myself in the case. Here's what we'll do, Mr. Wade. Macalister will continue to work the embezzlement angle, and I'll take over the murder investigation. We have every law enforcement agency in the province looking for Belanger, but we all have manpower problems. This isn't the only case we're working on. Most of us are working three or four cases at the same time. You're the only one who's working this one full-time. You'll have to let us know when you're on to something." He looked at me straight in the eyes. I knew he was thinking about our past relationship. So was I.

"That goes both ways," I said.

"If we're going to do this right and not get things fouled up, we're going to have to bury the past."

That was going to be hard for me to do. The past always has a grasp on you. Our shared past had been intensely personal, and I had been able to put it away to a limited degree. Now I needed to put it away for good. He was right; I didn't want to foul things up.

I returned his gaze, and our eyes locked onto each other's.

"Agreed," I said.

From there, I drove over to rue St. James, to the animal shelter. It was noisy, with dogs barking, and the smell reminded me of the new zoo in Granby that I had taken Angel to last year. I waited near the counter while a tall man in his fifties finished helping a young woman. A small cage sat on the counter with a little hairless dog curled in the corner, looking miserable.

"He'll come out of it, ma'am. Once you get him in the car and he realizes that he's going home with you, he'll come alive again. Mark my words, ma'am. Just mark my words."

I inched up to the counter after the woman left with her cage. I must have had a bewildered look on my face when the guy turned around to me after filing some paperwork in a cabinet.

"I can see this is your first time here at the shelter. Relax, and take a deep breath." He demonstrated, motioning with his hands for me to comply. "And let it out slowly."

I did.

"Good. Now, tell me all about it. What kind of little companion are you looking for? I can see you're a dog kind of man, right?"

"Actually, I'm looking for a cat. A little one."

"Ah, yes, a cat, of course," he said, ignoring his first assessment of me. "Let's go in the feline room and see what we have."

We walked to a door off to the side and went in. It immediately became quiet. There were rows of cages with every imaginable breed.

"I'll let you have a peek at what we have, sir, while I tend to a matter in the dog room. I won't be long."

I walked around the room, looking at them. Many of them were kittens. I guessed that when spring came and all the street cats started breeding in earnest, the shelter went on a collection mission. He returned sooner than I had anticipated.

"Now, have we found a little darling yet? Ah, yes, that Manx is so cute."

I was standing in front of a cat with no tail. That wasn't right. A cat needed a tail. Actually, it had one, but it looked as if someone had chopped most of it off.

"I don't think that one's quite right. I'm looking for a very young one. Something an older female cat can mother. It needs to have a tail."

"Ah, yes, I have just the one for you," he said. "Follow me."

I followed.

"Here's a lovely brown one with spots of black here and there. It's a Siamese."

I didn't think Antoinette would go for a cross-eyed one, so I asked the guy to show me another.

"We got this American longhair in just last week. Our vet thinks it's about three months old. The breed is one of the most popular ones. It's a he."

The kitten was standing on his hind legs with his paws up against the cage, assessing me. He was white with a fluffy brownish-black tail and a matching hat. He looked as if he could fit the bill. I hoped he saw me in the same light.

"Yes, I'll take this one." I pointed at it. "I think he'll do just fine."

"Little Henri. Very good choice, sir." The man was delighted with himself.

He put little Henri in a box just wide enough for him, with holes punched out. I filled out the paperwork, signed on the dotted line, and then reached into my wallet and put a ten-spot on the counter. When I got little Henri in the car, I took him out of the box. He explored the backseat and meowed all the way back to the office.

Antoinette was standing at the door when I went in. She took one look at what I had in my hand and hunched her back and hissed. I was a traitor. Not fazed by her reaction, I went to the couch and sat down with Henri on my lap. He squirmed and twisted in my hands, trying desperately to free himself. Antoinette looked at me as if I were trying to strangle him. At once, she became protective, jumping up onto the couch next to me and sniffing the new arrival. Henri sniffed back, and soon Antoinette started licking the smells of the shelter off him. Antoinette would be occupied mothering her new little kitten for some time.

While she was doing that, a thought entered my head. I needed to find the redheaded guy wearing the Panama fedora. I wanted to know exactly what he'd been arguing with Marguerite about that Sunday night at the Flamingo. Maybe Belanger hadn't killed Marguerite.

Maybe Carrottop had.

CHAPTER 13

I sat at my desk, updating my notes, pecking away on the Royal. Little Henri was racing around the office, exploring his new environment, twisting and bending and bumping into anything that stood in his way. Antoinette was following behind him, trying to paw him down enough to finish grooming him.

The late Sunday afternoon sun was streaming through the Venetian blinds, and the smoke from my pipe rose in its rays. I stopped typing and stared at the keys. I had a hard time wrapping my thoughts around Philippe Belanger. I didn't want to believe he was capable of killing anyone, but the evidence was dragging me in that direction. Some embezzlers do turn to murder, especially to cover their tracks. Even the most level-headed, mild-mannered suit-and-tie professionals find it impossible to grapple with a life turned upside down when you throw desperation into the mix. But most don't murder. It takes a special person to make that leap—someone who is already wired for it, someone who is already capable of murder but just hasn't had the right opportunity yet. From what I knew about him, Phillip Belanger didn't seem to be that kind of person. Yet

I'd been fooled before. Evidence doesn't lie, but I had to keep in mind that it could be misinterpreted. At that point, all the evidence was circumstantial. The case was somewhat solid for embezzlement but less so for the two murders. I still had my eye on Carrottop, at least for one of the murders.

There's a nice little Latin phrase I apply to cases whenever a curious sort of doubt appears to me: *Cui bono?* (Who benefits?). It's a principal that the probable responsibility for a crime lies with the person who has the most to gain from it. If you answer that question, you can just about wrap up a case, but it can take a good chunk of your time. If Belanger had committed either crime—embezzlement or murder—or both, then the answer was apparent. If he hadn't, then who would stand to benefit? Whether or not he was guilty of anything remained to be seen. I first had to find him.

I decided to push the case forward based on the uncertainty that Belanger had killed Trocadero because he'd found out Trocadero was setting him up to be captured, and Marguerite was somehow involved with Belanger. Maybe she was the blonde who had rented the room for him. That would also tie her to Trocadero. If she'd had plans to leave with Belanger, maybe she'd gotten cold feet, and Belanger had killed her to eliminate a coconspirator who knew too much. Whoever had shoved that knife upward into her heart knew her and wanted to make her death as painless as possible. I wondered how the redheaded Panama-wearing bozo was involved in all this. He knew both Marguerite and Carmine Galante, both of whom were associated with the gambling suite that Belanger had frequented. Maybe Ezra Adler knew more than he'd let on. It was time to pay him another visit.

That evening at 7:50, I pulled over a few storefronts down from the Montreal Pool Room, hoping Ezra would keep to his routine. The sun had just set, and the streetlights were on. The night had begun to cool to a pleasant temperature, so people were out and about. I didn't have to wait long. Ezra walked leisurely my way with his arms swinging at his sides, as if he didn't have a care in the world. He was wearing the same clothes he'd had on the last time I'd seen him. As he was about to enter the poolroom, I nudged the horn slightly to get his attention. He bent down a little and looked in my direction. I pushed down my hat, covering most of my face. He didn't know what I was driving, so he must have been curious about who'd beeped, because he walked over to the car. The window on the passenger side was down. He leaned in to see who was behind the wheel. Once he saw my smiling face, he grimaced.

"Jesus, not you."

"Hello, Ezra," I said. "Get in. We need to continue the discussion we had the other night."

"What—you're not done with the tough-guy stuff?"

"I am if you get in like a nice little boy. If you run, I'll go after you and finish that tie-twisting routine."

"You don't have to be nasty about it."

He grimaced again, fidgeted with his knot, and then he looked around as if he were trying to spot a constable. He gave up and looked in at me again at an angle with the classic unsure smile of resignation on his mug. He got in.

I had remembered to put a pack of cigarettes in the glove compartment of the Packard. I don't smoke cigarettes, but I keep a pack for those who do. His fingers were stained a yellowish orange, so I figured he did. I reached in, grabbed the pack, and then shook a cigarette halfway out at him. It was sort of my peace offering to show that I wasn't a terrible guy after all. Sometimes a cigarette helps calm an agitated moron like him down. I put the pack back into the glove compartment, took out a stick match, and gave it to him. He reached down, ran the match along his shoe, lit the cigarette, and then blew smoke out the window.

"So where did we leave off?" Ezra asked. His chest rose so much from a sigh that I thought he was going to have a heart attack.

I turned my head and looked at the side of his face. "Relax, Ezra. Take a deep drag, and relax." *Jeez*, I said to myself. *Where have I seen him before?* My inability to determine why he looked familiar was starting to bug me. "Marguerite. Tell me about a guy she knows. He has red hair, wears a Panama hat, and dresses like there's no tomorrow."

"You mean Johnny Como?"

"What's his line?"

"I don't know. He comes to the hotel a couple nights a week to gamble. He always has a roll on him this thick." Ezra held up a finger and thumb about two inches apart. "He loses a lot but always comes back. He's palsy-walsy with the boss." He took a drag from his cigarette.

"What about Marguerite? Is he palsy-walsy with her too?"

"He's head over heels for her. I don't know nothing besides that." He went into a pouting routine. His upper lip was thin and narrow, but his lower one was big and drooped as if he were pulling on it with his fingers.

"Someone rammed a knife into her last night. Was Johnny Como capable of that?"

He jerked his head in my direction. "What did you say?" He'd heard me, but his expression said that he didn't believe what I had just said.

"You heard me right. She's on ice at the city morgue. Could Como have done it?"

"Jesus, this is crazy. Marguerite's dead? Jesus." He shook his head. "Johnny Como was crazy about her. He wouldn't harm a hair on her head."

"Yeah, but he had no problem slapping her around, though."

"He did that?" He sounded shocked. "Well, there's a difference, you know. Slapping ain't the same as killing."

I had the sudden urge to resume the tie-twisting routine again. Little slaps here and there sometimes became a prelude to murder later on. I took out Belanger's picture and showed it to him again.

"You said he gambled at the hotel. Was he ever around them—Marguerite, Como, and Galante?"

"The three of them together? Never. I would have seen. He never talked to Marguerite as far as I know. Johnny was the one who was in love with her. She told me that herself. She wanted nothing to do with him."

"So Belanger and Marguerite never had anything going on?"

"Not that I know. If she had something for him, she kept it a secret."

That was a possibility.

"When does this Johnny Como come in? Which nights?"

"Nothing regular. Any night he wants."

"I'm going to be a regular there for a while. If you tip anyone off, we'll be having another conversation that I think you won't much care for."

"Listen, Mr. Wade. I'm just a well-paid doorman. I check people out when they come in. I don't want any trouble."

"I don't either, Ezra." I made eye contact with him.

I thought about Ruth. She had been a hardworking lady. It must have been a burden for her to have a son like this chump.

Everyone has someone who loves him or her, even the most ruthless mob bosses in New York. They kill or have someone kill for them, and then they sit down afterward to a plate of spaghetti and meatballs, fill their glasses with Chianti, and raise those glasses in a toast with those around them. They all have mothers who love them dearly. The mothers either don't know what their darling sons are up to or deny it. Either way, they still love them. It had been the same with Ruth. She must have loved this pile of excrement sitting next to me.

"When's your mother's funeral?"

Ruth had died on Friday. It dawned on me that the dead could not be buried on a Saturday, the Jewish Sabbath. That would have made the burial that day. I cursed myself for not remembering that. I'd wanted to attend the service.

"It was supposed to be today, but there was some problem they wouldn't tell me about. Now it's tomorrow at ten at the Baron de Hirsch Cemetery. I wanted to give her a fancy send-off—you know, an expensive casket with maybe some jewels set into it, maybe trimmed in a little gold and all—but Jewish law forbids it. All Jews leave this life in a plain wooden box, like we're all the same, rich and poor. Can you believe that? Can you believe that shit?"

My first impulse was to strangle him. This bloodsucking leech had lived off her for years, and now that she was dead, he wanted to fancy up the funeral and defy Jewish law by burying her in the equivalent of a Rolls-Royce. She was barely forty-eight hours dead, and he was ready to play another round of pool. He was staring out the windshield with the side of his face toward me. His hands were in his lap. It would have been easy for me to whack him in the head with my .45, throw him in the trunk, run him up to Mont Royal, and drop him off in the wooded area. It'd be just another murder, another unsolved crime.

I went with my second impulse. I looked at him with disgust. "Get out of the car, and go away, Ezra. Far away from me."

After Adler got out of the car, he must have changed his mind about playing pool, because he walked by the poolroom, heading toward rue Dorchester. Our little conversation had taken longer than I had anticipated, so I assumed he'd grab a taxi and go directly to the hotel. I drove over to the Flamingo and had a couple of drinks to think things through. The only thing I knew for certain was that I had to find Johnny Como. The Windsor Hotel was my only lead.

I was too wound up to sleep, so for the hell of it, I went to the Windsor. I got there just before midnight and gambled until four, when they closed. Johnny Como never showed up, and I lost two hundred smackers for my trouble.

CHAPTER 14

Early Monday morning, I phoned Bradford Wilcox and explained the situation to him. It was simple: Johnny Como had a connection to Marguerite, and I was certain she had some kind of connection to Belanger. The best and most cost-effective way to find Como was at room number 705 of the Windsor. I'd looked for his name in the public directory, and it wasn't listed. I could track him down eventually, but it might take longer than if I just waited for him to come gambling. I had thought about waiting for him outside the hotel and then following him when he came out again. I discounted that idea because I wanted to see him in action and observe whom he talked to while he was there. Wilcox okayed a nightly limit of one hundred dollars for me so I could play the part of a gambling fool. That would be worth it, he said, if I could recover the one hundred grand. "Anything over a hundred dollars will come out of your own pocket—and don't try to fudge your expense account!"

If I happened to win, he wanted a cut. The ruthless side of him came out every so often.

At ten o'clock, I found myself at the Baron de Hirsch Cemetery, attending Ruth Adler's funeral. Agnes T. Montjoy was there with others I assumed were the night cleaning crew. She was stunning and elegant in her black dress and pillbox hat. I liked her. I liked her a lot. I barely recognized the concierge in Ruth's apartment building because of the three-piece suit he was wearing. He wasn't stunning, but he was unquestionably handsome. Clothes certainly don't make the man or woman, but I'm always amazed at how they can force you to see another dimension of a person. All these people—who spent forty hours a week cleaning floors on their hands and knees or with mops and buckets, scrubbing toilet bowls, picking up garbage, and keeping the world sparkling clean for other people—were dressed in their finest for a send-off of one of their own. It was a testimony to their loyalty, to their faithfulness to each other, and to Ruth as well, a woman whom I'd known for years but whose last name I hadn't known until a few days ago. I felt ashamed of myself. Agnes T. Montjoy and the others had something important to teach me.

The service was short, sparsely attended, and sad. Besides the rabbi, Ezra was probably the only one in attendance who was Jewish. I sensed the rabbi—a pleasant young man in his thirties with a sharply trimmed, short black beard—would adjust for this, and he did. After he said, "*Baruch dayan emet*," he repeated it in English, "Blessed is the true Judge," and in French, "*Béni soit le tout puissant*." Then he told a story that anyone, regardless of his or her religion, would be able to understand. "As we try to make some sense of Ruth's sudden death, let me share a story from the Talmud." He cleared his throat with a fist to his mouth and then continued. "Once, a great teacher arrived in a city. His name was Rabbi Akiva. There he sought a place to rest, for he had traveled from a distant land and was weary. He went from person to person, from family to family, but no one would take him in for the night. To that, he said, 'All that God does, he does for the good.' Tired, he walked out of the city and into the nearby fields, where he would sleep on the cold, hard earth. He had with him a rooster, a donkey, and a lamp. Suddenly, a wind came and blew out the candle. A cat came and ate the rooster. A lion came and ate the donkey. Rabbi Akiva witnessed all of that and said, 'All that God does, he does for the good.' As all of that was happening, a foreign army had come into the city and killed the people.

"This story shows that bad things happen for a reason, even if we don't know what that reason is. Because of this truth, our sages tell us that we should always thank God for the bad as well as the good, even if we don't fully understand them. There is a season for everything, and we should be thankful for them all. Let us be thankful to God that we had the chance to know Ruth, for she brought joy and love into our lives."

I noticed during the service that Ezra was holding back tears. When it was his turn to drop soil onto the wooden coffin, he finally broke down and cried. Maybe the finality of Ruth's death had caught up to him. I almost felt sorry for him.

As I was walking back to my car, I glanced to my right at a clump of trees a little distance from where we'd all said our good-byes to Ruth. I noticed a man standing with his hands in his pockets, looking distraught. He didn't notice me.

It was Frederick Churchill.

I played the roulette wheel at the Windsor for the next three nights. I won and lost and then won and lost again. I kept track of the money carefully so I could have an accurate figure for my expense account. My overall losses were minimal because I was playing with the house money I had won. On Thursday night, Johnny Como finally showed up.

I looked up from behind the layout and over the shoulder of the croupier to see the three-piece pin-striped suit and Panama fedora. He gave his hat to Ezra, who briefly looked in my direction and then back again quickly. Como then walked toward Carmine Galante, who was sitting across the room in one of the plush armchairs, smoking a cigar. Como sat down next to him, and Galante offered him a cigar.

They sat there for close to an hour, drinking, puffing away, and chatting. I was about ten feet in front with my back to them, listening, but their voices were low, so I didn't hear much. From the tone, it seemed they knew each other fairly well. Their voices were soft and hushed, with occasional bursts of laughter that suggested familiarity. Como was either in the mob or was associated with it. No one talked to a mob boss like Galante with that kind of intimacy without some kind of connection.

Como didn't look as if he were going to gamble. If he decided to leave anytime soon, I wanted to be free to leave soon after him, so I cashed in my chips. I did a quick calculation and realized I had lost more than I'd won. That was fine with me, because I'd be reimbursed for most of it. Wilcox would be disappointed. At least I wasn't like the chumps in the lesser gambling establishments who sat at the wheel for ten hours straight, losing their shirts and maybe their pants, and then, just before they left, hit the magic number. They would leave with cocky grins on their faces, pleased with themselves that they'd beaten the house. Only much later, when they were telling their wives all about their good luck, would they realize they'd won back only a small fraction of what they'd lost. That was when the depression set in, and the drinking started all over again.

However, after a few days went by, their confidence would grow again, fueled by addiction, and they were right back at it. They wouldn't stop until they lost family, friends, jobs, and health. Even when they were sitting in the gutters of skid row, all they would think of was the next spin of the wheel or the next roll of the dice. Degenerate gamblers were like junkies who couldn't stay high; they kept right at it until they were dead. Once upon a time, I'd known someone like that. I didn't know if he'd ever made it to skid row or even if he was alive or dead, but I knew he'd caused a great deal of harm to a certain lady and their nine-year-old son.

I was pressing my luck by staying there. If I stayed much longer, Como was bound to recognize me. I had managed to keep myself behind others and out of his line of sight, but I couldn't do that indefinitely. It was quiet, with just a murmur of voices and the background music of a jazz record I couldn't identify. It stayed that way until a man wearing an expensive-looking black suit slapped his palms hard on the table to the right of me. For a split second, all heads turned in his direction. He pushed his chair back in anger and got up. He looked around and saw Galante to the left of me. He walked over to him, leaned down, and said something to him. Galante got up and placed an arm around his shoulders, and they walked to the hallway that I assumed led to the bedrooms. Galante motioned with his hand to a chestnut brunette who had been sitting in a chair off by herself. She got up and followed them down the hallway. Galante reappeared a moment later and walked over to Como. They spoke for a few seconds, and then Como got up, shook hands with him, and walked to the door. He got his hat from Ezra and left. I waited for about a minute and then walked over to Ezra. He gave me my hat with a pathetic, uncertain half grin on his face, and I left as well.

Once outside, I saw Como get into a taxi. I jogged to my car across the street and followed him to a house in Westmount, which was about a ten-minute drive from the hotel. From a safe distance away, I watched him pay the driver and walk up to a house set back from the street. I eased the car along with the lights off and parked directly in front of the house on the other side of the street. In the shadows, I watched him open the door and reach inside for the light switch. I thought about nailing him right then and there but decided to wait. After five minutes, the first-floor lights went off, and thirty seconds later, a light went on in a second-floor room facing the front. After another five minutes went by, the light went off, and the entire house was dark.

When catching someone off guard in his own home, the best and safest method is to wake him after he's been sleeping for about two hours. That way, you interrupt his dreams, and he doesn't know which way is up. He gets a nice little confused look on his face, and it takes him a few seconds to orient himself to what's going on. By then, it's too late, because you have him just where you want him, with his backside hanging in the wind as he helplessly looks into the dark barrel of a gun.

Como carried a gun of his own, and I didn't want to be surprised or have either of us get hurt. So I sat in my car for the next two hours, listening to an all-night station that played jazz and blues and planning out my early morning visit with Johnny Como.

When I thought I had waited long enough, I made my way up the long path to his house. I picked the lock using a penlight, turned the knob, and eased the door open. There was no indication that anyone else was in the house besides Como. The stairs going to the second floor were to the right. The house was old, so the steps would creak. I was careful to step on the outer edges, because there would be more support and less noise. The creaking was minimal. Once on the landing, I looked for a room that faced the front. The penlight gave me just enough light and no more. The door was open about halfway. The landing squeaked a little under my weight, which slowed down my progress. I took the .45 out of my shoulder holster, flipped the safety, and quietly eased a round into the chamber, cursing myself for not doing so earlier. Closer to the room, I heard Como snoring. His snores were the deep kind that I'd hoped to hear. It would take an earthquake to wake him up.

I stepped into the room a bit and looked around the edge of the door. As I did so, the door slammed back into me with so much force that it knocked the gun out of my hand and onto the floor by my foot. I moved my foot forward a little, trying to regain my balance, but the toe of my shoe hit the gun, which then spun into the room about seven feet in front of me. Before I had a chance to recover, Como was standing in front of me, aiming a revolver at me.

When you're in a pickle like that, you have to make a decision without much thinking. You could do nothing, hoping to talk your way out of it. However, with a character like Como, who I knew might be connected to the mob, I didn't think that was the most reasonable thing to do. Besides, we shared a little piece of bad history.

Looking back on it, what I did seems foolish, but I had no other option. I was convinced that when he realized who I was—which would take all of a few seconds—he'd plug me and then tell the cops I had broken into his house with the intent of plugging him.

Not giving him a moment to reflect, I put my head down low, making myself a smaller target, and ran toward him, aiming myself at his midsection. I grabbed him below his waist—around his hips and rear end—and forced him up, lifting him off his feet. I landed on top of him with all my 195 pounds. I had him by four inches and at least thirty pounds, so it wasn't a terribly difficult feat. He still hung on to his gun, so I reached both of my hands over to pry it loose. He brought his arm into himself with strength I didn't think he had, and then I felt his teeth sink into my wrist. That pissed me off, so I held his gun to the side with one hand and landed several well-placed blows to his nose with the other. His hand slackened, and I tore the gun out of it. I reared back for another series of blows, but he had placed both hands to his nose.

"All right, all right," he said. "Goddamn it, you broke my nose."

I stood up; grabbed him by the front of his silk pajamas, nearing lifting him off his feet; and threw him onto the bed. I walked a few yards, flipped the light on, and then recovered the two guns. There was a wooden high-backed chair near the window, so I sat down. I was tired and winded. He looked over at me, still holding his nose and blinking.

"Who the fuck are you anyway?" he asked. "What d'ya want with me?"

"Someone out of your past you didn't expect to see," I said.

He squinted, trying to clear his vision. Blood ran down his mouth and chin.

"Look a little closer, and you'll know why."

He looked at me hard. "Jesus, it's you," he finally said. "You caught me off guard that night. Maybe things would have been different if I'd been ready for you."

"Yeah, just like now, eh?"

He didn't say anything for about a minute. I reached over to a dresser beside me, grabbed a cloth off it, and threw it to him. He wiped his face.

"My nose was just starting to heal. Now you broke the goddamn thing for sure. What d'ya want with me? I didn't hurt her. I never would. You had no right to jump in."

"Yeah, well, she got hurt anyway, didn't she? Really hurt this time."

"I didn't kill her, if that's what you're thinking. I'd never do anything like that."

"What was Marguerite to you?"

"She was my girl. I loved her. If you think I killed her, you're an idiot."

Slowly, I brought my .45 up and pointed it directly at him. His eyebrows raised an inch.

"Broads are killed all the time by those who love them, Como." I moistened my lips with my tongue. "What did you say I was?"

"Jesus, don't shoot me. I take it back—you're not an idiot." His voice broke, high and squeaky. "I didn't kill her. I loved her. I looked out for her."

He was like all good punks and wise guys; when they think they're playing their last card, they get all gooey and weepy. I had no intention of shooting him, but he didn't know that. I snickered at him and then lowered the gun. His body slackened.

"What were you two arguing about that night at the Flamingo?"

Como didn't say anything right away. He just stared at me with a blank face. Then the lightbulb went on, and the blank look disappeared.

"I was trying to help her."

"By slapping her? Is that the way you help broads?"

"I was. I was trying to get her to stop—you know, stop doing what she was doing."

"I didn't know her, so I don't know what she was doing that needed stopping."

"I was trying to convince her to stop earning money the way she was. It broke my heart. It really did. But she didn't even want to talk about it."

I knew he was talking about Marguerite being a high-class call girl, so I let him continue.

"I think she would have, but she was so sucked in by Galante that she was afraid."

"What's he got to do with her?"

"He had her by the strings. She worked for him. Her and the two others. They're all locked into him. You want to know more, you better talk to Galante. And don't mention my name. And don't go thinking that he killed her. She was bringing in a lot of dough for his operation. The clients knew they didn't have to pay to have her. Galante was paying her plenty. She was just a little treat to bring in the gamblers. They couldn't have someone like her and the others elsewhere without paying up the wazoo. I couldn't get her to change her mind, because I couldn't find her a job that would pay that much. And besides, Galante wouldn't let her go anyway."

"The word is, she didn't like you very much. What makes you think she was your girl?"

"She would have been if I could've gotten her out of that business. I know she'd have come around eventually."

"Where can I find Galante somewhere away from the hotel? Does he have a favorite place to eat or drink? Where does he bunk down at night?"

"He eats lunch at Ruby Foo's every day at one like clockwork. I don't know where he lives. I heard he doesn't sleep in the same place for more than two nights in a row."

I pulled out the photo of Belanger and showed it to him. For a split second, a flash of recognition crossed his face. It was so slight that if I hadn't been looking directly at him, I wouldn't have caught it.

"Am I supposed to know him?"

"He gambles at the hotel."

"Not when I'm there."

I raised the .45 again and pointed it at him.

"You think I'm stupid enough to lie to you, given the circumstances? I'm telling you. I don't know who he is, because I never saw him before."

I did think he was stupid enough to lie to me, but I wasn't willing at that point to hurt him any more than I already had to get him to admit that he knew Belanger. The difference between the good guys and the bad guys is that the good guys will go only so far to get information. The bad guys will go as far as necessary.

I felt I'd gotten about as much information out of Johnny Como as I could, but I had something else to ask him before I left.

"One more question, and I'll leave you to your beauty sleep. What do you do that pays the mortgage on this place?" It was an older house, but it was in a rich neighborhood, and I was sure it had a nice market value attached to it.

Como looked toward the window for a few seconds in silence and then turned to me. "I help people fix things," he said, and then he wiped his bloody face again with the cloth.

"What kind of things?"

"Things. Like problems."

"With this?" I asked, holding up his revolver. He looked at it but didn't say anything. I took the bullets out of the gun and put them in my pocket. I threw the gun on the other side of the room, and it landed under a chest of drawers.

I got up and walked toward the door. "You'd better see a doctor. You don't look so good."

As I was walking down the hallway, I heard him mumbling something about his nose. His voice became fainter and fainter as I went down the stairs and out into the dark, cool Montreal morning.

CHAPTER 15

When I got back to the office, the first thing I did was feed the cats. Then I went to bed and got about four hours of uninterrupted sleep. That was three hours more than I usually got when I was working a case. At noon, I drove the borrowed Packard to the outskirts of the city, to the Decarie Strip and Ruby Foo's, passing the drive-in curb-service restaurants: Bonfire, Miss Montreal, the Orange Julep, and the Piazza Tomasso.

I pulled into the restaurant's parking lot and, after ten minutes, found a spot at the farthest end. As I'd expected, the lot was packed. I locked up the car and zigzagged my way to the front entrance. There were enough Cadillacs there to turn the lot into a used-car dealership. Beside the door, a billboard announced that Josh White would be appearing in the Black Sheep Room, starting on Sunday. I had seen him sing and bend a note or two there before. Not many things could make me tear up, but whenever I heard him playing his guitar and singing "Lord, I Want to Die Easy," he had me rolling on the floor and flailing my arms and legs in the bittersweet, euphoric intoxication of the soul. Okay, I'm exaggerating, but Josh White was a force to be reckoned with.

I'd eaten at Ruby Foo's many times before—and long enough to know some of the employees by name. Frank Goral, the maître d', greeted me as I walked in. I told him I was meeting someone there at one o'clock. "You may wish to wait in the cocktail lounge," he said with a smile and a long finger pointing to the right.

I bellied up to the bar, ordered a whiskey, and looked around. The place was crowded, but I didn't see anyone I knew. Ruby Foo's had three cocktail lounges and four dining rooms, with a seating capacity of six hundred. I hoped I wouldn't miss Carmine Galante.

Ruby Foo's was a place to see and be seen. While some people were eating their roast beef, Yorkshire pudding, or moo goo gai pan in the dining rooms or drinking in one of the cocktail lounges, others would be busy conducting the kind of business that made Montreal function and kept workers working. Jewish clothing manufacturers, Anglo insurance company executives, and French Canadian real-estate men and notaries constantly had their eyes peeled, scanning the dining room while sucking on sparerib bones or peering over their whiskey glasses.

Of course, there were other businessmen there conducting business that kept Montreal doing the jitterbug into the early morning hours. Galante was no doubt part of that and had been for the last few years. Why else would he come there every day? The egg rolls were good but not that good. I wondered if I was doing the right thing in confronting him about Marguerite and Belanger. Maybe *confronting* was the wrong word. You didn't confront someone from the mob if you had an ounce of sense in you, and you didn't try some stupid little song-and-dance number with him either. If I were going to talk to Galante, I had to be straight and up front with him and hope for the best. I was a private investigator on a case. I needed information. Galante would either give it to me or not. However, there was a certain amount of risk in approaching him, because if he perceived me as a threat of some kind, I'd be on his radar, and that wouldn't be a healthy place to be. Nevertheless, if you're ever going to accomplish anything in life, you have to get used to the risk factor, because it's always going to be there, rubbing shoulders with you and smirking.

At five minutes till one, I tossed back the rest of the whiskey and got up. I looked around for any familiar faces again, saw none, and then went into the nearest dining room. I stood at the entrance and looked for Galante but didn't see him. I climbed the stairs to the right of me to the second floor. When I got to the landing, I saw the back of a bald head of a small man sitting at the first table. Two gladiators in dark suits were flanking him. Both looked in my direction at the same time. I walked over to the table with one hand holding the rim of my hat at my waist and the other one inside the hat at the crown, out of sight, deferential-like. When I stopped beside Galante, the two goons pushed their chairs back in unison, reached inside their jackets, and held their hands in place. I had made a potentially fatal mistake by holding my hat as I did. I let the hat fall to my side with one hand and scratched the side of my jaw with the other, making both hands visible. *See? No gun, fellas!* Galante looked up at me nonchalantly with a short cigar in his mouth.

"Mr. Galante, I'm sorry to disturb you, but I wonder whether I could have five minutes of your time. My name is Bonifacio Edmondo Wade." For some stupid reason, I thought using my Italian first and middle names was a smart thing to do. It was supposed to mean "We don't know each other, but hey, we're goombahs, so relax!"

He glanced at his bodyguards and winked. Then he took the cigar out of his mouth and squinted up at me as if I had just told him that my name was Geronimo.

"What the fuck are Bonifacio and Edmondo doing with Wade? They don't go together very good, do they?"

"My mother was born in the old country. She married an Anglo-Saxon."

Galante glanced at the goons again and then angled his head at me and creased his forehead. "She married a what?"

"My father's family came from England. You can call me Eddie if you want."

"Okay, Eddie," he said, nodding and putting a little more emphasis on the first syllable of my name than I felt comfortable with. That wasn't a good sign. It was always a bad sign when someone said your name like that: "ED-dee," as in "What in the hell do you want with me, Eddie?" and "This better be good, Eddie, because if it isn't, Eddie, these two gentlemen will take care of you, Eddie."

"I'm a private investigator working on a case, and you might be able to help me with it." The two goons were still staring at me, but at least their hands were down at their sides. Galante narrowed his eyes at me. I was hoping he wouldn't recognize me from the Windsor.

"Now, why would I want to do something like that?"

"It involves two people you may know. Maybe another time would be better for you." I was uncomfortable now and had second thoughts, so I tried to worm my way out of the situation. I decided that approaching him hadn't been such a good idea after all.

"I ain't eating yet. You got me curious. I can't think of a single thing I could help you with, but you got me curious. You got five minutes to make me less curious." He looked at his bodyguards and motioned with his head. "Wait over there, boys." He indicated the top of the stairs about ten feet away.

They threw me nasty looks as they left.

"Sit down, and tell me all about it, Eddie." He looked tired and impatient. His face looked like a walnut with drooping eyes. His eyebrows were thick and black, and there was not a trace of hair on his head. I remembered Jake Asher telling me that he had moved up the ranks of one of New York's Italian mob families, from chauffeuring around the head of the family to being number-two man, by absolute ruthlessness.

This interview hadn't been one of my brightest ideas, but my feet were stuck in mud now. My opportunity to back away from it had ended with my drink downstairs. Maybe I should have just left, gotten in my car, and driven away. It was all water under the bridge now.

Dean Martin was being piped in. "That's Amore" made me feel a little better.

I pulled a chair out and sat down. I hoped I had my voice under control. "I'm investigating the murder of Marguerite Levesque." That was a half truth, but what did he know? "And I believe you knew her."

He looked at me but didn't say anything. I couldn't read his face.

"I think she may have been seeing a man who is of interest to me. His name is Philippe Belanger. I have a photo of him in my pocket, if I may."

He nodded at me. I started to reach inside my jacket but stopped as I looked over at the goons, who were standing with their arms crossed. They made a movement toward us. Galante must have seen my reaction, because he put his hand out to the side and waved them off. I slid the photo out and showed it to him.

"Never seen the man," he said.

"Can you tell me anything about Miss Levesque?"

"Don't know her either."

What do you do when you're interviewing a mob boss and you know he's lying?

"What did the guy do—bump her off?"

"That's what I'm trying to find out."

Well, there you have it. I'd been straight with Galante and gotten nowhere. I couldn't ask him any more questions about either of them without challenging his honesty, and I didn't think that was a wise thing to do.

Ruby Foo's must have had Dean Martin on a loop, because I noticed that he was still singing the same song. A cute little cigarette girl came over to the table. I knew her. Her name was Frances Lim.

"Why, Eddie Wade. How are you? Haven't seen you here for a while."

I smiled at her.

"Hello, Mr. Galante. Would you like a Cuban today?"

He said, "Certainly, my dear," and Frances gave him one. "Put it on my tab, gorgeous." He looked back at me. He was waiting for me to say something.

"Well, Mr. Galante, I guess that's all the questions I have for you." I got up and extended a hand. "Thanks for giving me the time."

"Sure, buddy, no sweat. Anytime at all. As they say here, bonne chance."

Unfortunately, I had to pass the two goons on my way downstairs. One of them stepped in front of me and grabbed my shirt and tie, bunching it up just below the knot.

"Don't ever do that again, Eddie. Understand?" The bodyguards worked for Galante. They spoke for him. It was sound advice.

"Loud and clear."

He let me go, and then, with both hands, he straightened out my tie and patted my shirt down. He gave me a little pat on the side of my face, smirked, and then winked at me. I didn't like that, but I wasn't prepared to do anything about it. *Maybe another time and another place.* I walked downstairs and out the door and got into my car.

I took out my leather-covered notebook and wrote down what had happened. What I found most interesting was that Galante had never asked me how I knew he was at the restaurant. Mob bosses didn't like surprises, and Galante hadn't been surprised when I'd come up to him at the table. He'd expected me. If that were the case, then Johnny Como no doubt had told him about me. Galante had known what I was going to ask him before I got the words out of my mouth. Galante knew both Marguerite and Belanger, and he'd lied about that. Marguerite had worked for him, and it was unlikely he wouldn't have recognized Belanger, because he had gambled on the seventh floor of the Windsor often.

I needed answers to a few questions: Did Galante know that Belanger embezzled his clients' funds? If so, did he know beforehand? If so, had Galante encouraged him to do it, maybe promising him a partnership in the gambling operation? And if so, did Galante know where Belanger and the money were? I didn't particularly like those questions, because if the answers were yes, then solving the case meant doing the death dance with the mob, and that, my friend, I did not like.

Bonne chance indeed.

CHAPTER 16

I took the rest of the afternoon off to do some personal business I had neglected that past week and then returned to my office. I opened the door, looked down, and saw little Henri and Antoinette looking up at me—or, rather, at the tins of cat food I was cradling in one arm.

Cats can see better than humans. They can also smell and hear better than we can. They've been endowed with certain senses so that they can survive in their natural environment. When they're on the big hunt, those senses, plus speed, all pull together as they pursue their supper. When humans took them inside and put a roof over their heads, we extended their lifespan, but we also turned them into loveable little domesticated, whining, peevish complainers. If they're no longer able to terrorize and kill other furry creatures, then we humans damn well had better provide them with nourishment at the right time of day, or we'll hear all about it.

I opened a tin and filled their bowls. They hunched over them and ate as if there were no tomorrow.

I picked up the mail off the floor below the mail slot and sorted through it. I found mostly bills, and I tossed them into my inbox. One envelope caught my attention, however. My name was written in cursive letters, without an address. There was no return address or stamp. The sender had put the letter in the mail slot. I tossed it onto the desk and got out a bottle of Canadian Club. I poured myself a finger, sat down, and filled a pipe. I stared down at my name on the envelope: Bonifacio Edmondo Wade. For a moment, it looked like someone else's name—someone I might have known years ago but had since lost contact with. I'd always admired others whose job was to catch the bad guys. They contributed to maintaining order in society. Without that order, society would have been a hellish place for us to exist in. I'd done my sharing of getting criminals off the streets, as much as my private license had allowed me to. But no one had told me that it would never end. The criminals I took off the streets were always replaced by others. The carousel kept spinning. There was no way to get off. It kept going faster and faster until everything was one big blur. You became dizzy. You fell and got up, and then you tried to hang on for dear life. At some point, you realized you were unable to distinguish the bad guys from yourself, because everyone had become distorted and contaminated—vague images melting into each other.

I picked up a letter opener, put the point into the corner of the envelope, and slid it across. I found one sheet of paper, neatly folded in thirds. I drank half the whiskey in my glass, lit my pipe, and read. The note was handwritten.

> Dear Mr. Wade,
>
> By now, you must realize that I know you're looking for me. I'm done. I'm finished. I can't continue on like this. It's more than I can take. I'm ready to give myself up, but only to you. I don't trust the police. I fear something will happen to

me if I walk in alone. Please meet me tonight at the corner of Saint-Vincent and Saint-Paul at 2:00 a.m. After I'm certain the police aren't there, I'll come to you with the money I stole and give myself up. But only to you.

Phil Belanger

I took out one of the memos I had with his handwriting and compared the two. They were the same. I puffed on my pipe and thought. The bowl was getting hot, so I set it down. *What are you after, Philippe Belanger? You want me dead. Is that it? You think that if I were out of the picture, your life would be easier, and you could make your escape. You tried to kill me once and failed, and now you want one more crack at me. You'll lure me in the middle of the night, pretend you're giving yourself up, and then shoot me in the head as you did Trocadero or stab me between the ribcage as you did Marguerite. Thanks, but no thanks. Mrs. Wade didn't raise a fool for a son.*

The case was expanding into something more complicated, unpredictable, and dangerous, and Belanger was still the centerpiece. Belanger had had contact with Trocadero, and Trocadero had been murdered. Belanger had known Marguerite—to what extent, I was uncertain—and Marguerite had been murdered. Belanger's pastime was gambling, and he'd gambled at Galante's high-stakes establishment for the well-to-do, protected by the police—the same place where Marguerite had worked as a prostitute. I wasn't sure how the money fit into everything, but maybe he owed Galante and couldn't pay him. The mob was not a bank with fixed interest rates. If you owed the mob money and couldn't pay, the interest climbed daily at astronomical rates. Maybe Belanger had panicked, and that was when he'd started to embezzle from his firm. If he'd had to pay

Galante the money he'd embezzled, he might be broke right now, in spite of what he'd written in the letter.

Or maybe Belanger wanted to use the money to partner up with Galante. I had to find someone close to the operation who might know something. Ezra Adler was just the doorman. I didn't think he'd know much. Marguerite had been much closer to things. She was probably servicing Galante in addition to the people who came to gamble. Maybe one of the other girls was as close. I'd have to go back to Adler for their names and pay them a visit.

I needed to clear my mind a bit, so I went to the Lion's Den next door for another drink and some conversation.

"It's the fault of those two bastards," Bruno said as he wiped the bar top dry.

"Who're you talking about?" I asked.

"Who do you think? That humorless, idiotic, fanatical prude Pacifique Plante and his stuffed-shirt sidekick, Jean Drapeau. Two peas in the same government pod." He threw the rag into a metal container under the bar.

"As I remember it," I said, "Montreal twenty years ago was a wild, out-of-control city with a high crime rate, just like today."

"Look, Eddie, you were just a punk kid twenty years ago. I already owned this bar and knew Montreal from a different angle. Sure, there was crime and corruption. But the police kept a lid on it. They didn't try to destroy it like these two dimwits are. The city back then had a certain rhythm to it. The criminals knew their place. It was safe to walk down a street and not be mugged."

"Yeah, as long as the police and city officials got their cuts." I upended the bottle of Molson I had been working on and finished it.

"Money well spent, if you ask me. It kept the ladies off the streets and inside their bordellos. People were free to gamble at hundreds of places everywhere in the city. The Yanks came running here with fists full of money. The nightclubs were jumping. You should have seen this place back then. Packed every night."

"You're right, Bruno. But there were a lot of lives ruined. Husbands gambled away their paychecks or spent them on prostitutes, and wives and children went without food." I wasn't a prude, but that was the way it was back then.

"There are always going to be schmucks, and they're always going to find a way to spend their money. But back then, the city was full of life. Now what do we have? The Civic Action League run by those crazies in the Public Morality Committee. And the police turned into a morality squad more concerned about people's souls than about keeping people safe. That asshole Plante shut down the brothels, drove half the women to New York, and closed down the bookies and lotteries. Well, most of them at least. If that wasn't bad enough, now he's going after the blind pigs and even the church bingo games. Montreal's getting a bad reputation as a clean city. It just ain't the same anymore. He and Drapeau are driving the money away. I can't remember the last time this place was so busy that I needed to hire extra help."

"Bruno, I'm not fourteen anymore. I know the city pretty well. Believe me when I say that all Plante managed to do was send it underground and replace it with a different public face. The money is still here; it's just harder to get at. Vice is alive and well, as it has always been in Montreal, except now the little lady's a bit disheveled."

"Don't use fancy words with me, Eddie. Montreal just ain't like it was."

"What is after twenty years?"

Bruno gave me a look that said, "You're still a punk kid. What do you know?" He went down to the other side of the bar, poured a beer for a customer, and then rang it up on the register. He reached into a cooler, took out another one, and held it up to me. I nodded. He brought it over, opened it, and set it in front of me.

"So who was the babe I saw in front of your door today?" he asked. "You doing a line with someone you haven't told me about?"

"Huh?"

"The babe! The broad!"

"I'm not seeing anyone. What're you talking about?"

"The woman I saw. Right after you left, around noon. I was sweeping the sidewalk at the entrance. I saw you leave in a hurry, so I didn't say anything. Then, a few minutes later, just as I was finishing up, this gal gets out of a car and goes to your door. I yell over that you weren't there. She doesn't say anything but slips something in your mail slot and then leaves."

"What'd she look like? What color was her hair?"

"I was close enough to realize that she was a genuine lollapalooza but too far away to see much. She had a scarf on her head and a blue dress that showed all the curves."

"What was she driving?"

"Listen, with a figure like hers, I didn't pay much attention to anything else. She must have left you something, though—in your mail slot."

"Yeah, I'll check it out. Maybe she was just a prospective client."

I clammed up for a while and thought. Maybe it wasn't Marguerite who had been helping Belanger. Maybe it had been this mystery woman all along. Maybe Belanger's connection to Marguerite didn't run deep. If that were true, then Belanger might not have killed her. I didn't want to change the way I looked at the case yet. I needed more evidence to back the theory up, but I had no way of finding out who this woman was. All I knew was that she had placed Belanger's letter in my mail slot. Bruno said something that interrupted my thoughts.

"What's that?" I said.

"I said you do know that you ain't going to find that Belanger fellow, don't you?"

"I'm going to give it the old college try."

"Yeah, but how're you going to do that on account of you ain't been to college?"

"A minor detail, Bruno. A minor detail." I took a long swig of beer.

"You know where he is? I'll tell you where he is. He's sitting in one of the bars across the street from police headquarters, having a nice martini and laughing at everyone. After he's done with his drink, he'll go to his room in the Ritz-Carlton and count all his money. He doesn't look like his old self, and he doesn't even look like his new self—you know, with the crew cut and glasses. That's on account of him having an Abercrombie suitcase full of disguises. Did I ever tell you about the guy who used to come here during the war when you were hiking through Europe?"

He'd told me the story many times, but he enjoyed telling it so much that I told him he hadn't.

"It was right after the draft started. Houde was released from internment by that time and was mayor again. Ah, I remember now. It was at the end of November '44, right about the time when the soldiers in BC were throwing a helluva fuss about the government sending conscripts overseas. You know, at that time, most of my customers were regulars. I knew everyone. One day this young guy comes in. Never seen him before. Nice-looking fellow with longish sandy-brown hair. Well dressed and polite. He orders a beer, drinks it while we talk hockey, and then leaves. The next day, another guy comes in. I'd never seen him before either, but he looks a little familiar—short hair, glasses, mustache. Two new customers in two days. That was unheard of in those days. He orders a beer, and we chat about something or other for a while. Nice young man. He leaves after twenty minutes. A couple of days go by, and another new customer comes in. Mucky hat, workman's clothes, and unshaven but very polite—a nice sort, you know? Orders the same brand of beer as the other new customers did earlier in the week. He gets up and goes to the loo, and in comes the feds—the RCMP. They're looking for a draft resister, and they show me a picture. It was the guy who came in four days earlier, the first one with the sandy-brown hair. Then I get the whole picture.

"All three new customers were the same guy. It's the guy in the loo; he's using disguises to keep one step ahead of the feds. He comes back, sits down, and finishes his beer a few feet away from where I'm talking to the cops. He even chimes in on the conversation. I don't think he ever got caught. I kept my trap shut. I figured he was using me to see if I could recognize him. It's amazing what a disguise can do."

Yeah, amazing, I thought.

CHAPTER 17

The next morning, I drove to Ezra Adler's apartment on rue Nicolet. Perry Como was singing "Wanted" on the Motorola. Perry wanted someone who'd stolen his heart; I wanted someone who'd embezzled money and then possibly murdered to cover his tracks. I had to get a handle on Belanger's gambling activities. I was sure Adler wouldn't know much, but maybe one of the ladies who provided entertainment to the gentlemen in room 705 of the Windsor would.

I rapped a few times on the door. When I didn't get an answer, I pounded harder. I heard a sleepy voice on the other side.

"Yeah, what do you want? Who is it?"

"The exterminator. I heard a rat's living here."

The door pulled back slowly, and I saw one of Adler's eyes looking at me over the chain.

"Oh, it's you."

"Let me in. I've got a question."

He closed the door and then opened it again after taking the chain off. I walked in. He was in his pajamas—pretty green ones—and his hair spiked out of his head. I felt about as welcome there as the cockroach I saw sitting on the top of his ice box. I made myself at home and sat down at the kitchen table. I looked around the room. The living room and kitchen formed one small room, with a bedroom angling off to the left. The place was a trash house and hadn't changed since I was last there. Adler sat down on the couch, about as far away from me as he could possibly be while still being in the same room.

"Let me ask you," I said. "With over fifteen grand in the bank, why do you live like this?"

"You came all the way over here to ask me that? You could've telegrammed me and saved on the gas." He cocked his head slightly at me and sighed. "The money's my retirement fund. I don't spend it on things I don't need. Besides, I'm used to living modestly. You don't like my place? Nobody invited you here. You can leave anytime it suits you."

Maybe he was still half asleep, or maybe my tough-guy routine was wearing thin on him, but his tone had shifted a bit since our previous encounters. Maybe he was trying his best to become a man.

"I need the names of the girls who work the seventh floor of the Windsor, and then I'll let you get back to your beauty rest."

"You ain't heard then? Nobody works the seventh floor anymore."

"How's that?"

"The joint was raided last night, just before I got there to open up. I pulled up in a taxi across the street like I always do, and the feds had Galante in cuffs, walking him out of the hotel. I saw the broads walking toward the hotel and flagged them down. We watched the whole show from the square across the street. They had the boss and his bodyguards."

"Who's they?"

"Like I said, the feds, the RCMP. Had they waited another half hour to raid the place, they would have had all of us."

"So the girls are okay."

"Right. They're fine, and I'm fine and dandy too. Now, what else do you want to know?"

"Don't be impolite, Ezra. It doesn't suit you."

He sat with his arms crossed over his stomach and his lower lip drooping.

"So what are their names?" I asked him.

"One's called Tangerine. That's what she goes by. I don't know her real name. The other just started. We were never formally introduced."

"Do you know where Tangerine lives?"

"We shared a taxi one night. The girls and I do that sometimes. The driver dropped her at the Morgan Curry Apartments. That's all I know. What do you want with her?"

"Careful, Ezra. If I told you, I'd have to kill you."

"You're a real card. I think you missed your calling. You should be on one of those radio shows. Maybe Bob Hope needs someone. I hear Hollywood has better weather than Montreal."

I let that go. Ezra Adler seemed to be inching up on manhood. I didn't want to get in his way.

"It's none of my business, but do you have a brother or a cousin? Your face looks familiar."

"You're right. It's none of your business. But the answer is no on both accounts. I don't have any relatives. So," he said, getting up, "if you don't have any more questions, can I show you where the door is?"

I got up and walked toward the door. "Thanks, but I can find it myself," I said. As I closed the door, I thought maybe there was some hope for Ezra after all.

As Bruno had reminded me, there was a long history in Montreal of the police tolerating criminal activity. Bruno thought it was a thing of the past. I knew better. Galante paying off the local police to keep his gambling den operating was one thing. It was the price of doing business in the city. But the feds were something else. I wouldn't say they were sparkling with moral virtue; they were as capable of taking bribes as any other organization. However, it was a little trickier with them. Galante had found that out the hard way.

I knew where the Morgan Curry Apartments were. The building was in a neighborhood that had six streets, and the people of Montreal had three different names for it, depending on where they lived. Most people in Mile End—or, more precisely, Little Italy, where I grew up—called it Victoriatown, named after the nearby Victoria Bridge. The closer to the neighborhood you got, the more likely you would call it Goose Village. The people who lived on those six streets simply referred to it as the Village. The Curry was the only apartment building there.

As a boy, I used to play basketball at the Mile End Boys' Club. During the winter months, our team was bussed over to the Village to play our worthy opponents at the Victoria Boys' Club. After games, we used to go Piche's at the corner of Forfar and Bridge for chocolate egg creams. The drinks had no eggs and no cream, but we loved them anyway.

Half of the people in the Village were Italians, with Irish, English, Polish, and Ukrainians rounding out the mix. The houses were old but well maintained. I became buddies with one of the players on the Victoria team, Oscar, and he'd invite me to his small apartment, where he lived with his sisters, brothers, and mother. His father, like my own, had grown restless and flown the coop. As I remembered it, the building had seven cold-water flats. It had been at least several decades since I'd been in that area of town and inside the Curry apartment building.

It was located a few blocks from Piche's on Bridge. The sun was shining brightly as I drove down the street, passing the Black Rock, which honored the thousands of Irish immigrants who were victims of typhus, or ship fever, in the middle of the last century. I was looking at Tangerine as a possible source of information about Belanger, so I didn't want to scare her off. I had to play my cards just right. Now that Galante was out of the picture and the gambling suite had been closed down, her income was going to take a hit. My guess was that she'd be looking for clients of her own. I pulled up in front of the building, got out of the car, and walked to the entrance. Seven mailboxes matched the seven apartments I remembered. Only three of the names could possibly be hers. I wrote them down.

Back in my car, I drove over to the Ritz-Carlton on Sherbooke and registered for a room for the night. It would cost me the equivalent of a week's salary, but that was fine. I'd put it on my expense account and let Brad pay for it. It was the cost of doing business.

It was nearing late afternoon, and I was starting to get hungry. I had too much to do for a sit-down meal, so I stopped at Fairmount on the way back to my office and bought a bagel and coffee to take with me. When I walked into my office,

Antoinette and Henri were on their backs on the couch, paws up. They turned their heads simultaneously to see who had disturbed their sleep and then closed their eyes again. These days, their only interest in me was as the source of their food. Bringing Henri into the fold had been a good idea. They were good company for each other.

I took my notebook out and flipped to the page where I'd written the names at the Curry apartments. I paged through the phone book while eating the bagel and sipping the coffee. I found telephone numbers for all three.

I filled my pipe and lit up while mentally rehearsing what I would say. I'd have to use the name Tangerine and not the names I'd found on the mailboxes; otherwise, she'd suspect something. A woman answered the first number I dialed and said there was no one named Tangerine there. I thanked her and then disconnected. I dialed the second number. Her name was Stéphanie Lapointe.

"Hello. May I speak to Tangerine, please?"

There was a long silence.

"Hello?" I said.

After a shorter silence, a voice said in French-accented English, "What do you want with her?"

"I was given this number by a short bald fellow who smoked cigars—last month at his establishment. I'm in Montreal a lot, and he said to call this number the next time I was in town. I'm calling to make an appointment with her for tonight if she's free. I'm leaving town again tomorrow morning."

There was another long pause. I gave her breathing room. With her boss arrested, she might be wary of the police. Freelancing was always riskier these days.

"I'll tell her. Where are you staying?"

"At the Ritz-Carlton, room 401."

"Okay, I'll tell her. If she's free, she'll want to meet you in the lobby. At what time?"

I thought I detected a slightly chirpier tone in her voice. The Ritz-Carlton meant money—a lot of money.

"Say, nine o'clock. I'll be the chap wearing a red tie, reading a newspaper, and smoking a pipe."

"Okay, but I make no promises."

"That's fine."

"Her fees start at a hundred, depending."

I didn't want to seem too eager. It might scare her off. She'd know all the routines. I knew that a fifty would buy the best in town.

"That kind of seems a little steep, don't you think?"

"Listen, take it or leave it. That's her price."

"Okay, okay, that's fine. I don't think the bald fellow would lead me astray."

I knew that the person I was talking to was Tangerine, and I knew she'd be there at nine. She was unemployed, so to speak, as of yesterday. A C-note with the prospect of more would be a lot of money for her.

I said good-bye, hung up the receiver, and blew smoke rings into the air.

CHAPTER 18

I sank into a rich brown leather chair, unfolded the late edition of the *Star*, and tamped my pipe. It was a quarter to nine, by my watch. There was a steady flow of the Saturday-night crowd in the lobby, walking in their finest under a gigantic crystal chandelier that probably cost the equivalent of fifty years of my salary. A red carpet was spread out on a portion of the highly polished marble floor, narrowing to the entrance. On the wall on the other side of the lobby was a five-foot-tall mirror with a gilt frame. Extending around its edges, gold flames blazed out in all directions. Even though I had my best suit on—the one I had bought at Morgan's for twenty-five bucks off the rack—I felt like a fish out of water. I didn't belong in the Ritz-Carlton. I knew it, and the people walking by me knew it. I was sure they pegged me for the house dick who was keeping a cool eye on things. What else could I have been in their eyes?

One headline stuck out like a sore thumb: "American Gangster Deported." I knew who the gangster was before I read the article. Carmine Galante had been arrested last night and deported that day as an undesirable. The article went on to say that Mr. Galante would be received in New York at LaGuardia

Airport by a welcoming committee made up of federal agents and the district attorney.

Good for him. Good for Montreal.

I was glad to have gotten the chance to meet him while he was staying in our fair city. However, his departure didn't mean we'd have less crime, less heroin trafficking, or fewer high-stakes gambling operations in the city. The Mafia was providing what people wanted. Others would take over where Galante left off. I was sure his Montreal counterpart, Vittorio Coppoletta, sweetly referred to as the Egg, had already looked into that. No one, not even the New York mob, did anything in this town without first getting the okay from the Egg.

I looked over the top of the paper and saw a woman sitting in the lobby across from me with one leg crossed over the other. She was looking into a small, round mirror, moving it around to check her hair. I'd caught only a glance of her that night at the Windsor, but it had been long enough for me to remember her face. Her eyes flickered over in my direction a few times. After a moment or two, she got up, readjusted her dress, and walked over to me, placing one high heel carefully in front of the other like a model. Her appearance—everything from her hairdo and makeup to her dress, jewelry, shoes, and handbag—blended in nicely there at the hotel. She would have stood out in any other place but not there. There she looked as if she belonged. She was one smart cookie. No one would have guessed she was a high-class prostitute who lived in a dump in Goose Village. Because Galante's clients at the Windsor had been wealthy, he must have paid a lot of money to see that his girls met their standards.

She sat down on a matching leather chair with an end table between us. Her hands grasped a small envelope purse with a brass clasp on it. She opened it and then put it on the table.

"Before we go up." She looked directly at me, then at the purse, and again at me.

I had a C-note in the upper pocket of my suit jacket. I didn't like taking my wallet out in public if I could help it, so I'd put it there before I left Mile End. I shielded myself with the newspaper and slipped the bill into her purse.

"Let me go up first. Room 401, right?" she said.

I hesitated.

"Listen, I know how this works here," she whispered. "We don't want anyone to be suspicious. Besides, I'm not going to run out on you. You have my number. It wouldn't be hard to find out where I live. Now, smile and tell me if I have the room number right."

I smiled and nodded.

"I'm going to walk out the front door and come back through the side entrance. I'll take the back stairway up and meet you on the fourth floor in fifteen minutes. Now, smile again, and shake my hand."

I did what I was told, and she picked up her purse and left. She was both elegant and smart.

When the elevator door opened, I found her waiting by my room. Plush gray-and-black carpet with specks of red ran the length of the hallway. With no one around, she was more relaxed and took on the demeanor of a street hooker, leaning her back against the door with a cigarette hanging out of her mouth. She looked like a street hooker, yes, but a chic one. In spite of this incongruence, she looked dazzling.

I unlocked the door and let her walk in before me.

"No rough stuff. Understand?" she said with her back to me, putting the cigarette in an ashtray. "And if I say stop, you stop. Those are my rules."

I locked the door. "Right," I said. "No problem."

When I'd reserved the room, I hadn't gone up to see it. While she walked over to a chair near the end of the bed, I looked around to see what fifty-five smackers had bought for the night. The carpet was thick and beige. The walls displayed a series of framed paintings, most likely reproductions. Off to my left was a chaise lounge upholstered in gold-and-black material. A large bureau with a mirror and padded bench lined one wall. On one side of it sat a bouquet of assorted cut flowers in a crystal vase. *Nice touch.* On the other side of the room was a king-size bed with a classy-looking red, black, and gold spread. I shifted my gaze to her. She had begun taking off her clothes. I thought she was going to ask me to unzip her dress, but she reached back herself and undid it. "You want me to play myself or someone else?" She slipped out of her dress and was down to her bra and panties.

I glanced at the door to make sure I had locked it and then went to the other side of the room and sat down in a chair. She was down to her bare skin by that time. I watched her pull the spread and sheet down on the bed. She hopped in, adjusted the pillows, sat with her back to the headboard, and pulled the sheet up to her neck. Then she looked over at me. "Huh?"

I hadn't said anything, and she was waiting for an answer. I didn't want to spook her, but at the same time, I needed to be direct. The room was large, and I was far enough from her so that she wouldn't feel I was a threat to her when I finally said something. I must have waited ten or fifteen seconds. I was struck by her beauty, and I knew that if I continued to stare at her without saying anything, she'd probably think she was in a locked room with a psycho.

"Actually, Stéphanie, I don't want you to be upset, but I didn't bring you here for that."

She sat up straight in the bed. "Hey, what's this all about? How'd you get my name? Did Carmine give it to you?" She looked nervous now and pulled the sheet up farther to her chin.

"All I want to do is talk."

She relaxed against the headboard again. "Oh jeez, it's like that, huh?" She lowered the sheet to her waist. "That's okay with me, but the price is the same. So talk away."

She must have thought I was some lonely traveling salesman whose equipment no longer functioned. All she had to do was sit and listen to my sorry little story about how life was sad and lonely, my marriage was in the gutter, and there was no one to listen to my deepest thoughts and secret desires except someone I paid to listen to them. It would be an easy night for her and some easy money.

"I don't want to talk about myself, Stéphanie. I want to talk about you." I got up, walked over to the far edge of the bed, and sat down. That was a foolish move; it was too fast. I had rushed it and made her feel threatened.

She jerked herself to an upright sitting position. "Don't call me that," she snapped. "My name's Tangerine, and I don't talk about myself. What's going on here? Who are you?" The sheet came down to her thighs, and she was holding a cute little four-inch blade. "If this is some kind of routine, buster, you better think twice. I'm getting up, putting on my clothes, and leaving, and if you try anything stupid, you're going to wish you hadn't."

I stood, put my hands up as if I had the barrel of a gun to my spine, and backed away from the bed. I carefully reached behind me and took out my wallet. I pulled another hundred-dollar bill and my business card out of it and placed them on the bed. "I'm going to sit in that chair again." I pointed to it. "Please put your clothes back on. My name is Eddie Wade. I'm a private investigator. You must have heard about Marguerite by now. I just want to ask you a few questions, and then I'll leave." I walked over to the chair and sat down.

She picked up my card and sat silently for a minute or so, looking at it and then at me, trying to wrap her brain around what I had just told her. I gave her the time she needed. I looked closely at her face. It was long and narrow. Her brows were thin and arched in the middle. The lids above her eyes were puffy, giving her a sleepy bedroom look. Her hair was black, was parted on the left side, and ran down to her shoulders in waves. Aside from the color of her hair, she was Lauren Bacall's double. She wasn't Hollywood gorgeous, but her looks would have had a casting director looking at her a second time when he wanted a mysterious, sensual face to play opposite Grant or Ladd.

She got up without a word. She wasn't embarrassed about being naked in front of me. She had probably been a working girl for a while, but she couldn't have been that old, maybe twenty-one. She had long pearl-white legs, a short waist, and small breasts that were in proportion to the rest of her. She put her bra and panties back on and then slipped into her dress. Her back was to me, so she must have believed I was who I claimed to be. As she was zipping up her dress, she said over her shoulder, "I felt so sorry for Marguerite. Maybe she had the wrong kind of guy. It happens sometimes. After I heard about her, I bought this knife for protection. I never worried about it before, but after, well ..." She reached over and grabbed the arm of the chair to balance herself and put her heels on. Then she walked over to me and turned around. "Finish it up, will ya?"

The zipper was about two inches from the top, so I finished the job.

She walked back to the bed and sat down. "We were close, Marguerite and me. I got sick when I heard she was murdered. Do you have any idea who killed her?"

"I'm trying to find out. I have an idea. Tell me more."

"We worked for Carmine, as you probably know. He took pretty good care of us. We mostly worked at the Windsor, because there were a lot of rich men coming in there to gamble. But if Carmine didn't like a guy, he wouldn't let him touch us. He'd let us work on our own, but he had so much business for us that it wasn't necessary. We were there most every night, so we'd have to arrange it in the day if we wanted to work outside the hotel."

"Did Marguerite ever vary her routine? Did she do anything recently that she wouldn't normally do?"

"Just one time. Carmine got Marguerite to do a favor for him. When he asks us to do a favor, it's really not that, you know, asking. But he almost never does. That's why I remember it."

"When was that?"

"It must have been—let's see—about three weeks ago. I don't remember exactly. He wanted her to rent a room somewhere, like at a rooming house, you know, under some guy's name. That's all. He gave her cash for it."

So it was Marguerite, I thought. *And Galante was in on it.*

"What was the name?"

"I don't remember it. Even if heard it, I wouldn't remember it."

"How do you know all this?"

"Marguerite told me. Like I said, we were close. We told each other everything."

"Did she tell you anything else recently, leading up to her death? Even something you might consider not too important?"

"I can't think of anything." She shook her head.

A thought occurred to me. It was a long shot, but I decided to ask her anyway.

"Did you ever see Galante work on his books—you know, for the gambling at the Windsor?"

"Oh yes, many, many times."

"Did he keep them in the suite?"

"It was just one, a ledger, but he sure did, and I doubt if the police will ever find it."

"Why's that?"

"They'd have to rip the place apart. He kept it in a safe."

"Where's it located?"

"Like I said, unless the cops dug up the whole place, they'd never find it. It's in the kitchen, where the crystal wine glasses are. Carmine had a safe put in and a false wall. With the glasses in front of it, you'd never know it was there. They'd really have to tear the place apart to find it, and then it would be tough."

I had other questions for her, but they could wait. I didn't want to overload her at that point. She'd become comfortable with me, and I wanted to keep it that way. However, I was curious about her name.

"Can I ask you a personal question?"

"You paid two hundred dollars and didn't get laid, so I suppose you could."

"How'd you get the name Tangerine?"

She grabbed her purse and took out a pack of cigarettes. She lit one and then put it in an ashtray. She looked toward the window, but the drapes were closed. Her eyes went to mine, then to the carpet, and then back up to me.

"No one ever asked me that before. You'll think it's kind of foolish—what did you say your name was?"

"Eddie, and I won't think any such thing."

"Okay, Eddie. You see, I'm from Notre-Dame-de-Portneuf, way out in the sticks. It's just a village. My father was a musician, playing with his band all over the province, so he was gone a lot. I suppose I was about twelve or so then. We had a lot of records in the house, the kind of music he played, so I grew up listening to it. There was one song I really liked that had been used in a movie. *The Fleet's In* was the name, with Dorothy Lamour and William Holden. Jimmy Dorsey played a song that captured my heart." She started to hum the tune. I recognized it. "Do you know it?"

"I do." I smiled. "It's 'Tangerine.'"

"Yes, yes, that's it! It's about this girl who makes women's heads turn, and the guys swoon over her. I knew all the words to it and went around the house singing it all the time. There was one line in particular that got me, and I'll never forget it. I'll sing it for you if you promise not to laugh."

"Cross my heart and hope to die."

She sang it. "'And I've seen times when Tangerine had the bourgeoisie believing she was queen.' I guess that coming from where I did, I wanted to become a queen. Six years later, I came to the big city to try it on for size. It's not like in the movies, Eddie. It's rough for a small-time girl from a village up north. I didn't become a queen. I guess I'm still working on it."

As I sat listening to her, I couldn't help but think of how many other bright and beautiful girls came to the big city for fame and fortune only to end up in a typing pool or in the red-light district. Montreal ate them up by the hundreds every year. Dear little Tangerine was just one of many. I could see she was intelligent; she was probably making a lot of money. I wondered if she knew that her looks were going to carry her just so far and that sooner or later, she'd be working the streets in skid row, selling herself for the loose change in someone's pocket.

"Anything else, Eddie?" She glanced at the bed and then back at me. "I don't think you got your two hundred dollars' worth. Besides, you're kind of cute."

God, how the angels of hell put temptation in front of me. This girl had something indefinable, and it got to me. She was wise in the ways of the world one shouldn't have been at her age, but there was a certain innocence about her that attracted me. She was lovely beyond the glossy pinup pictures in magazines on the racks of every street corner in the city. A voice whispered in my ear, *Go ahead, Eddie boy, and have her in that big, expensive bed you rented for the night. You'll be the latest on her list of men who've pushed her further and further along to nowheresville, where, eventually, for the price of a pack of cigarettes, she'll hoist her skirt in some dark alley for a quick jolt from some stinking, lice-infested moron. No, Eddie boy, you're better than that. This one is salvageable. Not all are, but this one is. Wake up, man! Stuff your ego, you pathetic little clown. A quickie, and you walk away so she can go on to the next? Is that what life has come down to for you?*

"I'll tell you what. I know a little place not far from here. Let's have a late supper and a drink, and we'll see what happens from there."

"Sure, Eddie, that's fine. I'm a little hungry anyway. Jeez, you're turning out to be a pretty nice guy."

I remembered that Marguerite had said something like that to me.

CHAPTER 19

I woke up Sunday morning with Tangerine on my mind.

She'd given me a good lead in the case. If I could get at Galante's ledger, maybe I could find something in there that would connect Phillip Belanger to the Windsor gambling operation. That was what should have been on my mind.

But it wasn't.

I had become smitten by her. After we left the Ritz, we walked south to Mountain and had a bite to eat at Café Martin. When we finished, neither one of us wanted the night to end, so she ordered a pink lady, and I had a brandy Alexander. We didn't talk about the case, Marguerite, or her background up north in a small French village. We talked about what she wanted out of life. Actually, she talked, and I listened. Her story was the usual one I'd heard too many times before. She had come to Montreal two and a half years ago at eighteen for a modeling career. The people at the agency she had gotten tied into had promised her a spectacular career, but she had to start at the bottom like everyone else. With her looks, they'd cleverly led her into being a high-class call girl, explaining to her that that was where her contacts would be. Shortly after, Galante had gotten his hands on her with more promises and big paychecks. Two and a half years later, she was still at the bottom, with no prospects. She had figured that out herself, so now she was saving her money, living low in Goose Village, and waiting until she had enough money for a McGill education and a future.

Tangerine was smart. She could do it. But I'd seen too many like her before. They never got out. They were still selling their bodies, but instead of selling them at the Windsor or the Ritz, they were doing it down by the docks for five bucks a shot—and they weren't getting any younger. If Tangerine were ever going to get out of that trap, it had to be soon; otherwise, she'd end up like the rest of them. When I woke up Sunday morning, my mind was in high gear, trying to figure out a way she could do it.

I spent most of the morning behind my Royal, typing up the notes I had written over the last week or so. The sun was streaming through the blinds, and Antoinette and Henri were chasing each other around the office. I put the pages in a file folder marked "Belanger" and filed it away. I grabbed a pipe out of the rack, filled my pouch with tobacco from the humidor, put my hat on, and made for the door. I had to see a man about a mission.

I pointed the Packard in the direction of Saint-Henri and stepped on the gas. I hadn't seen Jean-Paul Bonhomme for several years, and I hoped he still lived in his small redbrick house on rue Bourget, near the Lachine Canal. I needed to ask him for a favor. I'd discovered over the years that there was a trick about asking someone for a favor, especially if what you were going to ask was going to ruffle the feathers of several law enforcement agencies. If the person were indebted to you, he would more than likely be willing to stick his neck out to help you. However, under no circumstances should you ever bring up the aforementioned debt. It had to be unstated; otherwise, he'd resent you for asking, and you'd never regain the relationship you once had with him.

Jean-Paul was one of the cleverest safe crackers in Montreal. Some people had sharper senses than others. He was one of them. He had a golden ear. Like a canine, he could hear things before anyone else. He had learned his trade at the Wilson Safe Company in Philadelphia and worked for them for five years before moving back to Montreal. Then he'd gone into business for himself, freelancing in the world of crime.

He stayed away from banks—they were too risky, and there was too great a chance of being shot. He wasn't a violent criminal. His specialty was small businesses with modest amounts of cash on hand that didn't require a night watchman. He could get in and out with no fuss. He never got rich doing that, but it kept the wolves from the door, and he led a pretty good life, until he got caught—by me.

At one point, he started to hit jewelry stores—a whole slew of them. After a while, the owners got nervous, and Hemsleys, over on Sainte-Catherine and University, hired me. They hadn't yet been hit but figured they'd be next in line soon. We came up with a plan. It took several weeks, but sure enough, one day in the early morning hours, Jean-Paul appeared. I was sitting behind a desk, dozing a little, when I heard someone jimmying the lock on the back door. I got up and hid in lavatory in the back room with the door slightly ajar, just enough to be able to see the safe. I let him open it and grab the money before I busted him.

He did five years in Bordeaux and took it like a champ. I visited him when I could, and we became friends. There were no hard feelings. During one of my visits to the prison, he asked me to do a favor for him. He had a kid sister. She needed help staying on the straight and narrow. I told him I'd see what

I could do. She was streetwise and a little rough around the edges, but otherwise, she was a good kid. I got her a job and an apartment. I called on her from time to time and helped her with money once in a while. That was all she needed. She became a secretary at a big law firm and was doing well, though she was still rough around the edges. Jean-Paul never forgot that. I usually never ask for anything in return when I do a favor, but that day, I was forced to.

I found his house and knocked on the door. He gave me a bear hug when he saw me. He was skinny and probably weighed 140 pounds tops, but he looked the same as he had the last time I'd seen him. We chatted for a while over beers, and then I got around to what I had come for. I explained the situation while he sat listening. When I finished, he grimaced.

"Eddie, you know I'm retired. I've been a good boy. If something goes wrong, I'll end up back in the can for a long stretch. But you're a cleaver guy, so you got things figured out, eh?"

"As much as I can," I told him. "Nothing's a hundred percent foolproof. There's always a risk. Something could go wrong. But I'm putting myself on the line as well. The case is that important. You want odds? How about a ninety-five percent chance things will go as planned?"

"Coming from you, I'll take the risk. Do you know what kind of safe it is?"

"No."

"That will make a difference in how fast we get in and out of there."

"The hotel room is locked, and no one will be in it. The safe's behind a false wall. I'm told it'll be fairly easy to get to."

"Okay, but I think we still have to do the job as fast as we can. Getting away is sometimes harder than opening the safe, right, Eddie?" He winked, reminding me that I had caught him on his last job. "How many ways are there out of the room?"

"Two. The main door and the fire escape."

"Good. I don't like a one-exit job."

"What will you need?"

He got up, went to the other side of the room, and pulled back the carpet, revealing a floor safe. He opened it and brought out a small leather case.

"I have everything I need here. I keep it for old time's sake, as a reminder of my previous life. I've never been tempted. I didn't particularly like Bordeaux all that well. But I owe you, Eddie. I haven't forgotten what you did for me—for Amélie. Besides, if we get caught, we could be cell mates, eh? When's the big day?"

"Tonight."

"Oooh" was all he said.

As we drove to the hotel in the Packard, Jean-Paul explained his technique to me.

"You have to listen carefully," he said. "Only the most experienced can do that. You have to know what to listen for. There's a certain sound the tumblers make. You gotta have an ear for that. But there's also touch. When you dial the wheel in a certain way, you can feel the resistance. So it's sound and touch. You have to be cozy with the lock. And you gotta have patience. You can't rush it—just like with women, eh, Eddie?

"My ears ain't so good no more, so I use a stethoscope. If it's an easy lock, it could take an hour or more. Sometimes less. But the way I do it, it leaves no trace, and it leaves the safe in perfect condition. I'm quiet. No explosives. No noise. The biggest problem will be getting in and out of there without being seen."

"What if it's a difficult one?" I asked.

"Well, Eddie, it could take several hours or maybe never. But I will tell you this much—in all the years of my career, I've never come across a safe I couldn't open."

I parked the car a block away from the hotel. It was 3:05 in the morning by my watch. Jean-Paul emptied his case, putting the tools in the inside pockets of his jacket. It was the same jacket he had always used, with special pockets designed for each of his tools. That way, he had his arms free and his tools hidden. We walked over to the hotel and found a service entrance in the back that was locked. Jean-Paul opened it in less than fifteen seconds. We opened the door and stood there for a few minutes, listening. When we thought it was clear, we climbed the back service stairs to the seventh floor and went to room 705. He took a little tool from one of his pockets and used it on the lock. We went inside, and I turned on the light to discover the place was a mess from the police raid. They'd turned everything upside down. The roulette wheel was smashed. I started toward the kitchen, but Jean-Paul wanted to check out the fire escape first. "Once you break into a place," he told me, "the first thing you do is check out how you're going to get out." He opened a window and looked down. The fire escape led right down to the alley where the garbage cans were. There was no one there, and it was dark.

We went into the kitchen, found the cupboard where the wine glasses were kept, and carefully set the glasses on a countertop without making any noise. Jean-Paul pried the false backing off and looked at the safe. He turned to me, smiled, and gave me a thumbs-up. I made a series of hand gestures to let him know I was going back to the living room to turn off the main lights and listen at the door. He touched his forefinger to his thumb and gave a little jerk with his hand, indicating everything was okay.

I waited at the main door with my ear to it for the next forty minutes. Every so often, I turned around to listen toward the kitchen. Jean-Paul was working in complete silence. Finally, I heard him hissing at me. I walked back to the kitchen as he pulled the lever down on the safe and opened it. I shined a penlight in and saw a revolver sitting on top of the ledger I was after. I pulled the book out, set it on the counter, and opened it.

Holding the penlight in one hand, I ran a finger of the other down several columns of figures—amounts, each with a plus or minus beside it, along with dates. It was a record of money coming in and going out. I didn't see any names, but there were initials next to the numbers—a system to better hide anything that might be incriminating. If the law discovered a name in the ledger of an illegal business, that usually meant a nice, long vacation compliments of the government. Initials, on the other hand, were useless to a Crown attorney. They wouldn't hold up in court.

I flipped through the pages and found more of the same. When I came to the last page, where the most recent entries were, something caught my attention. The name Duke was written beside the amount of $95,000. Duke could be a first name, last name, or nickname. It could even be some kind of code. I pulled my notebook out of my jacket and wrote the name down, along with the amount and date.

Jean-Paul looked at his watch. I could tell he was getting antsy. I turned to replace the ledger in the safe, when I heard a key in the main door. I clicked off the penlight, and we stayed where we were but got down. The door opened, the overhead light went on, and I heard a female voice: "*Tabernac*!" That was an all-inclusive French Canadian word that could mean just about anything you wanted it to. The light went out again, and the door closed.

I whispered to Jean-Paul that it was probably the maid. "She'll call the main desk to report the condition of the room. They'll tell her that the police raided it a couple of days ago and left it like that." I told Jean-Paul we'd better go right away. I grabbed the ledger and used a handkerchief to wipe clean any Wade prints I'd left on it. I then put it back in the safe, placed the revolver where I'd found it, closed the door, pushed the handle up, and spun the dial. After wiping the safe down as well, I replaced the false wall, and then we both put the crystal glasses back. I told Jean-Paul that we'd better go down the fire escape in case someone decided to come up and have a look.

Once in the car, I tried giving Jean-Paul a hundred dollars for his time. He wouldn't take it.

CHAPTER 20

I got up early the next day. I stood in the middle of the storage room, a.k.a. my bedroom. I scratched my head. It had been fifteen days since I'd gotten the case, and I wasn't getting any closer to finding Philippe Belanger. I shuffled into the office and fed Antoinette and Henri. I then sat down at my desk, still in my T-shirt and drawers, and got the case file out to review and to add a few notes to it from the last few days.

Galante's ledger hadn't been all that interesting—not for the case, that was. If the police ever found it, they'd have a go at it and maybe find something useful for them. I picked up my notebook and paged through it to my last notes. There was one thing, however, that did stand out: the $95,000 entry with the name Duke beside it. Ninety-five grand was close enough to the one hundred grand that had gone missing from the brokerage firm. That alone might not have piqued my interest, but the date of the entry did—the entry had been made just before the embezzlement was discovered.

Money flowed in this city faster than booze after a Stanley Cup win. Some of it ended up in Galante's back pocket. The date could have been a coincidence—or not. The plus sign beside the entry could only mean that it was money going into the gambling operation. Duke was the big donor. Was he an indebted card player? A new partner of Galante? I discounted the bright idea that someone had used the money to pay off a debt. If so, I would have seen figures—minuses—that showed the debt along with the name Duke. There were no such entries. Besides, the name Duke appeared only one time. After dismissing the notion that Galante had some generous benefactor looking out for him, I concluded tentatively that Duke must have bought into the operation for that kind of money. It was unlikely that the name was legit. It could be a nickname or, just as likely, some kind of code for the unknown partner.

Perhaps Belanger, having gambled there for quite some time, had decided he wanted a cut of the action. Before the RCMP had busted the place, it must have been doing well, especially with city protection. Maybe Belanger had embezzled the money to buy in and planned to replace it when the profits started to roll in. *No one the wiser. Front money, plain and simple.* Then a client had decided to liquidate and thrown the earth off its axis—and the Belangers' lives out of whack.

Perhaps Belanger and Duke were the same person.

It was a fine hypothesis. I was proud of myself. It required a toast. I opened a drawer in my desk, pulled out a bottle of Canadian Club, and poured some into a stained coffee cup. I hoisted it to the gods, knocked it back, and then looked at my watch.

I took a quick shower, put my clothes on, prettied up in front of the mirror, grabbed my hat and pipe, and aimed myself at my car. I had to see a lady about a picture.

I drove down to rue Ontario and Bleury and pulled into the empty lot at the Bellevue Casino. It was closed at that time of the day, but most of the employees would be there getting ready for the doors to open and the crowds to come in. The front door was unlocked, so I went in. An old man wearing tan work pants, a matching shirt with the tail half out, and a rumpled fedora in worse condition than mine, a hat that must have been new when he was just a babe in the arms of his mother, was standing at the entrance, taking a smoke break. A mop and bucket were beside him. I asked him if Colette was there. He smiled and then chuckled to himself. His teeth were a light shade of brown. Was he laughing at me? Had I left a streak of toothpaste on my chin? I asked him again. He smiled again and then put the cigarette in his mouth. He threw one arm back over his shoulder, pointing behind him with his thumb. I walked down a hallway, leaving the old guy chuckling to himself.

A sign on the door read, “Knock First and Then Wait.” I knocked, and then I waited. I heard a female voice say, “Yeah, come on in. I’m not developing.”

I went in.

“Eddie Wade! Two times in one week. You want your picture taken or something? Oh, I remember now. You wanted to check on someone else’s, right?”

“Hey, what’s with the old guy with the mop?”

“Oh, that’s Charlie. What’d he do—laugh at you? Pay him no mind. He does that to everyone. He’s the boss’s great-uncle or something like that. He’s a little weird, but he’s harmless. He’s actually a sweetheart when you get to know him.”

“Right.” I took out the photo of Belanger and his wife and showed it to her. “I’d like to see whether you photographed this guy with a woman other than this one in the last few months.”

"Darling boy, do you know how many pictures I've taken in that time? How many people I've seen? Thousands!"

"How do you keep track of them? Do you keep them all—I mean the negatives—even if the person buys one?"

"Okay, here's how it works. I walk around the tables and dance floor every night with my camera. When I take a picture, I give the customer a number that also has the date on it. It corresponds to the roll of film in the camera. I tell him where to go if he wants a copy. Even if he buys one, I always develop a second one just in case he really likes it and wants another. You see those boxes over there?"

I turned around and saw dozens of them stacked on one another.

"Don't look frightened, Eddie. The boxes are all marked with the dates. Each box represents a month. So you take your little old behind over there, and look for the month you want. I've got a ton of work to do before we open. You'll find a table on the other side of the boxes to sit down at after you find the box you want. Just don't mess the place up too bad. Bonne chance." She flashed me a sympathetic smile.

I decided to start with last month first: May. I found the box easily enough, brought it to the table, and opened it. Each folder inside was labeled with the day of the month. Not knowing the date or whether they'd even been photographed, I started with the first of the month. I grabbed the folder and, resting it on my lap, went through the pictures quickly. The photos were all four by six inches, with the negatives fastened to the back. There must have been thirty or forty of them. *No, that's not it. No, no, no, no, no, no, and no again.* After I got to day fifteen, they all started to look alike. If I never saw another boozed-up, screwy-eyed, smiling face again, I'd be tickled pink.

On May 19, I struck gold. I stared hard at the photo, focusing my eyes on the details. The woman in the picture stared back at me. She was sitting at a table. One hand was out in front of her toward the camera; her fingers were spread out as if to block the shot. Her hand partially obscured her face, but there was enough of it, including those big blue eyes, to identify her. It was Juliette. There was a guy sitting next to her who had turned away from the camera. It wasn't Belanger. The photo gave the impression that the couple didn't want their picture taken. I pulled it out, set it aside, and then continued to look at the rest of the photographs in the folder.

After going through three more folders, I came across a photo of a well-dressed older couple with white hair. The guy had a cigar in his mouth, and his head was turned slightly up for the camera. What caught my attention was the couple sitting directly behind them. The woman was Juliette again, with her face to the camera. The camera lens was focused on the older couple, so she had come out a little blurry, but she was still recognizable. The guy next to her was looking in her direction. He was captured in profile, smiling at her. It was the same guy from the other photo.

I took the photos to Colette and gave her the first one. "Do you recognize this couple?"

"Oh yes, I remember now. They didn't want their picture taken and put up a big stink about it. She told me to destroy the negative. I apologized and said that I would, but I got so busy that I forgot."

I showed her the second one and pointed to the couple in the background.

"Yeah, that's them too. Actually, I don't remember them being in the picture. After all, I was shooting the old couple."

"Do they come in very frequently?"

"Once or twice a week, I guess. Maybe less."

I pulled out the photo of Belanger and Juliette again.

"Does this guy ever come with her?"

"Let's see. There are so many people who come here. Nope, never saw him before. But that doesn't mean he hasn't been here. I just don't remember him. She's always here with the guy in the picture—I mean the other picture. I don't go near them anymore. Come to think of it, I haven't seen them here lately. What kind of case are you working on, Eddie? Some kind of nasty love triangle? You little rascal you!"

"Do you mind if I take these two? I'll be sure to return them."

"Don't bother. I shouldn't have them, like I said."

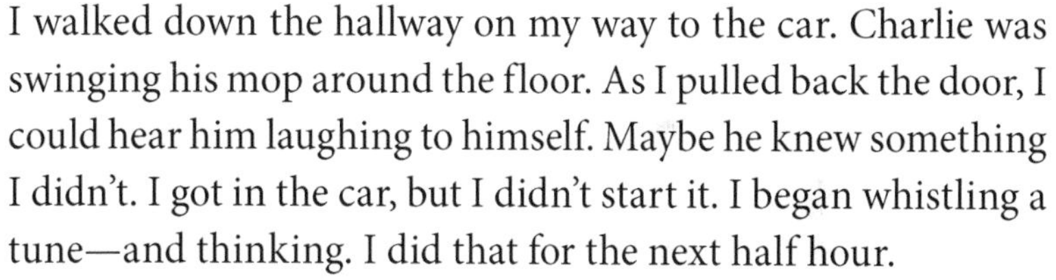

I walked down the hallway on my way to the car. Charlie was swinging his mop around the floor. As I pulled back the door, I could hear him laughing to himself. Maybe he knew something I didn't. I got in the car, but I didn't start it. I began whistling a tune—and thinking. I did that for the next half hour.

When something stinks that shouldn't stink, you want to know what it is. Maybe it's the garbage that you forgot to take out. Maybe a rat got trapped behind a wall and died. Anyway, you have to find the source of the smell in order to eliminate it.

I picked up one of the photos and looked at it for the umpteenth time. *Juliette, the stunning Greek goddess. Juliette, the hard-done-by wife. Juliette with those beautiful blue eyes of hers, looking into the camera. And beside her in profile, a man smiling at her.* I could imagine him being lovestruck. The look was unmistakable. I knew I could have been easily besotted with her.

And I wondered whether Michael Spence was.

CHAPTER 21

I found a parking space directly across the street from the Hardcastle Office Building, which housed Spence and Belanger Investment Brokerage. After I'd left the casino, I'd driven over to the Montreal Pool Room. I had been thinking about hot dogs all morning and into the afternoon. I'd had to satisfy the inexplicable urge that had been fueled by my recent visit there while looking for Ezra Adler. I knew the craving for a hot dog would go away eventually if I continued to ignore it, but while I was still driven by it, it was impossible to pretend otherwise. I wouldn't have been able to focus on the case.

The preoccupation with food that some people had must have stemmed from a deep-seated, innate, animalistic survival need handed down from our ancient ancestors. If they missed several opportunities to eat, they could become physically weak and mentally disoriented, falling prey to creatures with sharp teeth. If they missed too many chances, they could die. We hung on to that urge, even though food in plenty was now available twenty-four hours a day. Unless you were starving—and the craving for a certain food could fool you into believing you were—this obsession with one particular food was pointless. I wasn't even hungry.

I think the real point of that urge is a reminder that we're still a part of the animal world, where we once had to claw, bite, and draw blood in order to fill our stomachs. Now it's all linked to our taste buds, which are a blessing and a curse upon humanity. They allow us to enjoy our food, but they make pigs of us all. Anyway, I had downed three hot dogs, not one, enjoying every self-indulgent minute of it. The gods of gluttony were satisfied. I could now go back to work.

After I wiped the mustard and green relish off my chin and tie, I made a phone call from a booth outside. When Michael Spence answered, I hung up.

Now, sitting in my car across the street from Spence's building, I hoped that he hadn't left in the twelve minutes it had taken me to get there. I hate being lied to, especially by a client. Juliette Belanger and Michael Spence weren't my clients technically, but they were closely associated with the object of my investigation, Philippe Belanger. They had lied to me by omission; they'd forgotten to tell me that they liked to do the Lindy together at the Bellevue Casino.

I kept my eyes on the entrance to the office building. There was a steady flow of people entering and leaving. Did I now have to discount everything the two of them had told me? Perhaps they were having an affair and thought it wasn't any of my business. That was true; it wasn't any of my business. It wasn't a crime, after all. But I was curious. I wondered if they'd forgotten to tell me anything else or fed me any other lies. I decided to follow Spence around for a while to see where he'd lead me.

There was too much risk in following him on foot. He could easily spot me, so I had to do it in the Packard. I despised surveillance work, especially when I had to do it alone and in a car. It was a roll of the dice. The possibilities of wasted hours and wasted days were endless. In the end, you could have nothing to show for it. Furthermore, it was boring. You couldn't take your eyes off the target—in this case, the front entrance of the office building—because your target could be gone in a flash. Nevertheless, at times, surveillance was the only thing that got the job done.

So I sat in my car with my head twisted slightly in the direction of the entrance, waiting for Michael Spence to come through it. An hour went by and then another. There was no sign of him. It was 5:15, and unless he was working late, he should have been closing up shop and coming out anytime. At 5:55, the door opened, and I saw Spence exit and walk to his left. He made another left at rue Peel, and then he disappeared. I started my car and followed him.

As I turned, I saw him get into his car parked by Dominion Square, across the street from the Winsor Hotel. The car pulled away, stayed on Peel, and then made a left turn onto rue Sherbrooke, going west. I followed behind him at a safe distance. He turned left onto Atwater. He continued another four blocks before pulling up to a classy-looking apartment house in the middle of the block. I stopped about a half block from there. I watched him lock his car and go into the building. I knew he could be in for the night, but I decided to wait anyhow. I looked at my watch. I'd give him two hours before folding up my tent.

At a little after eight, just as I was halfway through mentally enumerating all the states in the American union, he came back out. He had changed his clothes. His threads were now more suitable for Montreal nightlife: a plaid jacket, no tie, brown slacks, brown-and-white shoes, and a Panama fedora. Dressed to kill, he was obviously stepping out for the night. I saw potential in this.

He got back into his car and eased it out of his parking spot, picking up speed. I started my car and followed him. He made a left turn onto Dorchester. So did I. He was four cars in front of me. I thought he might be going back to his office, but he drove right by it. Six blocks later, he turned left onto avenue du Parc. He drove north for about twelve minutes. Once past Mont Royal, he eased left onto chemin de la Sainte-Catherine. I knew where the rat was going. He pulled up to Juliette Belanger's house. I slowed down and then drove on.

It took me thirty minutes or so to get through the night traffic in town to Goose Village. I was hoping to catch Tangerine in her apartment. I used the drive time to consider the little game that Spence and Juliette were playing with me. There was something going on between them. It shouldn't have been any of my business, but it was. If their relationship had any bearing on my case, it was definitely my business. I stopped short of concluding anything for the time being. I needed to mull it over further.

Tangerine opened the door on my third knock.

"Eddie," she said, surprised. "How'd you find me?"

"With a compass and map. I borrowed them from the Canadian Forces."

She squinted at me askance.

"I drove you home the other night. Remember?"

"Ah, right, yes, you did. What do you need?" She looked at me with sleepy eyes. "Oh, sorry." She stepped back, pulling the door open wider. "Come in. Excuse me, but I fell asleep on the chesterfield while listening to Fibber McGee and Molly. I'm still a bit groggy."

I stepped in and closed the door behind me. She turned the radio off.

"A drink," I said.

"Huh?"

"You asked me what I needed."

"I did, didn't I?" She ran her fingers through her hair and then stretched herself out and yawned. "Beer's all I got. Go get yourself one in the fridge, and grab me one while you're at it." She walked over to the sofa and plunked herself down on one end, pulling her legs up with her knees to her chin.

I knew where the kitchen was, because I had been there before—long ago, when I was a punk kid playing basketball against the Victoria Boys' Club team. My friend Oscar had lived in that same apartment and had invited me up several times to see his model World War I biplanes hanging on wires from the ceiling. The apartment had looked much smaller then because it had been crammed with furniture, junk, sisters, brothers, and a mother.

I opened the fridge, retrieved two bottles of Labatt, found a bottle opener in a drawer, and wedged the caps off. I walked over to the sofa and gave her a beer, and then I sat on the other end. We both took long swigs.

"Thank you again for the lovely evening," she said, holding back a yawn. "It was very sweet of you. I don't meet many guys like you."

I raised my bottle in a toast and winked at her.

"Have you heard from the police? Have they found Marguerite's killer?"

"No, but they're working on a lead."

The more I looked at her, the more I realized just how stunning she was, even without all the makeup.

"That's why I'm here," I added.

Her former place of employment, the gambling suite at the Windsor Hotel, seemed like the center of something. I hadn't made all the connections at that point, so I didn't know what that something was, but the gambling operation seemed to be the focal point of an array of characters associated with my case. First, there was Marguerite, the hooker who'd worked for Galante. She could be tied to Philippe Belanger somehow. I had my doubts now because of the woman who had dropped his letter into my mail slot. Spence had told me he'd overheard Belanger mention her name during a conversation on the phone. He may or may not have been lying. She'd ended up dead. Then there was Johnny Como. He'd apparently had it hot for Marguerite, who hadn't returned his affections, and Como was tied to Galante in a way I had yet to discover. In addition, Belanger himself had gambled there. Then there was the mysterious Duke, who had forked over a sum of money to Galante, as evidenced by the ledger, maybe for a partnership in the operation. If you knocked off five grand, it matched the sum that Belanger had embezzled from his firm. I was still hanging my hat on the idea that Belanger might be Duke.

That brought me to Tangerine.

She knew where Galante had kept his ledger. If she told the police where it was, and if it contained incriminating evidence that could put some people away for a long time, then Tangerine might be in danger. If Belanger had killed Marguerite for whatever reason, maybe he wouldn't stop with her. Maybe he knew how close Tangerine had been to Marguerite. Tangerine had said they'd told each other everything. Maybe there were other things Tangerine knew that she was keeping to herself.

She looked at me, confused. "I don't get it. I told you all I knew about Marguerite."

"I know you did, but so many things have happened that I'd feel better if you stayed somewhere else other than here."

I didn't want to alarm her by telling her that she might be in danger, but she was alarmed nonetheless. She was fully awake now. She jumped up, nearly dropping the bottle of beer. "My God, are you saying that someone's out to get me like they got Marguerite?"

I got up and went to her in the middle of the room. "No, that's not what I meant. It's just that a lot has happened at the Windsor, and I think you should lie low for a while until things blow over."

"Don't lie to me, Eddie! I've had a funny feeling lately. Someone's after me. Tell me the truth."

"The truth is, I don't know."

"Oh jeez. Oh damn." She began pacing the room. "Oh jeez. Oh damn. What am I going to do?"

I stopped her after the fourth "Oh damn" and took her by the shoulders. "Look at me. Good. Now, do you have a safe place to stay?"

"No! I have nowhere to go."

"Okay, then you'll stay with me until the air is cleared. Nothing will happen to you. I won't let it."

She lowered her head.

"Look at me," I said, and she did. "Do you believe me?"

"Yes," she said reluctantly.

"Do you have a suitcase?"

"Do you want me to pack now?"

"Yes. Throw some things in it, and we'll leave when you're done."

I sat down on the chesterfield again and finished my beer while she packed. I hoped I wasn't overreacting, but it was better to play it safe. Tangerine was someone special. She was salvageable. She could brighten up the world a little if she had a bit of luck—if someone didn't stick a knife in her first.

CHAPTER 22

I felt the weight of the world on my chest.

I opened my eyes to discover that the weight was Antoinette. I reached over and gave her a good head rub. When I'd finished, she jumped off me and started to groom herself. Henri pawed his way over to her and did the same. I got up and stretched. Like a good boy, I had slept on the couch in my office, giving Tangerine my bed in the back room. A door separated us. I turned the knob on the radio and got the local news. I kept the volume low in case she was still sleeping.

After feeding the cats, I heard the door to my bedroom open.

"Sleep well?" I asked Tangerine. "Sorry about the radio." She looked disheveled. Her hair was tousled. I had given her my pajamas—my only pair—because I never wore them, and she had forgotten to pack her nightclothes. They looked funny on her—in a sexy way—because they were about two sizes too big for her. I could barely see her fingers, and her toes completely disappeared. They would have left a lot to the imagination if not for the fact that I'd already had a clear, unobstructed view of her in the room at the Ritz-Carlton.

"Good morning, Eddie." She yawned with an open hand covering her mouth. "No, that's fine. I was awake already. I tossed and turned for a while, probably because of the new bed. I slept like a baby after that, knowing that you were on the other side of the door." She grinned, her sleepy eyes examining me. "For protection, you know?"

I was in a T-shirt and underwear. I figured she wouldn't be too shocked by it, and she wasn't. "How about breakfast?" I asked.

"I could eat a cow," she answered.

"I don't have one at the moment. All I have is cat food. How about we go out?"

We took turns showering. I searched the rack for a suit with the least number of creases in it—an easy task since I had only two of them—and dressed. When Tangerine was ready, she came into the office area wearing a nice summer-weight light blue skirt, a white blouse, and black flats. Her hair was tied up in the back in a ponytail. She looked as if she were ready for classes at McGill. There was a chill in the morning air, so she went back to her suitcase and pulled out a sweater.

I decided to avoid the greasy spoon where I usually had my breakfast, so we walked south on rue Saint-Urban for five blocks to Beautys. It was a tiny place, but it was past the breakfast rush, so there were a few empty tables. Hymie, the owner, greeted us cheerfully at the door and showed us to a table by a window. I ate light, having only toast and coffee. Tangerine devoured the special: pancakes, eggs, bacon, toast, and coffee. When we'd finished, we leisurely strolled back to the office, each of us not saying much.

I showed her around the area a bit and then introduced her to Bruno next door at the Lion's Den. I gave him the lowdown on what was happening, so he could keep an eye out. I thought

Tangerine would be safe in that part of town, but you always have to prepare for the worst and hope for the best.

In the office, I handed her a key, told her not to answer the phone, showed her where the cat food was, and said that I should be back around six. "We should have supper together."

She was a little jumpy about being left alone, so I told her she was safe in that part of town and didn't have to worry (I let myself do all the worrying). However, if something came up that she wasn't comfortable with, she should go next door to Bruno. In case she couldn't for any reason, I left Bruno's telephone number with her.

Then I left.

On my way into town, I stopped at a Greek florist on Saint-Urban and picked up some cut flowers. I continued down to Dorchester and then turned right, going west. At that point, I had no idea where Philippe Belanger was. My investigation had hit a roadblock. Because every law enforcement agency in the province had his name and picture, including a description of his new appearance, he had probably dug a hole for himself somewhere in the city. He could hide out for quite some time, but eventually, he'd have to show his face again. Depending on his resources and connections, that could take weeks or months. If Brad kept me on the case that long, it would do my bank account a world of good, but it would tarnish my reputation. I had to come up with something fast.

The closest people to Belanger were his wife, Juliette, and his partner, Michael Spence. The buggers had lied to me. Now it was time to go after them. But first, I had to know more about their backgrounds. I turned left onto Mansfield, drove a half block, and then pulled the beast over. I got out of the car with the flowers and peered across the lawn at an impressive edifice: the Cathédrale Marie-Reine-du-Monde. It was the Roman Catholic archdiocese of Montreal. Its administrative building was on the other side of the cathedral, so I made my way over using the paved path.

As impressive as the cathedral was, the building where business was conducted and documents were filed was mundane by comparison and could have been taken for a provincial government building. I swung back the heavy door, walked down a long hallway, and opened the door to my right. A woman was sitting at her desk, eyeing me over her glasses.

"Eddie Wade, you rascal," she said. "I should be angry at you, and only the dear Lord knows why I'm not. I certainly don't."

"The Lord does know why, but he's not talking."

Fabienne Dumont must have been closer to seventy than sixty, but she looked twenty years younger and had the disposition of someone in her thirties. She was the secretary for the archdiocese. Her hair was cut short in the latest fashion; her dress was summery, with red, yellow, and purple flowers on it; and her face was beaming as she looked at what I was holding.

"The only time you visit me is when you want something. But you always bring me flowers, so I don't think I'll be mad at you."

"If I came around here for any other reason, the archbishop might get suspicious."

"Oh, don't worry about Cardinal Léger. He's never around here anyway. Come over here, and sit down. Let me have a good look at you. It's been awhile."

I sat down on the chair next to her desk and gave her the flowers.

"I'll be right back," she said. She got up and went to the back of the office, away from view, and returned a few minutes later with the flowers in a vase, which she set on the front of her desk. "There now. They're lovely. The colors are so vibrant. Thank you very much. Now tell me what I have to do for them." We both laughed at that. I felt a little embarrassed.

We talked for about ten minutes or so, catching up, before I brought up the subject. "Fabienne, I know you don't release information on people unless you have some kind of authorization to do so, but I'm really stuck on a case, and the information I need could be very useful."

"Just cough it up, Eddie darling. If you don't ask for what you want, how are you ever going to get it?" She gave me a quick wink.

"I'd like to see the marriage registration of a couple. I have no idea when they were married, but I'm guessing it was in the last fifteen years or so."

"I assume you have the happy couple's names. Oh, if you're investigating them, maybe they aren't so happy."

"Yes, of course. Philippe Belanger and his wife, Juliette."

"That name sounds familiar. Where have I heard it? The newspapers!" she said, clicking her fingers. "Oh my Lord, that's not the same—"

"I'm afraid it is. That's the case I'm working on."

"Okay, I'm not going to ask you any questions about that, because I know you'll give me your old song-and-dance routine." We laughed again.

She went into the back of the office again, this time to a wall lined with filing cabinets. She opened a drawer and hovered over it, flipping through files with her fingers. I heard her say, "Aha!" She left the drawer open and returned to her desk with a file folder. She sat down, opened it, and took out a single sheet of paper.

"You see how easy that was? Have a peek, and see if that's what you're after." She handed me the sheet.

It was the official document of the Belangers' marriage. After I read through it, I took my notebook out and jotted down a few things, including an address. I gave it back to her.

"Fabienne, you're a gem."

"Why don't you tell the cardinal that? Maybe he'll give me a raise. Next time you come, it had better be strictly social. On second thought, if it were, you might not bring flowers to bribe me. Forget the social part," she said with a wave of a hand.

We talked for another five minutes before I gave her a hug and left.

I made my way back to the Packard and sat there looking at my notebook. The marriage record listed Juliette's last name as Bergeron. The address was more than likely her parents'. Who better than they to tell me all about Juliette Belanger?

CHAPTER 23

I pulled up in front of the house and shut the engine off. It was mostly gray stone and situated in the middle of the block on avenue Isabella, between Lavoie and Légaré, just west of Saint Mary's hospital in Côte-des-Neiges. The modest-looking house was in a modest-looking neighborhood of mostly modest-looking apartment buildings. The Pontiac in front of the garage alleged that someone was home. I looked at the amber Indian head on the hood of the car and was briefly reminded of the tram murder case I had been involved with last year.

I sat in the car for a few minutes, going over in my head the routine I was going to use with the Bergerons. Their son-in-law had been charged with embezzlement, and I was investigating the case—looking for him and the money. Interviewing people who were close to a fugitive was standard procedure. There was nothing out of the ordinary there. I just couldn't tell them I was increasingly more interested in their deceptive, lying daughter than her husband.

I got out of the car and walked up to the entrance, straightening my tie during the journey. I rapped on the door with my knuckles decisively to suggest this was an official visit rather than a neighbor wanting to borrow a cup of sugar. The knocking sounded an alarm; a dog started barking. A man in his late fifties to early sixties pulled back the door and then bent over, holding the collar of a German shepherd. He looked up at me. "Don't mind him. Every time someone knocks on the door, he gets the idea that he's got a new playmate. He's pathetic as a guard dog. What can I do for you?" The man clicked his fingers, and the dog sat down but started whining. It sounded more like crying or moaning. His tail was thumping the floor nineteen to the dozen.

"My name is Eddie Wade. I'm investigating the case involving your son-in-law, Philippe Belanger. I wonder whether I could have a moment of your time."

"The police were here already. We don't know where he went."

"I'm sure you don't, Mr.—"

"Bergeron."

"Mr. Bergeron. I just wanted to have a little background information on him. It could be useful in resolving the case one way or another."

"Let me put Algernon out back so we can talk in peace."

He returned thirty seconds later with a woman who looked to be about his age.

"This is Helen, my wife."

I shook her hand and Mr. Bergeron's as well. He angled his head at me. I knew what the gesture meant. I took my wallet out and showed them my license. He looked at it and then at me.

"I hope I didn't offend you, young man. I just wanted to make certain you weren't a reporter. The police told us that the press can pull the wool over your eyes to get an interview. It was better for us if we didn't talk to them. You know, the publicity."

They showed me in. Helen Bergeron prepared some coffee, and then the three of us sat down in the living room.

"What exactly would you like to know about Philippe? We want to cooperate in any way we can. We want to help find him. We don't think he's capable of doing what the police said he did. We think he just panicked and ran—that's all. We're absolutely convinced he's innocent."

"Mr. Bergeron—"

"Please, just Sébastien," he said.

"Sébastien," I said, taking out my notebook, "I need to get a clear picture of the kind of person Philippe is. He's not making it easy for us to find him. If we could locate him, then I think we could clear all of this up. If I had more information about his personal background, it could help."

"I couldn't agree with you more, but you should really talk to Juliette. She obviously knows him best."

"I did that already, but she's been really traumatized by this whole thing. I didn't want to probe too deeply. She's pretty fragile these days." I sipped the coffee.

"Yes, we know. We've all been traumatized by this, but go ahead. Ask away."

"How long have you known Philippe?"

"Juliette met Phil at McGill when they were students," Helen said. "I think she said he was in one of her literature classes during their last year. At some point shortly after—my, it's been so long ago now that it's hard to know exactly when—she brought him home for supper. We could see even then that they had strong feelings for each other. Juliette said later that it was love at first sight."

"I suppose you want to know what our first impression was." Sébastien straightened his back. "Well, I can tell you it was favorable—highly favorable."

"Oh yes," Helen said, "we liked him from the very beginning. After that, Juliette started bringing him to the house almost every weekend. We grew to adore him almost like a son."

"When did they decide to get married?" I asked.

"The subject was brought up about six months later," Helen said. "We certainly approved, even though they hadn't known each other very long. You see, my husband and I married after knowing each other for only two months. Juliette and Phil had, at that time, known each other for three times as long. That's why we weren't concerned."

"We gave them our blessings," Sébastien said, "but we asked them to wait until they both finished their studies." He picked up his cup and made a slurping sound as he took a sip.

"Were they both in the same year?" I asked.

"Yes," Helen said. "Juliette was studying theater—you know, drama and acting—and Phil was studying finance. He also played on the hockey team." She looked at her husband. "I forgot what position, dear."

"Forward," he said forcibly. "Center, to be precise, and a damn good one at that."

I ignored that detail and followed up with a question about Juliette. "Acting?"

"Yes, she was a fantastic actress in her college days," Helen said. "One of her drama teachers told us that she had the right stuff for Hollywood or Broadway. She actually talked Phil into joining the drama club for their last play after the hockey season was over. He had a small part, but he did it well, and we enjoyed watching him onstage." She looked over to her husband. "Didn't we, dear?"

"Indeed we did," he said. "It was great to see the three of them together onstage, if only for one play."

"The three of them?" I took a few more sips of the coffee. It was good.

"Oh, excuse me," Sébastien said. "Yes, Philippe's partner, Michael, was in the drama club as well. I assume you met him already as part of the investigation."

"Michael Spence?" I asked for clarification.

"Yes, they were like three peas in a pod that last year," he said.

"Then Michael Spence knew your daughter at that time in college?"

"Oh, long before that." He waved a hand in front of him.

"Are you saying they were childhood friends?"

"Oh yes. He grew up in the neighborhood, five doors down on the other side of the row of apartment buildings. His parents moved out of the neighborhood awhile back. Actually, they moved to Toronto."

"Did he spend much time here with your family?"

"He practically lived here," Helen said. "Michael comes from a good family. The Spences couldn't have their own children, so they adopted Michael when he was a baby." She stopped abruptly and looked at her husband, her hand covering her mouth.

"I'm afraid that's confidential," Sébastien told me. "But now that you know, you must assure me that that information stays here."

"Of course," I said.

"The Spences confided in us right after the adoption and never told Michael, so he knows nothing about it. If he's going to know, it's got to come from his parents. You can understand that, right?"

"Yes, of course," I said. "It won't go into my report."

Helen looked relieved. "As I was going to say, they had a hard time with Michael growing up."

"How's that?"

"Well, he used to get into trouble. He hung out with the wrong crowd, especially in high school. We nearly forbade Juliette from seeing him, but he was such a nice boy to us and never caused us problems. He was always respectful to us and treated Juliette like a sister."

"You say that he used to get into trouble. Can you tell me something about that?"

"Well, there were so many times, but there was this one time—maybe I shouldn't talk about this, but there was this one time that he beat up a boy really badly. Nearly sent him to the hospital. We were all so shocked because he was never a violent boy. Michael spent six months in a home for juvenile delinquents for that."

"Why the beating?"

"The boy had called him a Jew," Sébastien said. "But Michael was just going through a phase, you know, like most boys, and he grew out of it. We had seen something very gentle in Michael. His getting into trouble and that fight were out of character for him. It wasn't him—the real him. And we were right. He turned into a very nice man. Yes, a very nice man indeed." He slanted his head at me. "I thought you wanted to know about Philippe?"

"Yes, of course," I said. "Just one more question, and I won't bother you anymore."

"You're not bothering us; let's get that straight," he said. "We just want to do what's right. We want to do all we can to help clear Philippe of that ridiculous charge."

"So do I, Mr. and Mrs. Bergeron. Do you have any idea how Philippe was able to start an investment firm with Michael at such a young age?"

Sébastien took another sip of coffee and leaned back on the couch. "Mr. Belanger, Philippe's father, worked as an investment banker. The family was quite well off. Mr. Belanger financed Phillip and Michael's brokerage firm after they graduated from McGill, out of his own pocket. Through his contacts, he even sent clients their way. The boys bought out a small existing firm whose owner was retiring. They worked their backsides off. They repaid the loan with interest and made the firm a success. The Belangers—poor souls—died in a car accident in the Swiss Alps. Phil inherited quite a lot from them. There was no need for him to embezzle. That's why we're convinced he's innocent. Excuse me, but Algernon's kicking up a storm out there. I'll be right back."

A minute later, the dog came galloping into the living room with his tongue hanging out and his tail slicing the air. He put his paws on one of my legs and started sniffing. He must have picked up the scent of Antoinette and Henri on my clothes.

"Down, Algernon!" Sébastien ordered. "Sit!" The dog got down immediately and sat in front of me. The whining started again. He made it clear: it was my fault he couldn't sniff.

I stood up, and Mr. and Mrs. Bergeron walked me to the door. I thanked them for their time and for the coffee. They seemed like a nice couple. I had gotten to like them in a short time.

I got in the car and pointed it in the direction of my Mile End office. Some of the pieces of the puzzle were beginning to fit. Of all the things the Bergerons had told me, one thing stood out above the rest: "They were like three peas in a pod." For the first time, I considered the idea that the three of them were in on the embezzlement together. The Bergerons had implied that Juliette and Michael had been like brother and sister growing up. Now it seemed that relationship had flowered into something different, and it was obvious that Juliette and Michael didn't want me to know about it.

If all three of them had participated in the main course, had Belanger known that his partner was getting a little dessert on the side? That matter deserved another look. However, none of my suspicions made any difference without evidence. I had to track down someone who had known them during their last year in college.

I knew just where to go.

* * *

My next step would have to wait until tomorrow.

I got back to my office lickety-split. Tangerine had been staying with me for about a day, and I felt I needed to spend some time with her to help her feel safe and make sure she was comfortable. This was a big change in her life. We went next door to the Den and had a beer, and Bruno updated us on the latest neighborhood gossip. By the time he was finished, we were both getting hungry, so we got into the Packard and headed south.

We had our supper in a Caribbean restaurant in Little Burgundy. It was small—with a capacity of maybe twenty people at most—but we didn't have a problem finding a table, as there was a constant flow of people in and out. We both ordered red beans and rice with chicken and relished every bite of it. We ate so much that we decided to walk it off. We went a few blocks east of the restaurant to the Atwater market.

The market was in a large pale yellow art deco building with a high tower. At that time of the year, most of the people who brought their fruits and vegetable there had small tables outside. Tangerine and I walked around them, eyeing everything. We wanted to share an apple but decided against it because we couldn't put anything else into our stomachs. We extended our walk about the neighborhood for another hour, until it started to get dark. We made our way back to the car and to Mile End again.

Antoinette and Henri greeted us at the door, as usual. Tangerine got a tin out of my desk drawer and scooped some food into their bowls. I, on the other hand, got some whiskey out of another drawer and poured a little into two glasses. We sat down on the couch, happy and exhausted. We chatted for the next half hour about nothing in particular. It was apparent to me that she was less tense than she'd been yesterday. She had smiled a lot on our little outing, and that was good.

When we were both tired of talking, she got up and turned the radio on. I picked up a copy of the *Gazette* I had bought that morning and paged through it. I read a few bylines—those of Jake Asher and a few other reporters I knew—and listened to her laugh at Jack Benny and Rochester going at it. I laughed a few times myself.

After we yawned a half dozen times, I turned the lights off, and we went to bed—she in the back room and I on the couch.

CHAPTER 24

I'd been on the case for seventeen days, and Philippe Belanger was still on the lam.

I was putting the case together in pieces, but it was taking me longer than it took the Creator to put together the earth, sun, moon, and stars. I was convinced that Belanger's wife and partner were somehow involved in the embezzlement, but without evidence, my suspicion meant nothing. I was also convinced that the big picture would soon appear—but only after I first gathered all the little pieces into a basket and sorted through them. On Wednesday, June 23, I drove over to McGill University, hoping I'd find another piece to put in my basket.

I stopped several students who were leisurely strolling on the campus and asked them where the theater department was. They turned around and pointed at a huge building topped with a cupola: the Arts Building, which faced rue Sherbrooke. Once inside, I looked at the directory on the wall beside the entrance and found the room number. The room was two flights up.

The secretary behind the desk was a skinny young broad with straight brown hair and glasses that had rhinestones along the sides. I flashed her a smile and asked if anyone who had taught drama classes back in the late '30s was still teaching there.

"Professor Chambers is the only one now." She flashed a smile back at me. "Professor Pritchard retired last year."

"Would he happen to be here today?"

"Wait a moment, and I'll check his office hours." She flipped through a few sheets on her desk, taking several quick glances at me as she did. The sun shone through the window and made her rhinestones dance. "Ah yes, you're lucky. He is in the building, but you'll probably find him in Moyse Hall with some students right now. He's working with a group during the summer for a special production. Just go back to the first floor, and look for the lobby. You'll see a sign."

I thanked her and went back downstairs.

I found the auditorium easily enough and pulled back the large, thick wooden door. I took a few steps inside and quietly eased the door shut behind me. One lone actor was on the proscenium, clearing his throat. It was dark except for a spotlight shining down on him. I heard a voice say, "Now, make this good. It's the end of the dream. You want the audience to leave feeling as if they themselves were in the dream as well."

The actor cleared his throat again and then recited his lines:

> If we shadows have offended,
> Think but this, and all is mended,
> That you have but slumber'd here
> While these visions did appear.
> And this weak and idle theme,
> No more yielding but a dream,
> Gentles, do not reprehend:
> if you pardon, we will mend:
> And, as I am an honest Puck,
> If we have unearned luck

Now to 'scape the serpent's tongue,
We will make amends ere long;
Else the Puck a liar call;
So, good night unto you all.
Give me your hands, if we be friends,
And Robin shall restore amends.

"Bravo! Bravo!" the other voice said. "Well done, Chad. Lights, please! Now, everyone come out. Good. Full dress rehearsal tomorrow at two o'clock sharp. No running the streets tonight, I'm afraid. And no alcohol. Make sure you get a good night's sleep. Now, off you go. Skedaddle!"

They skedaddled behind the wings, leaving the stage bare. I could see the back of the head of the disembodied voice sitting in the middle of a row five rows up from the stage. I walked down to him, forcing a cough as I did so as not to startle him. He looked over his shoulder at me.

"Professor Chambers?"

"Yes. Ambrose Chambers here. Can I help you?"

He was older than I'd thought he'd be, probably in his early to midseventies. He had longish, curly white hair, and even though he was sitting down, I could see that he was fit. His face was long and narrow, and his eyebrows were bushy. He wore a light blue shirt with the sleeves rolled up, open at the collar, and a nice tweed vest. His jacket, also tweed, was draped over the seat next to him. He looked as if he had forgotten to shave that morning. It was now early afternoon. Maybe he was the type who needed to shave three times a day in order to look clean. He slid his glasses down his nose and looked over them at me.

"My name is Eddie Wade, and I'm a private investigator." I showed him my license. "I realize you're busy, but I was wondering whether I could have a moment of your time."

"By Jupiter, I hope I'm not in any trouble." He chuckled and ran a hand over his stubble.

"No, no, it's nothing like that."

"Actually, I'm free for the rest of the day. It's the summer session, so the academic pace slows down a bit. Can we talk here, or do you prefer my office? Actually, I believe we'd have a modicum of privacy here. You can choose." His accent was British but watered down, probably from living in Canada for decades.

"Actually, here is fine, and I'll try not to take too much of your time." I sat down in the same row, leaving two seats between us. "I'm working on a case that may involve two of your former students."

"My word, are they in some kind of trouble?"

I wasn't in any position to give him the details of the case and told him so. "I hope you can appreciate that."

"Of course, of course. Which students are you talking about?"

"They were members of the drama club in the late thirties. I believe they also took theater classes from you. Juliette Bergeron and Michael Spence."

"How could I forget them? Best raw talent I've seen in all my years of directing plays here."

"They were that good, eh?"

"As I said, the best. I know a few people in New York who produce plays—mostly off-Broadway productions. During their last year at McGill, I contacted one of the producers about them. We set up an audition for them. I thought they'd be excited about it. Very few actors get that opportunity."

"They turned it down?"

"Flat. They didn't even want to discuss it. Said they had other ambitions—acting was only a pastime for them in college. It was a shame."

"How long were they your students?"

"For nearly three years. Which was my luck, working with such talent. I can't take too much credit, though. They were good from the very beginning, even before I got my hands on them. Innate talent—both of them."

"Were you able to help them along?"

"I was, but as I said, they already had the raw talent, so it was easy on my part. I teach method acting, developed by Lee Strasberg. He trained some of the best actors in America—still does."

"I'm not familiar with him."

"Strasberg's method emphasized the practice of connecting to a character by having the actor or actress draw on personal emotions and memories. He developed a set of exercises and practices that included both sense memory and affective memory. I won't bore you with the details, but the exercises essentially require the actor to call on the memory of details of his personal life from a similar situation and then import those feelings to those of his character. An actor is essentially pretending to be someone else. To give a character authenticity, the actor must use his own experiences and emotions and then impart them to his character. That's the basic idea, but it's much more involved than that." He stood up and stretched. "Excuse me, but I've been sitting here for the last three hours." He was much taller than I'd thought—six foot three at least. He sat down again. He had to twist his legs to the left a bit to fit in the seat.

"And Juliette and Michael were good at that?"

"Oh, yes indeed. Especially Duke."

My heart stopped. When it started again, I said, "Duke?"

"Oh, forgive me. I meant Michael. We called him Duke those years because he was obsessed with Humphrey Bogart's character in *The Petrified Forest.* You know, the movie. I believe it was in 1936 when it first came out. It was a joke at first, but the nickname stuck. Duke Mantee was the character's name, but if you ask me, I think Michael was probably reacting to Bogart's acting, because it was he who breathed life into Mantee. Howard and Davis were great, but Bogie shined!"

"I'm not familiar with the movie. Who was Duke Mantee?"

"The antagonist. A ruthless gangster who was fleeing the police. Bogart is, in fact, a method actor—and a fine one at that. I always felt he was a bit cold-blooded down deep." He chuckled for a few seconds. "He played Duke so well."

"How long has it been since you last had contact with either Juliette or Michael?"

"Not since they left McGill and took my dream of turning them into stars with them. I don't exaggerate when I say that they could have been onstage on Broadway or on the big screen in Hollywood. I hope that they're all right and that they're not in any trouble. Did they ever get married?"

"Why do you ask?"

"Well, they did have quite a romance going."

"They did, but to different people."

"I see."

"I'll leave it at that, if there's nothing else you can tell me."

"I can't think of anything else. They kept their personal lives to themselves, rigidly so, so there's nothing I can tell you on that score. Except the romance thing. That was obvious to everyone."

"I appreciate your time."

I left the auditorium, exited the building, and found a wooden bench to sit down on. My suspicion was confirmed: Spence was in on this caper, and maybe Juliette was as well. Maybe the three of them were in it together. However, the name Duke in Galante's ledger wasn't evidence that would hold up in court.

Whenever a crime is committed involving more than one person, especially if the crime involves a lot of money, it's not uncommon for one criminal to squeeze the other out of the picture. Why share the pot when you don't have to? I wondered if Spence had put the squeeze on Belanger and maybe even set him up to take the fall alone.

I took out my pipe and filled it from my pouch. I put a match to the tobacco and started to puff. As I was looking over the top of the bowl, I noticed an older gentleman walking toward the Arts Building, where I had been. He turned right at the building and walked up the steps. When I had looked at the directory earlier, I'd noticed that the philosophy department was also housed in the building. The guy I had met in Dominion Square while waiting for Ezra Adler to come out of the Windsor hadn't been lying to me. He'd said he was the department chair of philosophy at McGill. I had seen him once after that, at Ruth Adler's funeral.

Now I was looking at Frederick Churchill for a third time.

I went to a phone booth across Sherbrooke and called Jake Asher at the *Gazette*. I told him I wanted to meet him at Slitkin's and Slotkin's in fifteen minutes if he was free. He was. There were so many threads running through this case that I wanted to make sure I wasn't losing sight of any of them.

One of those threads was Johnny Como. I needed to know more about him. He had known one of the murder victims, Marguerite, and he was connected to Carmine Galante in some way. It seemed that all roads led to the gambling suite at the Windsor Hotel. Belanger had gambled there, and it looked as if Michael Spence, under the name of Duke, had given Galante the embezzled money for a cut of the action, maybe to expand the racket. The case was far more complex than I'd thought. Spence, Belanger, Belanger's wife, dead Marguerite, dead Manny Trocadero, and Johnny Como—how did they all fit together? I had to get evidence that would stand up in court. However, there were still a lot of unanswered questions.

I found Asher waiting for me in a booth.

"Sorry I'm late, Jake." I slipped into the seat opposite him. "No time to socialize this time."

"That's what my wife said this morning."

"Tell me what you know about a Johnny Como."

"You really are something, Eddie. Don't I even get a beer?"

I pulled out two bits and put it on the table.

"Order one when I'm gone. I don't have time to drink one with you. Now, about Como."

"Never met him. I only heard rumors."

"What rumors?"

"That he does favors for the mob."

"What kind of favors?"

"Well, let's put it this way: he's an independent disposal company."

"That little runt?"

"You don't need size when you carry heat. All you need are a little guts and an ice-cold disposition."

"You heard that Galante was deported, right?"

He looked at me with distain. "It was my byline you read, Eddie!"

"Okay, thanks, Jake." I stood up. "Got to go."

"You couldn't have asked me about Como on the phone?"

"I wouldn't have been able to buy you a beer."

I left Asher looking a little ticked off at me and went to the phone booth outside in front of the restaurant. I dropped a dime and called Juliette Belanger. She picked up immediately. When I'd finished talking to her, I called Michael Spence at his office. We talked for about thirty seconds before I hung up.

Even with a lack of evidence at that point, I was bound and determined to bring this case to a head and to nail them to a cross.

CHAPTER 25

"You see," she said, "I've got this big, long list of things I should never have done in my life. I keep it handy so I can look at it once in a while."

"I've got a longer one," I said. "Besides, at your age, yours can't be too long."

"Is that right?" She turned her head my way. "You'd be surprised."

I had gotten up early Thursday morning, gone to the greasy spoon, and bought some coffee to go. By the time I'd returned, Tangerine had gotten up, showered, and dressed. She had been sitting on the couch, playing with the cats, when I opened the door to my office.

"I suppose that the longer you live, the longer your list becomes, eh?" she said.

"I suppose."

I was falling for her more than ever now. I looked at her. Her head was down. Henri was sprawled on her lap, and she was petting the length of his body, her fingers gliding over his fur. I could hear him purring even from where I was.

Everyone is imprisoned by something. If someone else doesn't impose a prison on us, we impose one on ourselves. We can do our time and hope to be paroled eventually, or we can try to escape. Tangerine needed to escape from her prison, but she needed help. The problem was that she didn't recognize it. She was beautiful, and she was making a lot of money by selling herself. She thought she could end it when she had enough money saved and then traverse to a different life. She wasn't old enough or experienced enough to realize that wasn't how it worked.

"Upsy-daisy!" She lifted Henri up over her head. "You're a cutie. Do you know that?" She set him on the floor, and he skittered away. She picked up her paper coffee cup and held it on her lap.

She could set herself up in a thousand classy hotels in a thousand different cities, and the men she'd have wouldn't care whether she lived or died. The cold, hard truth was that they wouldn't care a dime's worth about her. They would see her only as a means to satisfy their own fantasies. All her problems wouldn't mean a thing to them, because they'd think of only one thing, and they'd flash enough cash in her face that eventually, she wouldn't even care about herself. The men would keep coming, the cash would keep flowing, and neither would stop until she lost her looks and the innocent sparkle in her eyes—but by then, it'd be too late. She'd be relegated to the red-light district, leaning against a decaying building with a cigarette hanging from her mouth, selling herself for whatever she could get.

"Listen, Tangerine," I said, working up the courage to broach the subject. "I've been thinking about getting an answering service. I miss too many important calls. Business has been pretty good for quite some time, so I can afford a service now."

She looked at me with a blank stare, waiting for something more.

"But I decided against it."

"Oh. So what about all those calls you'll miss?"

"Well, I made a big decision. I'm going to hire a secretary. Besides answering the phone, I have enough work for her to do around the office. She'd be my sidekick, so to speak. We'd work together on cases. She'd be in the office, and I'd be out in the field."

"Ah, that's nifty. A girl would be lucky to work with you."

"It's something that I've been thinking about for quite some time."

"That's great."

"Yes, it is."

"You're going to hire someone right away?"

"Well, yes, very soon." I sipped my coffee. "The reason I'm bringing it up is because I want you to come work for me."

Her eyebrows arched, and her eyes widened. Her mouth was agape. "You want *me* to be your secretary?" She pointed a finger at herself. "Eddie, you're a darling, but I really don't think you can afford me." She shook her head, holding back a laugh. "I'm making a lot of money, and well, I can't afford—"

"Wait now. Just hear me out. Let's say I could match what you average in a week. Would you consider working for me then?"

"But, Eddie, that's a lot of money."

"Would you?"

"I don't know. You just sprang this on me."

"I'm not asking you to decide now. I'm just asking you whether you would consider it."

"Well, I don't know. I guess I'd have to think about it first. This is so sudden."

"Okay, swell. Here's something else to think about. As I said, you'd be working with me on cases. If you wanted to, you could even stay here in the back room to save on expenses. You wouldn't have to pay rent. You could save as much money as you are now. Probably more. And you could get out of the business now, which is what you wanted to do eventually."

She drew her legs up and wrapped her arms around them, resting her chin on her knees.

"I wouldn't want you to start until the case I'm working on is done," I said. "But you'd be on the payroll starting now. I could start breaking you in."

"Oh, I just don't know, Eddie. My life isn't exactly the best right now, but this would be a big change for me."

"I'll tell you what. We could have a trial period—let's say for a month. At the end of that period, if either you or I have any reason not to continue the arrangement, then it's done. No questions—just done. What do you say?"

"Oh, I just don't know, Eddie," she said again.

"Will you consider it?"

"I can do that. I'll consider it."

"Good."

A few minutes went by in silence. She kept her chin on her knees, looking down. The gears in her brain were well oiled and rotating. She was considering my proposal. Slowly, she lifted her head and looked at me.

"Eddie?"

"Yeah?"

"Would you start calling me Stéphanie if I came to work for you?"

"I could do that," I said.

"Okay." She put her chin on her knees again, deep in thought.

The day before, I had phoned Juliette Belanger and asked her to meet me at Dinty Moore's diner on Sainte-Catherine that day at five in the afternoon. Then I'd phoned Michael Spence and asked him to do the same, only at five fifteen. I wanted to update them on the case. I'd not told them that the other would also be there.

To hell with updating them on the case—I wanted to put the squeeze on them and see how they'd react when they suddenly saw one another in my presence. I wanted them to know that I was close to breaking the case. I wanted to force them to do something stupid. I'd have my eye on them from now on. They'd been slick. They'd been leading me around like a dog on a leash. Now it was my turn. I wasn't going to get anything from them unless I opened the right door—or blew the hinges off the frame.

I hadn't picked Dinty Moore's because of their famous corned beef and cabbage; I had picked it because I knew how the diner was laid out. I had reserved the first table next to the entrance. Most people didn't want to sit there. When you walked in, you had to go down a short hallway and then turn left into the diner. The table I had reserved was right there. If you were sitting at that table, you had a clear, unobstructed view of the people coming in. When you came in, it was the first table you'd see. You'd have to walk either to the left or right of it to get to the other tables. During the supper rush, it was usually the last table anyone took.

I was there a little before the hour. At five o'clock on the dot, Juliette came in and saw me right away. I stood up. She was wearing black slacks with a white blouse under a gray sweater. Her appearance was understated, as usual, which made her look even more gorgeous than she was.

"Thank you for coming, Juliette. Sorry I had to drag you out, but I didn't want to use the phone." I pulled a chair out for her—a chair directly in view of the entrance. I sat down next to her and angled my chair a bit so that I had the same view. She seemed to be in good form.

"Thank you, Eddie. Actually, I was going downtown anyway to do some errands, so this isn't an inconvenience at all."

We each ordered a gin and tonic, and after the waiter brought them, I asked her how she was doing.

"Under the circumstances, I'm doing as well as can be expected." She paused long enough to sip her drink. She ran her tongue across her lips. "Let me ask you, Eddie—why was it necessary for you to interview my parents?"

I looked at her. She had doll eyes, nice blue ones—beautiful even. I looked closely at them, and they looked back at me. I couldn't penetrate them, because there was nothing behind them. I was glad the Bergerons had told her I'd been there. I hoped they'd told her every word that was said.

"In an investigation like this, it's standard procedure to interview everyone who knows the person being investigated. Each person can have a different slant on a case. They're a lovely couple—your parents."

"And what slant did the lovely couple have?" Her voice took on an edge that I hadn't heard from her before.

"They're convinced that your husband is innocent."

"They told me that you asked about M—" Before she could say any more, Michael Spence walked in.

Their eyes locked onto each other.

My eyes shifted between the two. The blood drained from their faces. Because they were good actors, I knew it would be just a matter of seconds before they composed themselves. But for the moment, they registered shock and surprise that couldn't be hidden, and the look on each face was exaggerated, not like that of two friends unexpectedly coming across each other while walking down a street. No, it wasn't like that at all. It was more like when the police were interrogating a criminal who'd been denying he'd committed a crime, and then they brought in a confessed coconspirator that the criminal didn't know had been arrested. It was that kind of shock.

"Juliette," Spence said as he walked to the table, "I didn't know you were going to be here." He shifted his gaze to me. "Eddie, you didn't tell me." He sat down at the table.

"Sorry. My fault. I thought it would save me some time to talk to both of you at the same time. And I really didn't want to do this on the phone."

They both looked directly at me, avoiding even a glance at each other. I caught the attention of the waiter. He took Spence's order and left.

"I won't take too much of your time. I just wanted to update you on the case. First of all, I have a definite lead on Philippe. He's keeping a very low profile. But I want you to know that I'm making real progress on the case."

"Progress on what exactly?" Spence asked. "What do you have? Do you know where he is?"

Spence had regained control over himself. Juliette also seemed more relaxed now. However, there was an edge to both of them that they couldn't conceal. The tendons in their necks were twisting into taut cables, but their faces showed no sign of stress. My aim was to push them closer to the edge.

"Sorry, but I can't share the details. As a private investigator, I'm obliged to share them only with the person who hired me. If I did otherwise, I'd open myself up to a lawsuit. I could lose my license. You see, I signed a contract."

Juliette spoke up. "But why did you have us meet you here if you weren't going to tell us anything?"

"Two reasons. One, I wanted to let you know that I'm on the verge of breaking this case. If I had to guess, I would say in a matter of days. That should give you a measure of consolation."

The waiter brought Spence his drink. He picked it up and downed half of it. He made a face as if he had drunk strychnine.

"Things are suddenly coming into focus," I said. "I can now see how this all went down. I just have to shove a few more pieces into place, and then I'll have the whole picture."

They were staring at me intently, hanging on my every word.

"And you can't even give us a clue about this?" Spence asked.

"Sorry. Not even a clue. But I'll let you know this much: whatever you thought about the case, scrap it. The case took several different turns. Things are not what they appear to be." I paused briefly to let that sink in. Then I said, "Go outside, and pick up a rock—any rock. Examine it. Turn it in your hand. One side will be clean, but the other side is always going to have dirt on it. Know what I mean?"

Juliette's reaction was slow and measured. "Does this mean you think my husband is innocent?"

"Sorry again. You'll know in a few days. The second reason I asked you to meet me is more serious. As you know, several people I believe are linked to this case ended up dead. I don't know for certain who killed them. To be on the safe side, both of you should be careful. I can't say with certainty that the killing is done."

"But you thought Phil might have killed one of them, possibly both," Spence said. "Are you saying that he might come after us?"

Although it was never obvious, there was a secret dialogue going on between them. It was as if we were playing a parlor game.

"I have no evidence that would stand up in court that he killed anyone. What I'm saying is that both of you should find ways to protect yourselves. The police aren't going to help, because there's been no direct threat to your lives."

For the second time since this charade had started, both of them looked at the other, making eye contact.

As planned, I got up abruptly, laid a five on the table, and put my hat on. "I suspect the next time you'll be contacted, it'll be by the police. They'll fill you in on the details. Sorry that I have to leave in such a hurry."

I walked the few yards to where the hallway began and glanced back for just a second. Both were still at the table, looking in my direction. Ugliness rose like a poisonous vapor, spreading to the far corners of the diner, contaminating everything.

I made my way down the hallway and out the door. Outside, I paused to suck in the fresh air.

Late that night, I drove over to Johnny Como's house in Westmount. I wanted to have one more go at him. If he were a freelance button man, as Jake Asher had said, then I wasn't ruling him out for the murder of Trocadero. He'd convinced me that he probably wouldn't have killed Marguerite. At any rate, he was part of the web, the center of which was the gambling suite. I knew the only way I could get him to say any more than he already had was to lay into him with classic biblical vengeance. I had to make him believe I wouldn't hesitate to put a bullet in his head. Power is a vacuum; you have to walk in and take it—even from a button man.

I parked the Packard across the street and down a half block and walked back. There were no lights on inside the house. He could have been inside, sleeping, but I doubted it. Most likely, he was cruising the nightclub scene, which meant I might have a long wait. The last time I'd been there, he had taken a taxi home. Maybe he didn't own a car. I doubted that as well. If he took a taxi home that night, the element of surprise would be gone. I'd have to take him inside the house, as I had before. I preferred to do my business with him outside in his car—if he had one. I'd have to prepare for both possibilities.

I was standing in a short alleyway directly across the street from his house, with a huge elm tree overhanging the street to the left. There were apartment buildings on either side of it, and I could see a lot of dark, shadowy areas around. Most of the lights in the buildings were off. I found a spot where I could see him pull up, just out of the way of the light cast by an overhead streetlamp. There was no driveway at his house, so if he'd driven, he'd have to park his car at the curb. From that distance, it would take me all of four seconds to run to his car. If he took a taxi, I'd go to plan B.

I waited for two hours. There was no sign of him. The street all the way down the block was dark between the overhead lamps, and it was quiet. Another hour went by. I was becoming annoyed. I decided I'd wait until four o'clock, and if he hadn't showed up by then, I'd have to go inside the house, because he'd most likely be sleeping. Remembering what had happened the last time, I wasn't looking forward to that. Como was a skinny little guy, but he was dangerous.

Forty-five minutes later, I heard the engine of a car. It stopped just to the left of the alleyway. I leaned down to have a look and saw Como sitting behind the wheel with his white Panama fedora cocked to one side on his head. The elm blocked most of his view of me. I took my .45 caliber out and chambered a round. I heard the engine die. As he opened the door, I was already there to greet him. I flung the door back farther and pointed my gun at his face. "Slide over to the passenger seat, Johnny," I said. "One way or another, this won't take long. And keep your paws where I can see them."

He inched himself across the seat, and I took his place behind the wheel, angling my body to face him.

"You lead a dangerous life, Wade. You've been lucky—twice lucky. Maybe your luck is running out."

"The hell you say."

"The hell I say."

He had the savage look of casual indifference. He had cold killer eyes for a little runt.

"Don't get snotty with me, Johnny boy. It doesn't suit you." I pointed the gun at him from a safe distance in case he decided to try something unhealthy. "Maybe your friends should start arranging your memorial service. I could get them a discount from a friend I know."

"That's reckless talk. If you shoot that gun, the lights will go on in the apartments here, and you're going to have two dozen witnesses on your hands."

"I'd be out of here before they're even out of bed. Cooperate, and we can avoid all that."

"Whaddaya want? I told you everything I know about Marguerite. I didn't kill her."

"I want to know something you haven't told me. Did you kill Manny Trocadero?"

"You think I'd tell you if I did?" He snickered.

"I see that you know him, eh?"

"Who doesn't know that two-bit confidence man?"

"So?"

"So whaddaya going to do—arrest me if I did?" He threw his head back and laughed. "The fuzz would probably pin a medal on me and throw me a party."

"I want to know who Trocadero was working with—who got him to hand me that routine."

"Sorry, fella. Can't help you there. I don't know nothing about no routine."

"Was it Belanger?"

"I don't know what you're talking about. Your ears plugged or something?"

I took the safety off the pistol and cocked the hammer.

"I'm telling you I don't know. If you want me to make something up, tell me. I'll make something up."

"Were Galante and Spence partners in that gambling operation at the Windsor?"

"Galante and who?"

"You heard me. Michael Spence—Duke!"

"I don't know that either."

"For a guy who gets around, you don't know very much, do you?"

"I know plenty, just not what you're after."

I was exasperated. I had no intention of shooting him, and I didn't want to rough him up. I made one more play.

"I know you know Belanger. You can walk away from all of this in one piece. Just tell me where he is. Where's he hiding out?"

He didn't say anything for a few moments. I could tell the wheels were spinning. He was considering his options—his way out of all this. Finally, he said, "I don't know, but you won't find him."

"Why? Did he leave the city?"

"You'll have to ask his pretty little wife that ques—" He chopped the last word off with a butcher knife.

"What does she have to do with this?"

"I ain't saying anything else. Wave that piece around all you want. I ain't saying anything else."

He was pushing the limits, and I was getting angrier by the second. He knew something, but he was never going to tell. I switched the gun to my left hand and extended my right arm, aiming my fist at his nose.

"Jesus." He leaned into the car door. His hands went toward his nose and quivered in front of him, as if he were trying to shake water from his fingertips. He said something guttural and inarticulate. His voice turned into a sickly rasp.

"You got the jitters, Johnny?"

"The third time with the nose, you crazy bastard! Plug me. Plug me, but I ain't saying anything more."

I went roaming in my head and got lost. The jungle trail went nowhere. There was too much brush to cut through. I opened the door, got out, and leaned into the open window. "It's been a pleasure, Johnny," I said. "Have the doctor send me the bill."

"Next time you point that gun at me, asshole, you better pull the trigger," he said, holding his nose. "You better be looking over your shoulder from now on." His voice was adenoidal.

"You're killing me, man." I laughed. "You're killing me."

I walked to my car, got in, and drove off to my office.

CHAPTER 26

On Friday morning, Tangerine and I walked down to the local greasy spoon for a light breakfast. She was reticent and introspective, which wasn't like her. I hoped she was mulling over my offer to work for me. On the way back to my office, neither of us spoke.

Once inside, I put on a tie, told her I'd be back at the end of the day, and left her with the cats. I drove north on the Main until I got to rue Dante. I turned right and continued for five blocks to avenue Henri-Julien. I parked the car at the curb, got out, and walked to the rectory behind the Church of the Madonna della Difesa.

I was in the heart of my old stomping grounds in Little Italy. That had been my parish when my mother and I had lived a ten-minute walk away. I had stayed away from there for years because of the ghosts. There were many of them—too many for me to handle. I didn't like them, and I didn't like being back there now.

I pressed the doorbell on the rectory and then stared at my shoes. I had forgotten to polish them, but they didn't look too bad. After a few moments, the door swung open, and an ancient nun appeared. I looked down at her. She was no taller than four foot five. She wore a black habit that came down below her shoes. A veil covered her head, and a white guimpe of starched linen ran down either side of her face, making it look puffy. It covered her neck and spread out below it to form a bib. A silver cross hung from a black cord around her neck. A rosary of wooden beads and metal links dangled from a cloth belt at her waist, suspended by small hooks. She held her hands together in front of her. There was a gold ring on her left hand. She was married to someone or something: God the Father, Christ, the Church, the order, or maybe the rector. I didn't know. Perhaps the ring was a symbol of her fidelity to the resident ghosts there. Her face had deep, leathery trails running in all directions. I supposed that her job was to mind the parish priest, who was probably half her age and twice as healthy. She looked up at me.

"Yes?" she said. "How may I help you?"

"I'm here to see Father Joseph Segretti."

"Do you have an appointment?"

"I don't. I was just driving by and thought I might catch him in."

"Oh, young man." She lowered her voice and leaned into me. Her tone took on a hint of conspiracy and confidentiality. "That's a bit chancy. He has so many duties that I find it difficult to keep track of him. He's supposed to let me know where he goes in case someone is looking for him." She looked to either side of her and then back at me. "But he seldom does. I have to know where he is in case there's an emergency. I had to resort to having him write it down on a chart I made especially for him. Just one moment. I'll take a peek at it."

She seemed like a nice old lady. She took her calling seriously. I wondered whether she'd been there when I was a kid. She didn't look familiar, but of course, my time there had been many years ago.

She returned a minute later. "If the chart is correct and he wasn't trying to fool me, he should be in the church. I wouldn't know why, because nothing is scheduled there until the noon mass."

"That's fine. I'll walk over and have a peek myself."

"You do that. Good-bye, young man." She closed the door. There was a smile and a wink in her voice.

I walked to the front of the church facing Henri-Julien and hesitated at the door. I hadn't been inside it since I finished high school and moved out of the neighborhood. I opened one of the doors and went inside. It was semidark and smelled of incense. I wasn't surprised to find the ghosts there, as if they'd been waiting for me to return after all those years. I closed my eyes and let them flow over me. I stood there for about a minute, taking deep breaths, until I realized I was still standing upright with my shoes firmly planted on the tiles. I was still Eddie Wade, but I was no longer the little kid I used to be. Maybe the ghosts hadn't recognized me.

I continued on through another set of doors and stopped. Father Segretti was in the second pew in front of the altar under the apse. His back was to me. I didn't think he'd heard me come in, because he hadn't looked back. He was sitting instead of kneeling, but maybe he was praying nevertheless. I hesitated to disturb him. Maybe he wasn't praying; maybe he was just talking to the ghosts. They had been his too, after all. I dropped my car keys, which I had been holding, and reached down to pick them up. The priest turned around and looked my way. We were too far apart, so I knew he didn't recognize me.

"Father Segretti?" I said.

He got up and started down the aisle toward me. "Yes? Can I help you with something?"

I didn't answer him but instead let him continue walking. When he got about ten feet away, I said, "Ciao, *amico*! Ciao, Little Joey!"

He stopped dead in his tracks and squinted at me. "Is this who I think it is? Bonifacio? Eddie Wade?"

"Ciao, Joey!" I said.

He raced down the aisle, and we embraced each other.

"*Come stai*?" I asked.

"*Bene, bene, grazie*! *E tu*?"

"*Così e così*."

"How long has it been? Jeez, you look great, Eddie."

"So do you. I've never seen you with a collar on." I grabbed his cheek with my thumb and fingers and shook it a little, just like his mother used to do. "My little Joey!" As a kid, he'd been short and small framed, but he'd grown into a tall, muscular man nearly as big as I. His black hair was combed straight back, and his thin mustache gave him a Hollywood look. He was a handsome man, and I couldn't help but think of all the women he missed out on.

We went outside and sat down on a bench in the side garden. We talked. He talked mostly about the seminary, and I talked mostly about catching bad guys. We talked nonstop. It had been close to twenty years since we had last seen each other.

"I thought for sure I'd see you in the papers, winning the heavyweight championship," he said.

"I thought for sure I'd see you in the papers, receiving the papal tiara," I said.

Our conversation went on like that for the next hour. The joking back and forth felt good. When our reunion had run its course and our conversation started to wane, I broached the subject.

"Joey, I came here today because your name came up in an investigation."

"Really?" He was shocked. "Tell me more."

"I'm working on the Philippe Belanger case."

"I see."

They were two simple words: *I see*. However, something was off; something wasn't right about the way he'd said them.

"I know that he and his wife attend Mass at this parish and that Philippe and you are friends. Can you possibly tell me anything that would help me on this case? Anything he may have confided in you? Even something that you may consider inconsequential. *Potresti aiutarmi*? Could you help me, Joey?"

He stood up, facing away from me, and ran both hands over his hair. He stared off to his left and sighed. Then he turned around, planted a shoe on the bench, and leaned an arm on his leg. "Eddie, I don't know what to say. I've been going through hell ever since I read about Phil in the papers. I was just thinking about him as you walked into the church."

"Then you know something that could help me."

"I don't know how much it could help, but yes, I know something."

I cocked my head to the side and waited for him to continue.

"Phil talked to me about, well, what turned out to be his problem. He told me quite a bit about it before he was arrested and the story broke in the papers."

I waited again for him to continue. After a few long moments, he did.

"But he talked to me in the confessional. As you know, Eddie, in the church, we have something called the seal of the confessional. As a priest, I am obligated never to disclose anything said by any penitent during the course of the sacrament of penance. This is an absolute that even the civil authorities recognize."

"Is there any way around it?" I asked.

"I'm afraid not, Eddie."

"And what you know—do you think it could have a bearing on the case?"

"I'm not sure. But if I had to guess, I would say yes, it could."

"Think of it this way, Joey. When we catch Belanger—and we will eventually—he could be sent to Bordeaux for a very long time. If you have information that could throw some light on the case but you don't share it with the police, you'd have to live with that for the rest of your life. He'll be an old man by the time he gets out of stir. He might also stand trial for murder. It could mean the death penalty, if he's found guilty. If he's innocent, and you held back ..." I felt bad about using guilt to spur him on, but at that point, I had no choice.

Father Segretti said nothing. He looked down at his shoes. Unlike mine, they had a nice gleam to them.

"Can the church give some kind of dispensation in special cases?" I asked.

He looked back at me. "In theory, yes, they can, but they rarely do. If I talked to you about what Phil told me in the confessional and I had to testify in court, I could be defrocked by the archbishop."

Several minutes went by in silence.

"Can you wait here for a bit? I want to run this by Father Mazzoni. He's the rector. He's also my confessor and spiritual adviser, and he's well versed in canon law."

"I can wait as long as you need me to," I said.

"*Torno subito.*"

"*Buona fortuna*!"

Joey had been a good, honest kid when growing up—and he had paid a price for it. Bullies had often teased him, but he had always taken it like a man. The bullying had always made me angry. On several occasions, I had intervened with my fists on his behalf, and I'd usually gotten a lecture from him that violence never solved anything. He had been wrong, though. The harassment had eventually stopped, at least when I was around him.

I took out my pipe, filled it, and puffed away. A half hour went by. I wondered what exactly Belanger had told him. From Joey's reaction, I sensed it hadn't been a confession to embezzlement. I started to consider the possibilities, when Joey returned, interrupting my thoughts.

"Sorry to keep you waiting, Eddie," he said while sitting down. "I had a talk with Father Mazzoni."

"And?"

"He reminded me of the duties and responsibilities of my vocation and of the consequences I could face if I broke the seal of the confessional. He had no authority to grant me a dispensation, but he did suggest I could take my case to the archbishop. All this involves canon law, you see. It could take weeks or longer before a decision was made."

"So that's not good news."

"I stressed the urgency of the matter. At the end, he suggested I use my conscience and pray."

"Well, I guess that's it, eh?"

"I took him up on that suggestion, and as I was walking from the rectory, I used my conscience and prayed. Do you have a notebook, Eddie?"

"Yes."

"Then get it out."

I reached into my jacket for it. After all these years, Joey hadn't changed. He was still very much the man.

He was silent for a while, collecting his thoughts.

"Now that I think about it, I really don't have much, Eddie, but it may be useful. Phil talked to me about this only once, but he was very troubled about it. It had to do with his work. He believed that someone was manipulating his clients' portfolios. He had discovered missing funds from quite a few of them. He'd gone over those portfolios again and again with the same results: missing funds. He said that the only other person who could have done that was his partner, Michael Spence. There were notes in those folders, apparently about each financial transaction. They were written in his own handwriting, but he didn't remember writing them. That made him think there was something wrong with him. He thought he might be losing his mind or having a nervous breakdown from too much work. He felt terrible about thinking his partner might be embezzling funds from his clients. He wanted absolution from me for thinking ill of his partner. That's about it. As I said, it wasn't much."

"Actually, Joey, it's quite a lot. The way the case is going, I don't think it will end up in court, so you won't have to testify. Please know that I'll keep your name out of it."

"But if it does come to a trial, I will testify. Phil is innocent of the charges against him. I'd have to testify; morally, I'd have no choice."

After talking with him for another ten minutes or so, I walked back to my car. I got behind the wheel, when a sickening thought assailed me.

Philippe Belanger might be dead.

Instead of going back to my office, I drove straight to Griffintown. I had been thinking about Ruth Adler. Ezra was supposed to take care of her personal belongings and the furniture. I didn't trust him to do that. It was really none of my business. It wasn't my responsibility, and I had no right to see that her ungrateful lump of a son did it. But that was too bad. I was going to see that it got done anyway.

My talk with Joey Segretti confirmed what had been twisting around inside my head. I had been caught in one huge whirlpool of deception and violence, a not-too-unfamiliar landscape in which nothing was what it appeared to be. I decided to take some time to figure out how to bring this case to a close. I wanted Michael Spence and Juliette Belanger to stew in their cauldron for a while. I had planted the seeds of suspicion. They knew I was onto something. I hoped now that out of a sense of desperation, they would do something stupid. I still didn't have enough solid evidence to put Spence away for good, but I was approaching it. He was never going to confess.

I still couldn't figure out what Juliette's role in all this was, but I was certain she had one. I had been set up from the beginning like some two-bit patsy; I just didn't know how. And I had nothing linking Spence to the murders.

I pulled up in front of Ruth's apartment building on rue Saint-Martin. The concierge was sitting outside on a lawn chair, reading a paper. He wore a white T-shirt and gray work paints. I got out of the car, and we shook hands. I told him why I had come. He said he hadn't seen Ezra since the funeral, but I shouldn't worry, because he wasn't going to rent out Ruth's apartment for a few months. Her things could stay where they were.

He was a genuinely nice man, a rarity. His name was Gus. I invited him to have a beer with me. He folded the paper and put it under his arm, and we crossed the street to a dumpy public house. We ordered two Molsons.

"Here's to Ruthy." He hoisted his bottle.

"To Ruthy," I said.

He was a baseball fan. The Royals were having a great season so far, and we both agreed that it was because of Max Macon, the manager. This season had started off just as it had in 1946, when they'd won the Governor's Cup after defeating Syracuse.

"That was a great season, Eddie. Do you remember that they had that colored player with them?"

"How could I forget? He's been playing up a storm with Brooklyn," I said. "Jackie Robinson can hit, field the ball, and run like no one I ever saw."

We talked baseball for a while, until I brought up Ruth again.

"She never married then?" I asked while filling and then lighting my pipe.

"She never talked about a husband, but there had to be someone in her life to plant the seed. I'm just glad she found a little happiness at the end. Too bad the old ticker gave out."

"How's that? What happiness?"

"Well, during the last year, she had a—what do you call it? A gentleman caller."

"Really?" I said, surprised. "I hope it was good for her. Tell me more; I'm curious."

"She never talked about it to me, but this guy would pick her up in a shiny black Buick maybe once a week, on her day off. I don't think he ever went into the apartment. She always came down to him. He would get out of the car and open the door for her. A real gentleman. From the way he dressed, I think he had a few bucks, if you know what I mean."

"Unbelievable," I said. "Who would have thought?"

"He would always greet her with one of those double kisses on the cheeks, like the French do. I have to tell you, Eddie, it made my heart warm to see them together. A real gentleman, he was."

At that point, I was really curious. "So Ruth had a gentleman caller who had some cabbage. What did he look like? Did you see him close up?"

"Oh, he was always dressed to the nines—three-piece suit, shoes polished. Even wore a gold watch chain. Ruthy always lit up whenever he came."

Something clicked in me.

"How about his face and hair?"

"What are you doing—writing a book?" he asked, and we both laughed. "Gray hair, bushy mustache, bushy eyebrows, glasses. Oh, and he smoked a pipe like you."

"Well, anyway, I'm also glad that she found a little happiness in her life. She certainly deserved it."

We hoisted our bottles again to Ruthy.

"We have to do this again, Gus," I said, putting enough change on the bar for the beers and a tip. He agreed.

I got back in the car and drove to my office to see Tangerine and the cats. I thought about the gentleman caller. He had to have been Frederick Churchill. When I'd seen him at Ruth's funeral, I hadn't been able to figure out why he was there. Now I knew. But something wasn't right. Churchill had been married. His wife had died five years ago, he'd told me. If he were going to start a new relationship, it was unlikely he would start one with a charwoman whose son was involved in criminal activities. But he might not have known that. Besides, Ruth was out of his class.

I suspected that their relationship went way back. Of course, that was none of my business. But I was curious enough to find out.

CHAPTER 27

I got up early Saturday morning and decided to skip breakfast. I explained to Tangerine that I had an interview to conduct but said I'd be back shortly after noon. She wasn't thrilled. She had hoped we'd do something together that day. I promised we'd go to the botanical garden and maybe wander around La Fontaine Park or take in an afternoon Royals game. She still hadn't mentioned my offer.

I drove to Sherbrooke and parked at the curb across from the Arts Building at McGill. The last time I was there, I had seen Frederick Churchill walk into that building. It was the weekend; if he wasn't there, I'd have to track him down somehow.

Once inside, I found the office number of the philosophy department and walked up to the second floor. Instead of knocking, I tried the doorknob. It was open. There was no one behind the secretary's desk. To my immediate right, I saw Churchill's name in bold black letters on a door. I walked over to it and knocked. I heard his voice say, "Yes?" on the other side. He spoke only one word, but it sounded hollow and isolated, tinged with despair. I opened the door. He was sitting behind his desk. His suit coat and hat were hanging on a wooden stand by the door. His sleeves were rolled up, exposing the gray hairs on his forearms. His pipe was blazing away, filling the office with sweet-scented tobacco. He looked at me quizzically and sadly, and then my face registered.

"You're the guy I met at Dominion Square that morning," he said with a sudden shift of spirit.

"I was hoping to catch you in. I remembered that you told me you worked at McGill. Do you mind if I come in?"

"Of course not. Come, come. Grab a chair. I told you that I work at McGill?" He got up from behind his desk and pulled out another chair in front, and we both sat down, facing each other. "I practically live here. Let's see. Wade, isn't it? Eddie Wade, if I remember correctly."

"Your memory is good. I mentioned it only once, and that was a few weeks ago."

"I'm certainly glad to see you again," he said. He seemed to mean it. "We had a great chat that morning. Thank you again. And I appreciated your indulgence. I was letting off a little steam, if you remember. But what brings you here?"

"What I didn't mention that morning was that I'm a private investigator. I'm working on a case. Because of confidentiality, I'm not able to tell you anything about it."

"That's fine, but how is this relevant to me?"

"The case involves someone you know—someone you knew, that is," I said, bending the truth a little. "Her name is Ruth Adler."

He looked at me with compunction. His face paled as the blood drained from it, perhaps from the sudden shock of hearing her name. As if he were anticipating a hailstorm of memories crashing down on him, fear competed with misery in his face. His face then flushed. The veins on his nose turned a rich purplish color. All that happened within a few seconds. After

I'd had my talk with Gus last night, I'd thought Frederick's relationship with Ruth wasn't a new one. I had a feeling now that I was right.

He continued to look at me but said nothing. He had composed himself.

"I saw you at her funeral," I said. "And I have reason to believe that you had been seeing her socially for the last year."

"Good God, how did you find out about that?" His shock was genuine.

"Sorry. That's part of the investigation," I said, lying to him. I didn't feel good about doing that. Why was I there in the first place—out of some morbid curiosity? I had no moral or legal right to be asking him questions about his personal life. Frankly, I felt like a bug, and I deserved to feel that way. Nevertheless, something—call it a gut feeling, or call it intuition—compelled me to stick my nose where it didn't belong. "I came here to ask you some questions about Ruth. You don't have to talk to me if you choose not to; that's your right. You yourself are not part of the investigation, and you're not in any kind of trouble. I can only rely on your sense of decency and on any feelings that you may have had for Ruth."

He got up and took a few steps to the front of his desk. He put his pipe down and leaned on the desk with both hands, his head hanging down. He stayed that way for about a minute, not saying anything. It became obvious to me that he was a man with a great burden. He turned around; went back to his chair; sat down again, crossing one leg over the other; and relit his pipe.

"You know, I could tell you that the relationship I had with Ruth is none of your business. I could ask you to leave. If you persisted, I could simply lie to you—feed you some cockamamie story that you would end up believing."

"That's right; you could do all those things." I felt like an interloper intruding in his memories, a place I had no right to be.

"I don't think I will, though. I like you. I can't say that about too many people I associate with. You know, horseshit is the preferred language of our time. But you're different. You speak from the heart. I heard you that morning. I trust you."

I didn't say anything.

"I can't for the life of me understand how I could be helpful to you. I don't even how what this is all about. But I suppose it doesn't matter anymore. None of it. What kind of information about Ruth do you want?"

I took out my notebook and a pen. "I hope you don't mind."

"Certainly not. Write away."

"First of all, is your son still missing?"

"He is."

"I'm sorry for that. I'm sure it's causing you a great deal of pain." I paused briefly before continuing. "When we were talking that morning in the square, you suggested that his sins were your punishment for a past transgression—a repayment for something you may have done in the past. Might that have anything to do with Ruth?"

He looked sad as I spoke, his eyes tearing. "I can answer that question, but in order to do so, I have to start at the beginning. Starting anywhere else would be an injustice to Ruth. Lord knows she's experienced enough unfairness in her lifetime."

"Certainly."

"Ruth and I met in high school. We fell in love almost immediately. We planned to get married as soon as we graduated; it was that serious. My parents were Anglo-Protestant and very rich. They forbade me to marry her because she was Jewish. They forced us to stop seeing each other, even though we were very much in love. Unfortunately, neither one of us had the strength to fight against their threats. They put pressure on us out of their own fears. Ruth and I certainly didn't have any. My father owned the Churchill Box Company. He threatened to cut me out of his will. We had no choice other than to end it. After I graduated, I went to work for him for the summer, but my heart wasn't in it. I left in the fall for the university. But by that time, Ruth was already pregnant."

A cold insect crawled up my spine from the small of my back to the nape of my neck. I braced myself for what would come next.

"Ruth's parents were poor. She lived in a black-market baby house for the duration of the pregnancy, where she was looked after rather well. It was there that Ruth gave birth to baby boys. They arranged to have the twins adopted—illegally, of course. At her age, Ruth had no say in it.

"The first baby's delivery was normal, but the second one was difficult. The doctor said there was insufficient oxygen to the brain—an umbilical cord prolapse, I think he told Ruth. The baby was sure to be mentally disabled to some degree. She would have to keep the second child; they couldn't adopt him out. Ruth's parents refused to take her back because of the baby. At the age of eighteen, she found herself an unwed mother. She named the boy Ezra. She gave his brother the name of Jacob, although she knew she would never see him again. As it turned out, Ezra showed no signs of being disabled. However, Ruth always treated him as if he were, lovingly protecting him from the outside world. Because of this protection, Ezra never really grew up to be a self-sufficient man."

I had a few thousand questions to ask Frederick at that point, but I didn't want to stop him.

"I may have been a terrible young man, but I still loved Ruth. I kept in close contact with her on the sly as much as I was able and even gave her money for herself and the child. However, she would never take it, even though it would have provided her with more comforts than what she had. If she wasn't good enough for the Churchill family, then she wanted nothing from them, from me. She broke my heart, and I deserved it. As I don't know what your investigation is all about, do you want to know more? Shall I continue?"

"Yes, please continue." I felt remorseful that I was having him dredge up the past, but at the same time, I was exhilarated by what I was finding out.

"Jacob was adopted by an employee of my father's company. He had no idea he was adopting the baby of the owner's son. Nor did my father. I was the twins' father, and I dearly loved their mother, yet I was unable to take responsibility for any of it. I tried, but maybe I didn't try hard enough. Maybe I wasn't man enough. Jacob's adoptive parents gave him the name of Michael. I knew the father from work but only from his reputation. By all accounts, he was a good, honest man, so I knew that Jacob would be treated well and cared for."

"Do you remember the adoptive parents' name?"

"How could I ever forget? They were raising my son, for God's sake—something I should have been doing myself. Their names were Thomas and Margret Spence. They lived in Côte-des-Neiges, but I believe they moved out of the province not long ago."

My mind was spinning. Ezra had looked familiar to me, but I hadn't made the connection to Michael Spence.

"Though they had little money, they always looked after Jacob—I mean Michael—well. As I hinted at, I kept track of them. I hired a private investigator. Once a month, I would put cash in an envelope and have a messenger service deliver it to their house, with the strict admonishment to the service never to disclose who'd sent it. I did that until Michael finished high school. During all of that time, Ruth would never take a dime from me. When my father died, I inherited the business, but I sold it. Money has never been an issue for me."

"Why did you start to see Ruth again, if I may ask?"

"My wife died. I mentioned that to you. I had a wonderful life with her and loved her very much. But as the years passed, I grew lonelier. A house that was once full of joy suddenly became empty, with no one to come home to. That is a terrible thing. I wouldn't wish it on my worst enemy. About a year ago, I decided to see Ruth again. She consented. We went out to dinner frequently and for walks in the park. My love for her sparked again. Months went by before I asked her to marry me. She wouldn't give me an answer. She seemed content with the life she had created for herself. I begged her. She told me that she had to think about it. Before her answer came, she died."

"How much do you know about Ezra?"

"Enough. By the way you're asking that question, I trust you do as well."

I nodded.

"That morning, in Dominion Square, I didn't just happen to be there. I had known that Ezra was involved in some way with criminal activities, as indicated in the investigator's reports, but I didn't know the details. I still don't. That morning, I was waiting for him to come out of the Windsor. I was going to tell him that I was his father and that I wanted to help him. After our chat—yours and mine—I determined that it was probably a stupid idea. I had no way to gauge his reaction. I didn't know whether he was violent or not. I had wanted to help him financially since he was born. He would have had the right not to believe me, though. Do you how frustrating it was for me to want to assume my fatherly responsibilities for him and be denied that?"

I told him I couldn't imagine, as I was not a parent myself.

"I don't blame Ruth, though. The Churchills put her in that position. I, of course, include myself. She had her pride and did the best she could. It was a terrible situation that didn't have to happen."

"And your other son?"

"He became a bright, decent investment broker. Part owner of his own firm. I have his parents to thank for that. The word *adoptive* is a misnomer. They were his parents in the truest sense of the word."

"But you supported him financially."

"Money doesn't raise children. It provides some comforts, but it doesn't tuck a child in at night or guide a child morally. Parents do those things. The Spences were there for Michael. I wasn't."

"Not by your own choosing."

"Don't attempt to lessen the impact my decisions caused, Eddie. It all had to do with choice; never doubt that. And we Churchills made some bad choices."

"Do you read the daily newspapers?"

"You're alluding to the Belanger case, of course. Yes, I've been following it. I'm sure Michael's beside himself."

I was unable to tell him the facts in the case, but even if I could have, I didn't think I had the guts to explain that his son wasn't decent at all but was an embezzler and possibly a murderer. Eventually, he'd read about that in the papers, and I didn't want to be around to see it.

"I'm sure he is," I said.

He looked at me askance. "You're not involved in the case, are you?"

"No, of course not, but I've been following it in the *Gazette*."

He looked at his watch. "I'm meeting with a graduate student in five minutes. Are you in need of more information about Ruth? We could arrange another time. Later today if you want."

"No, I think you pretty much covered it."

He tamped his pipe and relit it, sending a cloud of smoke around him. "Since you were a bit philosophical when we last met, let me return it in kind." He looked down at his hand holding the pipe for a moment and then back up at me. "The world has a myriad of wonders and exquisite splendor with which to lavish yourself. Enjoy every sublime minute of it, Eddie. Ravish those moments, because they'll come at a cost, purchased by days of pain, distress, grief, and sorrow. There's no escaping that. So just appreciate what you have around you, be grateful for it, and seek out a bit of happiness along the way. You deserve that."

As I crossed Sherbrooke to my car, I thought about how much I liked Frederick Churchill. He was a man in pain; the past would forever haunt him. His experiences as a young man with Ruth would never be burned away in some kind of ash heap; the residue would never scatter forever into the universe. They were instead flushed into his psyche and left there to fester, rising to the surface on occasion to remind him that his past was just a blink away.

On the way back to my office, I stopped at Schwartz's on the Main and bought two smoked meat sandwiches and a half pint of potato salad. I knew the manager, so he let me take a couple of forks with me if I promised to return them, which I did. I was going to call Tangerine from there, but I remembered that I had told her not to answer the phone.

I discovered that she wasn't at the office, so I went next door to the Lion's Den. She and Bruno were yakking away at the bar. I told Bruno I wanted to borrow her for a few hours, and we left with as little fanfare as possible.

I drove us back to Sherbrooke and parked the car beside La Fontaine Park. We got out, and I carried our lunch under one arm. The sky was blue with few clouds, and there was a soft breeze. It was a good day that needed to be used. We walked up a wide path under a canopy of giant trees and listened to the birds chirping.

"I've never been here before," Tangerine said. She slid one hand into mine and held my arm with her other one, leaning her head against my shoulder. "It's beautiful."

"My mother took me here a few times when I was a kid," I said. "She'd make a lunch for us, and we'd take the tram from Little Italy. It always seemed like an adventure to me, almost like going to a foreign land."

"I never heard you mention her before. Is she still alive?"

She was right; I hadn't mentioned her before. I wanted this to be a happy few hours for Tangerine. She'd had a tough life, and I didn't know how the next few weeks would go for her. *So right now, no sadness and no sorrowful thoughts.* Now wasn't the time to tell her about my mother.

"She passed away while I was in Europe during the war. She left me with a lot of happy memories, some of them from right here in the park."

"That's good, Eddie." She smiled up at me.

We passed a young couple sitting on a bench. The woman was holding a child maybe a year old on her lap, playing with him. As we walked by them, I saw Tangerine twist her head slightly over her shoulder, looking at them. Her eyes had a longing in them. I hoped it was for a life different from the one she had been living. I still believed she was salvageable. She had a raw and rare sense of self-worth that I hadn't seen in other prostitutes, but it was myopic, and she needed a little help, an opportunity to change directions. However, she had to make the decision. I couldn't force her, because if I did, it wouldn't last.

We made our way around the lake to a small waterfall and a bridge, an area called Lover's Point. There weren't many lovers there at that time of day. We found a spot under a tree and ate our lunch. After that, we walked some more and talked about nothing in particular. A few times, I told her some stories that made her laugh. Other times, we just said silly things and giggled like kids. She was as happy and relaxed as I'd seen her.

I thought about the advice Frederick Churchill had given me that morning. He'd said I should lavish myself with the wonders and exquisite—what was the word he'd used?—*splendor* of the world. I should enjoy every sublime minute of it and be grateful for it. As I looked at Tangerine, I couldn't help but think that that was exactly what I was doing.

I looked at my watch. We'd stayed much longer than I had planned. The sky caught fire across the west and purpled in the east. We walked back to the car, hand in hand.

CHAPTER 28

Joshua! Joshua!
Joshua fought the battle of Jericho, Jericho, Jericho.
Joshua fought the battle of Jericho,
and the walls came tumbling down!

I thought I heard the phone ringing, but I had been possessed by a demon, and it wouldn't let go of me. I couldn't move.

You may talk about the men of Gideon,
you may talk about the men of Saul,
but there's none like good old Joshua
and the battle of Jericho!

The phone was ringing. Maybe it had been ringing all my life or maybe for just a few minutes. I couldn't tell. I couldn't get that song out of my head.

Right up to the walls of Jericho
they marched with spear in hand;
"Go blow those ram horns," Joshua cried,

"'cause the battle is in my hand,
'cause the battle is in my hand,
'cause the battle is—"

I twitched and then squirmed. I rolled onto my side. Finally, I got off the couch and stumbled my way to the desk. I picked the receiver up but couldn't say anything.

Jericho, Jericho …

"Eddie!" a voice said. "Eddie, are you there?"

"'Cause the battle is in my hand,
'cause the battle is—"

"Yeah, it's me," I mumbled. "Who's this?"

"Brad Wilcox. Are you awake? Go run some cold water over your head. I'll wait."

"No, I'm fine. What time is it?" I rubbed an eye with a knuckle.

"It's four twelve ante meridiem on Sunday. As far as I know, you're in Mile End, and I'm at home in Westmount. We're still in the Dominion of Canada. I've got some news that can't wait."

"Did the walls come tumbling down?" The words came out slow and slurred.

"What?" he asked. After a moment of silence, he added, "Something like that. Are you awake enough to engage in a rather simple but important discourse?"

"Discourse away."

"The Hardcastle Office Building on Dorchester is up in flames as we speak. You should get yourself over there right away."

"Why is that any of my business?" I yawned out the words.

"Obviously, you're not awake yet. I'll indulge you and repeat what I just said. The Hardcastle Office Building is up—"

I suddenly woke up. "Jesus, that's Michael Spence's building!"

"Voilà! I know the building management people. We insure a lot of clients there. Someone from the office called me ten minutes ago, but I wasn't given any details, and that's why you need to put your clothes on and get down there fast, while the blaze is still blazing away. Talk to whoever is in charge of the fire brigade. Find out as much as you can."

> And the walls came tumbling down!
> And the walls came tumbling down!

Fully engaged now, I said, "I'm on my way," and I slammed the receiver down.

I gathered my clothes off a chair and began dressing. As I did, a movement at the door to my bedroom caught my attention. Tangerine was standing silhouetted in the doorway.

"Flip the light on, will you?" I said to her.

She turned it on and then scratched her head.

"Sorry I woke you. It's sort of an emergency. I have to go into town."

I didn't tell her the nature of the emergency. I wanted to keep her as far away from this case as possible. I still hadn't put everything together yet, and the less she knew about the case the better. She waved her fingers at me, yawned, and went back to bed. I finished dressing; grabbed my notebook, keys, hat, and pipe; locked the door behind me; tugged on the knob once to make sure it was locked; and then headed for my car with that persistent demon still very much persisting.

"Go blow those ram horns," Joshua cried,

"'cause the battle is in my hand."

I had the old Packard up to fifty-six miles per hour going south on rue Saint-Urbain into town. The street was empty, with only the occasional car going north. It wasn't often that I saw the streets of Montreal that desolate. I could imagine how they'd look under a Soviet missile attack. I didn't have to stretch my imagination too far. We were close enough to the United States. Eighty percent of Canadians lived within a hundred miles of the border. We had signed a defense treaty with the Americans. If they fell, we got to fall with them.

I eased up on the gas a block before approaching Dorchester. As I turned right, I encountered a considerable number of vehicles on the street, so I went the speed limit the rest of the way. The street was blocked at Metcalfe, so I pulled over, parked the car, and walked the rest of the way. A slew of fire engines and police vehicles were on Dorchester between Peel and Stanley. A small crowd had formed—probably people who were going to work nearby. Uniformed officers were stretched around the area, telling people to stay on the other side of the wooden sawhorses stenciled with "Police Line—Do Not Cross." I heard one constable say to a woman, "Lady, can't you read? It says if you cross the barrier again, I'm going to get very angry!"

In front of the building was a hook-and-ladder truck. A fireman was in the bucket about five stories high, hosing the building down. Three other hoses aimed up from street level. No flames were visible, but a lot of smoke was billowing out the windows. It looked as if the brigade had the fire under control, limiting the damage to the top two stories. I noticed the fire inspector, Pierre Simard, standing by one of the smaller fire engines, writing something down on a clipboard. I had worked with him on an arson case several years ago, but maybe he wouldn't remember me. It was going to be difficult to get past the officers, so I reached inside my jacket pocket, pulled out my phony press card, and stuck it in my hat.

I squeezed between two sawhorses under the watchful eyes of one of the constables, making sure the white card was visible, and made my way over to the inspector.

"Inspector Simard," I said.

He looked up from his clipboard and ran a finger across his mustache. He squinted and made some sort of sound in his throat. "Wade, isn't it?"

"That's right. We worked on a case together awhile back."

His eyes meandered to my hat. "Change professions?" As I was trying to think up an answer, he said, "Your press card is blank, a sure sign that you're still a private license. Why are you interested in this?"

"There's a person with an office on the top floor who's under investigation."

"By whom? The police?"

"And by me."

"Love to stand here and chat, but as you can see, I'm a little tied up right now. I can answer a couple of questions, but be quick about it."

"Have you been able to make any assessments yet?"

"Not many. We have to get in there and poke around first. But I can tell you this much with a degree of certainty: the fire started on the top floor. If it had started just below that, it would have worked itself down much faster than it did." He pointed up at the building. "Count three floors down from the top. We stopped the fire before it reached there. If the fire had started on the second floor from the top, it would have spread far below that point by the time we got here."

"Electrical?"

"Unlikely. The building was inspected three months ago. I did it myself. The wiring was still in excellent condition. Sorry, Mr. Wade, but I've got to cut this short." He walked over to a fireman who looked like the person in charge. They glanced down at the inspector's clipboard and up again at the building, pointing at something. I turned around and walked between the barriers to the other side of Dorchester.

As I watched the streams of water smacking the building, I thought about Michael Spence. I had put some pressure on him to get him to do something stupid. Maybe this was it. Maybe the audit had missed some incriminating evidence in his files that would lead to him. Maybe there was so much of it that he'd felt he didn't have the time to fudge it all. Setting fire to the office would have been easier and faster. Maybe he'd felt that the hammer was going to drop on him soon.

I looked toward my right at the crowd and saw him. Michael Spence was looking up at the top floor, perhaps hoping his files were now burned to ash and watered down to an unrecognizable heap of nothing. I put two fingers to my lips and whistled to get his attention. He saw me. I waved him over.

He shouldered his way through the crowd. He was out of breath by the time he got to me. "Eddie, I'm surprised to see you here. How'd you find out?"

"Brad Wilcox called me. It looks like the fire started on your floor."

"The wiring is ancient. I've talked to the management company about it, but they just put me off. I told them I'd move if they didn't replace it. All my client files are gone now. I don't know what I'm going to do."

"Aren't files like that supposed to be kept in a fireproof cabinet or walk-in safe?"

"Yes, we do have a walk-in, but I took all the files out to go over them. I had to call all the clients to reassure them that their investments were safe. I was going to put them back when I finished."

"Listen, the fire inspector isn't going to know anything about the fire until they get in there. There's nothing we can do here. Let's go down the street to an all-nighter and have a coffee."

We walked several blocks to a diner and sat in a booth. I motioned to the waitress behind the counter for a pot of coffee and two cups. She brought them over lickety-split.

Michael Spence looked melancholy. Maybe it was real, or maybe he remembered his training in method acting. A little of Lee Strasberg goes a long way.

"First the embezzlement," he moaned, "and now this. I'm ruined, Eddie." He looked down at his coffee but didn't drink any of it.

"If we find Belanger and prove he stole the money, your firm will be reimbursed."

"That may be so, but with the fire now—"

"If it proves to be the wiring, there will also be a payout on a fire claim."

He perked up. "I hadn't thought about that. But yes, you're right."

I had given him high hopes of recouping his losses. Now it was time to put the squeeze on him. If he'd been stupid enough to set fire to his office, maybe he'd be stupid enough to do something else. *Twist the knot, Eddie. Cut off the oxygen.*

> They marched with spear in hand;
> "Go blow those ram horns," Joshua cried,
> "'cause the battle is in my hand."
> And the walls came tumbling down!

"Spence, now that we have time to talk, there's something I'd like to discuss with you."

"What is it?" he asked. "Sounds serious."

"Well, it depends on how you take it."

"Go ahead." He sipped his coffee.

"Whenever a case is investigated, whether by me or by the police, we have to look into the backgrounds of the people who are associated with the suspect. It's just standard procedure." I picked up my cup, took a few sips from it, and put it down, giving him time to absorb what I'd just said. I ran my finger across my lips. He was watching my every movement. "There's something I have to tell you, Spence, that you have a right to know."

"Jeez, Eddie, now you're giving me the chills."

"During the course of the investigation, I found out that you were adopted and that your mother recently passed away."

"Adopted? Oh, you must be mistaken," he said. He suppressed a laugh and then added, "My parents are alive and living in Toronto. I talked to my mother just last week."

"I meant your real mother. Her name was Ruth Adler. I knew her. She was a wonderful woman."

"Listen, you must have gotten this wrong. It's probably another Michael Spence. It's a common name, after all. Besides, my parents certainly would have told me if they had adopted me—if not as a child, then certainly as an adult."

"I'm sure they had their reasons for not telling you. The adoption was an illegal one. The authorities call it a black-market adoption. Maybe that had something to do with it. Perhaps they were frightened that some sort of legal action would be filed against them if it came out."

His tone became more serious. "I assume you have some sort of proof of this?"

"Just hear me out first. Your mother gave birth to twins, so you have a brother. Your mother had to keep him because there was a problem with the birth, and they didn't think he was adoptable. They were wrong. He's fine, and as far as I know, he doesn't know he has a brother."

"You're serious about this, aren't you?"

"I am. Your father is alive, and he knows about you. As a matter of fact, he sent money to your parents once a month for your support while you were growing up. He sent it anonymously, of course. Your adoptive parents had no idea where the money was coming from."

He shifted his position in the booth and then diverted his gaze from me. After a moment, he looked at me again. "This is a lot to take in. So what's his name? Does he live in Montreal?"

"Are you interested in contacting him?"

"I don't know. Maybe. Sure. Why not?"

"I'm not able to tell you his name, but I can pass that on to him. Whether he contacts you or not is up to him. I have to respect that."

"Do you know where my real mother is buried?"

"Yes, at the Baron de Hirsch Cemetery."

"That can't be right. That's a Jewish cemetery."

"That's where she's buried. I attended her funeral."

"You're telling me—"

"Half Jewish. Your father's background is English Protestant."

"Jesus, Mary, and Joseph," he said.

I was going to mention that they were also Jewish, but I decided not to.

"And I have a brother? Do you know anything about him?"

"More than I want to know. His name is Ezra Adler. He resembles you but in a rough sort of way. I'm afraid his story isn't a good one. He's been involved in criminal activity. Up until recently, he worked for a New York mobster named Carmine Galante."

Not even the best of actors can suppress genuine surprise upon hearing unexpected news. His face told me a multitude.

And the walls came tumbling down.

"Galante had been in town for the last few years. One of his operations was a gambling suite in the Windsor Hotel. Your brother was the well-paid doorman. That's where Belanger gambled. I believe the money he embezzled went to Galante to buy in on a partnership. The operation was busted by the RCMP recently, and Galante was deported. But I saw his ledger. I think Belanger was using the name of Duke. I'm about to get my hands on something that will prove this one way or another. I should be breaking this case in the next day or two." When I said the name Duke, I saw him wince slightly. He couldn't hide that either.

"Have you told anyone about this besides me?" His voice was calm and controlled now.

"No. I haven't written up my report yet. No one knows about it."

His face relaxed for the first time. We chatted for a few more minutes and finished our coffee.

"Will you let me know?" he said.

"About what?"

"The Galante thing—whether he ended up with the money."

"You'll be the first I tell."

We got up and left the diner, each going our own way. I'd lit the fuse. I'd just have to wait to see how long it took for the dynamite to explode.

Joshua fought the battle of Jericho,

and the walls came tumbling down!

Later that afternoon, I called Frederick Churchill at his office. I wasn't exactly sure why I did. I liked the old guy. Perhaps I looked at him as the father I never had. He was a decent fellow who didn't deserve to be deceived by me or anyone else. He had the right to be told the truth about Michael Spence. I knew he could handle it, as he'd handled so much in his life already. We agreed to meet at Dominion Square at seven, where we'd first met that morning, which now seemed an eternity ago.

When I arrived at ten minutes till the hour, he was already there.

"Hope I haven't kept you waiting," I said.

"You haven't. Besides, I'm early, as you can see. We both are."

I took out my pipe, filled it, and put a match to the tobacco. Frederick had been smoking his already.

"I'll get right to the point, Fred." I blew some smoke into the breeze. "I talked to Michael this morning. I explained the whole thing to him."

He wasn't surprised or angry. If anything, he seemed relieved. "How'd he take it? Did you tell him who his father was?"

"I left your name out of it. That part is none of my business. At first, he was surprised. By the time I left, he accepted that he had been adopted. He wants to meet you. I told him I'd pass that on to you. He doesn't know anything about you."

He puffed on his pipe and was silent for a long moment before he spoke. "Eddie, I haven't been entirely truthful with you."

I didn't say anything. I knew he hadn't been, but that was fine with me. He had a right to his own past.

"Do you remember that I said I hired an investigator?"

I nodded.

"Well, I didn't tell you the whole story. He's an old friend. We've known each other for years. He was the means by which I kept track of my sons. He'd been providing me information for years. I told you that I knew Ezra had been involved in some criminal activities, but I said I didn't know the details. Well, I do. Ezra was working for Carmine Galante, some kind of crime boss in the city. My friend told me he was from the mob in New York. I had to see this for myself, so for many months, several times a week, I came here and sat on this same bench. My friend was correct about Ezra. He was involved with this criminal. But I also learned something else."

I had a feeling I knew what he was about to say, so I didn't interrupt him.

"It's about Michael. I also saw him come and go from the Windsor. One night, I saw him walk out of the hotel with Galante. It was obvious they knew each other well. My suspicions grew. I had my friend tail Michael for months after that, and what I learned wasn't good."

"Does it have to do with Philippe Belanger's wife?"

"Unfortunately, indeed it does. They were seeing each other behind her husband's back. When the story broke about the embezzlement and Belanger disappeared, my imagination ran wild. I didn't like what I was thinking. I cursed myself for having those thoughts, but it didn't change the facts. That's when I concluded that Michael may have been involved in the theft and that Juliette Belanger had also been in on it. God only knows what happened to her husband."

"I haven't been entirely truthful with you either," I said. "I am working on the Belanger case. I had the same suspicions as you, and I'm close to getting the evidence. Have you read the paper this morning?"

"You're referring to the fire in Michael's building."

"I think he may have started it to destroy evidence that might incriminate him."

"Good Lord, is there no end to this?" he said in almost a whisper, as if to himself. He looked at the entrance of the Windsor across the street and narrowed his eyes. "So Michael and Ezra must have known each other. Do you think—"

"No, they didn't know they were brothers. When I told Michael about the adoption this morning and said he has a twin brother, his reaction was genuine."

"So what are we going to do about this?"

"I've been putting a lot of pressure on both Michael and Juliette in the last few days to force their hand. I let them know without saying as much that I suspected them. They'll need to deal with me soon—before I go to the police and before I file a report. I think I'm going to receive a phone call any time now. They're going to want to meet me somewhere."

"Are they capable of violence?"

"I think they're capable of anything."

"You should let the police handle this then."

"They're not going to confess to them, so there's no point. All the evidence that could stand up in court still leads to Belanger." I was silent for a moment, mulling something over, and then I said, "I think I can get a confession out of them."

"But you said they're capable of anything. You could be putting your life in danger."

"Yeah," I said, "I could be. It won't be the first time, and it certainly won't be the last."

A boreal chickadee heckled me from the branch of a nearby linden, throwing insults down on me. I told him to mind his manners, but he wasn't listening.

CHAPTER 29

I didn't have to wait long. The phone rang early the next morning.

Tangerine and I had just returned to the office after having a good feed at the greasy spoon. I had wanted to walk down to Beautys for breakfast, but she'd insisted on the neighborhood haunt. She liked the way they fried the potatoes in lots of butter. I liked them too, but last year, I had decided I'd better start watching what I ate. I was self-employed and in good physical condition. I needed to stay that way. Once a week, I eat whatever I want. The rest of the time, I eat like a monk in a monastery—well, mostly. Tangerine, however, was slim and trim, and she was a decade or more away from having to worry about her figure.

She sat on the couch, playing with the cats on her lap. I liked her laugh. It made me feel good inside, for her as well as for me. She was getting used to the routine, but I sensed she was getting impatient with being cooped up in the office. She did go out, though, for walks and for her meals, and she was becoming a regular next door at the Lion's Den. She and Bruno had buddied up. He'd told me a few days ago that Tangerine made him feel young again. I was pleased with that.

I sat behind my desk, sorting through old mail with my checkbook out. Because I had been wrapped up in the case, I had forgotten to pay some bills. I was writing a check to the Quebec Hydroelectric Commission, when the phone rang.

"Wade Detective Agency." I leaned back in my chair.

"Oh, Eddie. I'm glad I caught you in. This is Juliette Belanger. I tried earlier, but there was no answer. You're a hard man to reach."

"I'm working on that," I said. "What can I do for you?"

"Listen, I'm going to take the tram to Cartierville to visit a friend for the day. I was wondering whether you'd be available later in the day for a visit. I thought it would be a good opportunity to have a nice chat. I really do need to think about something other than this whole disastrous tragedy. Would you have the time tonight?"

"What time did you have in mind?"

"Let's say eight o'clock. There's a bench just outside the entrance to Belmont. We could meet there. Perhaps I could catch a lift with you back to Outremont, seeing your office is close by."

Something in the tone of her voice caught my attention. It was subtle, but it was there. It was an artful mix of male arrogance and female cajolery. Hedy Lamarr would have been impressed by her.

"It would be my pleasure, Juliette. See you then." I hung up the receiver.

What was it that Sir Walter Scott once wrote? "Oh, what a tangled web we weave, when first we practice to deceive!"

Cartierville was about a forty-five-minute drive from my office. I left early because I had to stop somewhere first, and then I took my time. I drove north on the Main and thought about Juliette Belanger. She'd had me fooled. She was good. Almost everything I'd known about her had been wrong. I had made some assumptions about her based on my observations, but like the actress she was, she had fooled me. She had wrapped herself around me in the guise of another person.

I didn't know how this was going to play out, because I didn't know what game she was playing. I didn't know what she wanted or whether Spence was going to show up to play with us. My thoughts were bouncing off the bumpers of a pinball machine. I was waiting for the bells, flashes, and blinking lights, but there weren't any. My best guess was that she wanted me dead. That would solve their problems—hers and Spence's. They were desperate. With me out of the picture, it was unlikely they'd ever be caught, because for the police, all roads led to Philippe Belanger as the embezzler and the murderer.

I turned left onto Gouin and kept driving. I looked into the rearview mirror and saw a car behind me. It was keeping a safe distance between us and had been following me since I left Mile End. Maybe I was becoming paranoid; maybe it was just going in my direction and not following me at all.

Investigative work usually involved a certain amount of risk. This case hadn't involved much when I'd first taken it on. As it had developed and spread its wings, so had the risk. I confess that I have a morbid attraction to people and situations that are dangerous. Listen, I had a boxing career, and I volunteered for combat duty during the war. What more can I say? I've been an investigator since the war ended. I have nothing to complain about. I could have said to Juliette that I wasn't available to meet her. I could have turned over the Belanger file to Bradford

Wilcox and told him I'd done my best. I could have provided Lt. Max Drummond with more information about the case, shared my suspicions about the two, and called it a day. But I hadn't done any of those things. I took my right hand off the wheel and patted my semiautomatic tucked under my left arm, and then I took a deep breath and told myself to stop whining.

I slowed down, made a sharp right turn onto rue Lachapelle, and followed the road for a quarter of a mile. The car behind me made the same turn but then pulled off to the side of the road and parked. Apparently, I was getting paranoid. Belmont Park was situated to my right on the banks of Riviere des Prairies. I drove around the lot several times before finding a parking space. They had a good crowd there for a Monday night. They probably had a special attraction or a good band at the dance hall to draw more people in on a night that was usually slow. *Summer fun!*

The sun was off to the west and dying. I got out of the car, took my sunglasses off, and threw them onto the seat. I was early—on purpose. I wanted to scout out the area before Juliette arrived and see whether she'd bring a little surprise with her. A large maple tree shaded the edge of the east end of the parking lot. I walked over to it and leaned against it. I listened to the unmistakable roar of the Cyclone, the wooden roller coaster that ran at an astronomical speed. I heard the laughter, shouting, and screaming of children, no doubt scared out of their wits. Over all the noise was an incessant, maniacal female laugh. Inevitably, my thoughts turned back several decades to my mother and our first visit there.

After my father ditched us both in Brooklyn for a better life, my mother returned to Montreal with me, her nine-year-old son, in tow. That first summer back—I suppose to take our minds off the miserable situation we had found ourselves in—my mother took me to Belmont Park, and she did so every summer until I was well into my teens and suddenly felt it was too childish for me. It was my first trip there that I remembered the most. We took the number 65 tram from downtown to the 48 in Montreal West and then on to the Garland Terminus off Decarie, where we changed to the green number 17 Cartierville car for an awe-inspiring journey. To me, at the time, it felt like an excursion into some faraway foreign land. Finally, we pulled up to the Cartierville Terminus and got off. The anticipation I had felt during the trip only intensified when I heard the din from the park.

As we waited in line for our tickets between two huge towers on either side of us—perhaps an entrance to a castle—with a sign above that screamed, "Parc Belmont Park," we could hear the distinctive, disembodied laughter of some unknown female voice. The excitement I felt was almost unbearable. It was so strong that once we had our tickets, I made a beeline to the nearest toilet.

After a good, long pee, as soon as I got out of the restroom and took my mother's hand, I saw the source of the laughter that seemed to drown out everything else. I looked up at a five-foot papier-mâché (of course, I didn't know what the material was at the time) lady who bore a striking resemblance to the crazy woman down the block from us, who threw chestnuts at my friends and me while laughing hysterically. There were several different names for her: *la grosse femme*, *la grosse femme qui rit*, or *la bonne femme qui rit* if you were French or simply the Laughing Lady if you were English. When I was older and could go to the park by myself with my friends, we started calling her Laughing Sal.

She wore a colorful flowery dress with long sleeves and a black necklace. She had shaggy, straw-like hair that came down to her eyes, with a hat pinned to the back of her head. She had rouged cheeks, exaggerated thick black eyelashes, and bright red lips. Her perpetual smile exposed a missing tooth. As she laughed, her head bobbed back and forth, her body bowed and then straightened at intervals, and her arms flailed. I knew she wasn't real, but I was young and innocent enough to be able to pretend that she was. That made all the difference. Hearing her laughing now gave me a reassuring feeling that after all these years, something constant remained in the universe. *Good for you, Laughing Sal. Good for you.*

Belmont was an amusement park, and they did their best to amuse me on that first visit. I had every right to be excited, and I was. It was an excitement that had been building up for years, because when we'd lived in Brooklyn, I had begged my father many times to take us to Coney Island, but he never had.

We lined up at another ticket booth and bought a strip of fifteen-cent tickets, which got me on a pony, a boat, the train, and the bumper cars alone, but I wouldn't venture on the Cyclone without my mother sitting beside me. Also, my mother had to go with me in the haunted house, because it was too frightening for me alone. The car pushed us back and forth on the tracks in darkness, and we always anticipated creatures, such as the giant tiki gods and the shivering Indians, thrusting out at us and scaring the pants off me.

At some point, we took a break from the excitement to have lunch. My mother, having packed a bag for the day's outing as a way to save money, spread a blanket beneath the same tree I was now standing under. She retrieved from the bag our lunch: fried-egg sandwiches with yellow mustard, kosher dill pickles, baked beans bathed in maple syrup, and potato chips. Somehow, the food tasted better outdoors. Since this was an outing, for dessert, she bought us a special treat: honey-glazed doughnuts.

After lunch, my mother leaned her back against the tree as I sprawled out on the blanket. She talked about how things were going to be better for us. I don't remember her ever mentioning my father again for as long as we lived together. I was terribly sleepy-eyed at that point, but I refused to fall off into dreamland, because so much more fun awaited us. I blinked my eyes and hummed, hoping to keep awake. My mother had a good laugh.

After the rest, we went back at it again. I rode on the carousel and the Ferris wheel; had a dip in the pool (I wore my swimming trunks under my pants, which was a problem after the swim); rode the boat and train again and, of course, the Whip and the Wild Mouse, which was not a good idea after eating lunch, as I found out. Toward nightfall, when we were both exhausted, we walked around the spectacularly lit midway to see the freak sideshows. They were exhibits of unfortunate people with rare biological deformities—freaks of nature, if you will—and extraordinary diseases and conditions. Looking back at them as an adult, I was saddened to think they had been displayed like that. I still remember the canvas sign flapping in the wind: Human Freaks. But as a nine-year-old, I was completely awed by the sight of them: the Siamese twins; the bearded woman; the woman with three legs; the alligator man (just an ordinary guy with a skin disease); the wolf man with a hairy face; the armless and legless man billed as the snake man, who squirmed back and forth on the wooden floor (I later found out he had lost his extremities in the Great War); the man with carbuncles on his face and head (he scared the hell out of me); the African woman with humungous legs and feet (a disease I later found out was called elephantiasis); and the five-hundred-pound woman dressed in a diaper and a bonnet (the world's largest baby). I looked over at the park and hoped they had retired the show.

Both of us were completely drained by the time it was dark. We went back to the tram station and boarded the number 17 back home. The seats on the tram weren't all that comfortable, but in spite of that, I could have slept for a week. The motion of the tram was calming, soothing, and reassuring. The steel wheels grating on the rails, the rhythmic *clump-clump-clump* sound, the jerking of the car, the occasional bell—it was a recurring symphony. I watched the heads of the passengers jerking from side to side. Each time the tram stopped to pick up passengers, there was a piercing squeal as the motorman moved the lever again, allowing air to reenter the brake lines for a smooth stop.

I looked over toward Lachapelle Bridge, which connected Montreal Island to Chomedey, and saw Juliette Belanger walking toward the bench where we were to meet. She was alone. I looked at my watch and was surprised to see that it was 8:37. I had lost track of the time. In another fifteen minutes, it would be dark, save for the lights spilling over from the park.

She walked over to the bench, sat down, reached into her purse, and took something out. I imagined it being a gun. It wasn't. She took out a mirror and lipstick. She looked into the mirror, raced the greasepaint over her lips, and gave herself a sucked-in bite, spreading the fresh lipstick. I looked to the left toward the bridge and saw a couple strolling hand in hand. I then eyeballed the area. I saw no sign of Michael Spence. The din from the park was lower now. It would be closing in about an hour. The parking lot was filling up with people, and I could hear engines coming alive.

I walked over to her and approached the bench from behind. She heard me as I got closer. She swung her head around. She was wearing a pale yellow dress, which went well with her blonde hair and gorgeous blue eyes.

"Hi, Eddie," she said.

"Hi, Juliette."

We both said, "Sorry I'm late," at the same time and then laughed.

"Nice evening, eh?" she said.

"Lovely." I sat down next to her but not too close. "How was your day?" I hadn't deluded myself into believing she had come that far to visit a friend. Her sole reason for being there was me. Maybe I should have felt special, but I didn't.

She threw her head back, and her hair settled as if it had a memory of its own. "Oh, I had a wonderful day," she said. "It was so nice to leave everything behind and not have to think about anything else."

She droned on for the next five minutes about her friend and what they'd done that day. I listened, nodding and agreeing at the appropriate times, making the obligatory gestures and expressions. She was animated—or perhaps simply nervous. When she ran out of gas, I started gabbing, mostly about how I used to come to Belmont as a kid. I couldn't think of anything else to say. The conversation was forced, and it was uncomfortable. By the time I finished, it was dark, the park had closed, and most of the cars in the lot were gone. There was a long moment of silence between us, interrupted only by my question.

"So who's your friend?"

She looked at me, uncertain what I meant. "Which friend?"

"The one you talked about for five minutes but never mentioned her name." I made a point of sounding accusatory. Juliette was a cute little package, and I wondered how to open her up.

"Oh," she said. There was a long pause. Then the conductor rapped his baton, and the music started again, but this time, it was a different tune. "Is there something wrong?" She cocked her head slightly to the side.

"There's nothing wrong. You never mentioned her name."

"You wouldn't know her if I had." She glanced at her watch.

"I get around. How would you know?"

"You sound testy, Eddie. Are you testy?"

"I'm not testy. I just wanted to know the name of your friend that you spent the day with. That's all."

She didn't say anything for quite some time. Instead, she stared at me curiously. Her eyes were fixed, and her mouth was set; her face was a blank easel. Then her lips spread into a wide grin. "Let's walk down to the river. I'll tell you her name on the way. It's lovely down there." She started to get up, but I grabbed her arm. She eased herself back down. "You're hurting my arm, Eddie. There is something wrong with you. What is it?" She glanced at her watch again.

"Got a date?"

"That's not funny. What's the matter with you?"

"Where is he, Juliette?" I asked.

This time, the silence was longer and palpable. However, she was poised and cool, which made me feel slightly oafish. Subtle and complex women sometimes made me feel that way, especially if they wanted to kill me. She glanced at her watch again and then up at me.

"You mean Phil?" she finally said. "Oh, you can stop looking for him now. It doesn't matter." She said it in such a self-assured way that it gave me a sudden chill.

"Who killed him—you or Spence?"

"Neither of us, but he's dead nevertheless."

"You had him killed then."

"By an acquaintance of yours."

"Johnny Como?"

She smiled but didn't say anything.

"I didn't hear what you said."

"That's because I didn't say anything."

"You and Spence hired Johnny Como to kill your husband, Philippe Belanger. Say it. I want to hear you say the words."

Instead of saying anything, she looked up over my head, behind me. I turned around, and Michael Spence was holding a gun, pointing it at me.

"Okay, I'll say it," Juliette said. "Michael and I hired Johnny Como to do away with my darling husband, Philippe Belanger. That's why you don't have to look for him anymore. Satisfied?"

Spence walked around to my right. Juliette leaned over to me and ran her long fingers through my hair. My hat fell to the ground. Talking to Spence but staring at me with those lovely blue eyes of hers, she said, "Sorry, Michael. Little Eddie boy here wouldn't walk down to the river with me. Such a shame. It's so nice and dark down there. Maybe you could persuade him to now." She eased herself closer to me, and with her face just inches from mine, she said, "Eddie, could you be persuaded to take a little stroll down by the river with us? Would you be open to that idea? It's lovely down there; it really is." Before I could say anything, she spoke again. "You know what your problem is, Eddie? You're a dangerous idealist. You just don't know when to fold up shop and call it a day."

"You know," I said, "I spent the better part of three weeks chasing my tail. You could at least give me a break and tell me how you arranged all this before you slug me over the head and throw me in the river."

As cool and collected as Juliette was, I could see that Spence was nervous. That would have been fine with me, but I wasn't thrilled with him being twitchy and holding a gun on me at the same time.

"Let's cut this bullshit and get it done," Spence said. "Get up, and start walking, Wade. But first, pull your gun out, nice and easy. I know you're reckless, but I don't think you're a fool."

I eased my gun out of the holster and handed it to Spence. Then I looked at Juliette, hoping for the best. I sensed she wanted to tell all; she would derive satisfaction from my knowing exactly how they'd manipulated me.

"You heard what the man said, Eddie," she said. "Get up."

"So he's in charge, eh? I never would have thought you were the kind to take orders from anyone."

"You're playing that old game, Eddie. It won't work with us. Better do as the man said."

"What if I don't? What if I just sit here? You're going to shoot me? There are still workers in the park. They'll hear the shot."

Spence walked over to me, grabbed the back of my neck, and drove the barrel of his gun into the side of my head. "Let's just find out exactly what I'll do. You can die now, or you can get up and walk down to the river and live for another five minutes. Your choice."

Living for another five minutes seemed like a good option for me. I'd always said that discretion was the better part of valor. I got up and started to walk toward the bridge with the pair of them on either side of me. Juliette's ego must have needed a boost, because along the way, she explained exactly how she and Spence had managed the whole scheme—in detail. Spence, calmer now, even chimed in, filling in certain aspects that Juliette neglected. By the time we were under the bridge, I had the whole story. What I didn't have, however, was a clear idea of how I was going to stay alive.

I stood with my arms raised at the elbows. Spence was in front of me, and Juliette stood directly behind me. As I had turned around to face Spence a moment ago, out of the corner of my eye, I had seen Juliette pick up a large rock with sharp edges. It must have weighed five pounds.

After having survived the war in Europe, I didn't particularly want my life to end that way. Juliette wasn't the problem; I could take care of her with little effort. The difficulty was Spence, with the barrel of his gun pointing at me. If I could somehow get him to move toward me another foot or so, I'd have a chance to knock the gun out of his hand. The way he was standing and holding the piece was amateurish. I wasn't convinced he even knew how to fire it. But from that distance, it didn't matter. I had to goad him so he'd come closer to me. I figured this was my last chance.

"You're a coward, Spence—a driveling little mommy's boy. You couldn't punch your way out of a paper sack. You have to let a woman do your dirty work for you. You don't have the guts to take a swing at a real man, because you know you'd land on your ass."

He stared at me, his eyes menacing, his arm extended, still pointing the gun at me. His shoes were firmly in place on the ground. He wasn't going to come any closer to me. "You caused us problems, Wade. It's going to be a pleasure to see you float away in the river." He looked over my shoulder at Juliette and nodded.

Just as he did, a voice said, "Drop the gun, Michael."

The voice was familiar.

Spence jerked his head to his left toward the voice, his arm still extended. I knew that the rock Juliette was holding would soon find its target, so as Spence turned toward the voice, I dove toward the bank, out of harm's way. I heard two shots fired nearly simultaneously. I looked toward Spence. He had dropped down to one knee, holding his empty gun hand. I got up, ran over to him, and picked up the piece. My .45 was sticking out of his belt in the front. I got that as well. I suddenly remembered Juliette. I looked behind me. She was lying on her back with her arms at her sides. I walked over to her and knelt down. The streetlight above provided enough light for me to see a small bullet hole in the center of her forehead, no doubt put there by Spence's gun. Blood pooled around her head. Her eyes were wide open. She was staring the long blue stare. I brushed away some of the blonde hairs from her forehead. There was no need to check her pulse.

As I bent over her, I felt a hand on my shoulder. I jerked, thinking it was Spence's. It wasn't. I looked up at its owner and said, "Thanks. You saved my life."

"You're welcome, Eddie." He held a gun at his side. "I'm glad you weren't harmed. You're a good man."

I rose, and we walked over to Spence. The man looked down at him. Spence was now on both knees, holding his hand, obviously in pain. For a few seconds, the two men stared into each other's eyes. Then the man walked toward Belmont, fading more and more into the night.

CHAPTER 30

"This one here," he said, pointing at a framed photo, "is Eddie knocking out Joe Brigham in the second round." They shuffled down the wall a few steps and stopped. He pointed a chubby finger at another one. "And this one here is Eddie knocking out Kid Silverman in the sixth. Eddie earned his money in that fight." He grinned. "The Kid had him on the ropes a couple of times before he went down." He put his fists up to protect his face, hunched over, and then bobbed and weaved with his back to the imaginary ropes. "Then Eddie lands a right uppercut right here, like in the picture." He threw his head back and pointed a finger under his chin. "Lou Griffin told me after the fight that he didn't see the punch, but he could hear the Kid's body hit the canvas from the last row."

"Enough already!" I said to Bruno. I was sitting at the bar in the Lion's Den with a pint of Molson between my hands. "I'm sure she's thoroughly bored."

Bruno had been giving Tangerine the grand tour of his boxing photographs that lined the walls of the Den. He'd taken a good number of them at the Forum in the short-lived glory days of my boxing career before the war. Bruno was fanatical about boxing, and he had traveled all over Canada and the United States to see matches. He would purchase ringside seats and take pictures of the fighters with his Speed Graphic—bought specifically for that purpose. His photos were as professional as any sports photographer's. He had a special eye for photography, catching the fighters at the right times with the right punches and at the right angles. For the last year, I had been trying to convince him that his photos would make a great book and that he should be looking for a publisher. So far, he'd been content to show them off on the walls of the Den, especially to first-time customers.

I didn't know whether Tangerine was particularly interested in boxing, so I intervened on her behalf before Bruno got to the three photos coming up next of Graziano versus Zale. He would feel obligated to tell her the stories behind the photos, which would take up the next twenty minutes at least.

"Let's go back to the bar," Bruno told Tangerine as they walked back to me. His arm was around her shoulders. "Next time, I'll tell you about these three." He pointed behind them.

Bruno went behind the bar, and Tangerine sat down beside me. The brown Emerson Bakelite radio squeezed between the bottles of liquor on the shelf behind Bruno was on low, playing a Sinatra tune.

"I wasn't bored," she said to me. "Bruno's pictures are very interesting."

I glanced up at Bruno and caught him smiling, something he rarely did.

"And you were very handsome as a young man," she added. "Of course, you still are."

My nose had been rearranged on my face several times during my brief career and didn't look particularly pretty. But what's the old saw? Flattery will get you everywhere. Bruno took our empty glasses, filled them from the tap, and brought them back.

It was a slow night at the Den, even for a Tuesday; only three other drinkers were there besides us. They were in the back, talking up a storm, still arguing about the Canadiens' loss two months ago to Detroit in the play-offs. Bruno and Tangerine wanted to hear the details of the Belanger caper. After the shooting at Belmont last night, I had called the police as well as Jake Asher. I'd wanted to give him a jump on the story before the other papers got their hands on it. Jake had the byline in the *Gazette* (the paper had to stop the presses in order to get the story out in time for the morning edition), but the article was short, giving only the bare facts of the case. There would be a follow-up article with more details tomorrow. They could sell more papers by stringing the story out. Neither Bruno nor Tangerine wanted to wait. So far, I'd told them only that I was lucky to be alive and that someone had saved me.

Bruno excused himself and went into the back room. I gulped a few mouthfuls of my beer and then looked over at Tangerine. She was looking down at her beer and tapping her fingertips on the bar. She glanced sideways at me briefly and smiled but didn't say anything. There wasn't any tension between us, but I could tell from her eyes and her expression that she was thinking about something and on the verge of making a decision. I thought about bringing up the subject that we were both avoiding, but I didn't. She knew what she had to decide, and I had to give her the room to do it without putting any pressure on her. It had to be her decision, not mine. I couldn't force it.

Bruno came back and set a plate of sandwiches on the bar between Tangerine and me. "For those of us who are starving," Bruno said. "Ham and French Canadian cheddar with mustard on pumpernickel. The house specialty." The sandwiches were quartered and stacked high. He grabbed one and bit into it. We did the same, with Oscar Peterson now playing in the background with his magical fingers on the piano keys.

We ate in silence for a few minutes. Bruno then ran a napkin across his mouth, scratched his bald head, and adjusted his new glasses. "So who actually stole the cabbage, Eddie?" he asked, referring to the Belanger case. "The paper didn't say."

I took another bite of my sandwich and washed it down with some beer. "Michael Spence," I said. "He'd cooked Belanger's files and siphoned off the money little by little over time."

"And Belanger's little wifey helped him?" Bruno asked.

"She played her part. She'd practiced her husband's handwriting for months and had it down pat. She wrote the notes on each fraudulent transaction Spence made. At some point, Belanger discovered the discrepancies and the notes. He first suspected Spence but then concluded that he must have made all those transactions himself and just didn't remember them. Juliette's handwriting was so like his that it even fooled him. He thought he was going out of his mind—you know, like crazy. He convinced himself that he was having a nervous breakdown."

"So where's Belanger now?" Tangerine asked.

"He's dead," I said.

They were both shocked. They looked at each other and then at me.

I glanced at Tangerine. "You remember Johnny Como from the gambling operation, right?"

She nodded.

I looked over at Bruno. "He's a professional hit man."

Tangerine registered shock again. She hadn't known that. She'd thought he was just a gambler, a friend of her boss.

"Spence hired him through Carmine Galante. Como killed Belanger after he was released on bail, and then he drove his body up north somewhere and buried it. Como was arrested early this morning and is now sitting in a cell at police headquarters."

Tangerine was surprised again. "So Carmine knew all about this?"

"He did," I said. "Spence used the money to buy into the gambling operation. He and Galante had plans to expand it. But Spence had to cover his tracks. He had to make it seem as if Belanger had stolen the money and was on the lam. He hired a two-bit criminal named Manny Trocadero to contact me with phony information about seeing Belanger. After he did that, Trocadero became a loose end, so Spence got Como to kill him as well, making it seem as if Belanger had done it. All with Galante's seal of approval."

"I never thought Carmine was an angel," Tangerine said, "but I had no idea he could do something like that."

"Believe me," I said. "He's done much worse in New York."

Tangerine's brows were drawn inward; her look was serious. Her jawline was rigid, and her mouth took on a severity I hadn't seen before. I hoped she was thinking about her involvement at the gambling suite—not just about the illegal gambling, the illegal prostitution, or even the murders but about the particular road she was on. She was on a long, narrow road leading to a place she hadn't considered in her wildest dreams or nightmares. I also hoped she was thinking about Marguerite.

"Galante told Marguerite to rent a room under Belanger's name in a sleazy rooming house," I said, "which she did. But Spence got a little nervous about her. She belonged to Galante, but he felt she was also a loose end. She didn't know much about what was happening, but she knew enough. Spence couldn't ask

Como to kill her, because Como loved her, and he couldn't get the okay from Galante, so he did it himself."

Bruno took off his glasses and knuckled his eyes. I looked at my watch. It was getting late, and we were all tired.

"So, Eddie," Bruno said, "what I don't get is how you know all about this."

"Before I drove out to Belmont Park, I stopped by police headquarters and told Lieutenant Drummond what was going down. I told him I thought I could get a confession, so he wired me up. He said he'd keep his cars far away from the area so they wouldn't alert Juliette and Spence, and he couldn't guarantee my safety. After the cat was out of the bag, I told Spence and Juliette that if I were going to die, I at least deserved to know how they'd set the whole thing up. They spilled their guts, and they were pretty damn proud of themselves. The only thing that worried me was how I would stay alive."

"Jesus," Bruno said. "Their whole scheme must have taken some planning."

I glanced at Tangerine. She was staring down at her beer, in her own little world.

"Probably the better part of a year." I looked over at him. "Spence had a bad feeling about me from the beginning. At one point, as the investigation was just gaining steam, he wore a fedora and thick black glasses and took a few potshots at me one night in a car, pretending to be Belanger, trying to discourage me from continuing the investigation. He and Juliette made a good team. She even wrote the note from Belanger to me, wanting to meet me somewhere. You saw her slipping it in my mail slot that day. She also wrote the one that Trocadero used as proof that he knew where Belanger was. I'd been comparing her own handwriting, not Belanger's. She told me that even if I had dug through her husband's files and come up with something old that he'd written, the writing still would have looked the same to me."

There was a moment of silence. Bruno yawned, which made me yawn. Tangerine continued to stare at her beer. I was tired of talking.

"Let's say we call it a night," I said.

Bruno agreed but then said, "Just one more question. Who saved your rear end?"

I didn't answer right away. That information wasn't going to be in the papers, and I wasn't sure I wanted to tell them. I had lied to the police about it.

After Juliette was shot, while Spence was on the ground, holding his hand, I told Frederick Churchill to give me his gun and leave. I said I would tell the police I had used it in self-defense. If Spence said otherwise, I'd call him a liar. He had lied so much already that it was unlikely the police would believe him. The investigator that Churchill had snooping around had given him some startling facts about Spence and Juliette. He had come to his own conclusions. The last time I had seen Churchill—at Dominion Square—he'd thought I might be in danger, so he'd followed me out to Cartierville the next day. I hadn't known it at the time. He had seen everything as it was going down. As we got down to the river, he had feared that Spence was going to shoot me. As he'd told Spence to drop his gun, I'd dived for cover. He'd fired at Spence, hitting him in the hand. Spence's gun must have had a hair trigger, because it had gone off as he was shot, killing Juliette, who had been in his line of fire. For a brief moment, Churchill had stood over his son, their eyes locked onto one another. Spence had had no idea he was looking up at his father.

I looked at Bruno. Tangerine had turned her head toward me.

"I saved myself. Don't you know I'm Superman?"

They both frowned at each other.

"What about the dough?" Bruno asked. "Did you ever get it back?"

"You said that was the last question. Read about it in the morning edition."

They glared at me.

"Okay, but then I'm going next door to drop dead on the couch for at least a week." I tipped my glass back and drank the last of the beer. "When the RCMC raided the gambling suite, they found the money in Galante's desk drawer. They thought it was profit from the operation. When the city police lifted the APB on Belanger this morning, the feds called them. After listening to Spence's and Juliette's confessions, they put two and two together. There's no way to trace the cash with certainty, but they decided to treat it as the embezzled funds. The investors will be reimbursed, and Brad Wilcox will have to cough up only the five grand that was missing. Maybe Spence and Juliette spent it on one last good time."

"That's a sad story, Eddie," Bruno said. "I'm glad you came out of it in one piece. It would have been a pain in the ass—" He stopped and looked at Tangerine. "Sorry," he said sheepishly, and then he turned to me again. "It would have been a pain in my behind to have to find someone else to rent your office if you were dead."

I grinned at him.

Tangerine seemed to perk up. "I'm glad you're in one piece too." She swung her head toward Bruno and said, "Did you know that Eddie hired a secretary? She starts tomorrow!"

Bruno didn't look impressed. "It's about time. Does that mean I don't have to look after you anymore?" he asked me.

"It means," I said, "that I'm going to have a wonderful young woman looking after me from now on." I turned to Tangerine. "Right, Stéphanie?"

"You're right, Eddie," she said. "So very right."

Printed in the United States
By Bookmasters